THE GOOD NIGHTS
DREAMS OF DESTINY

JAAFAR CHARAFEDDINE

© **Copyright 2025 - All rights reserved.**

The content contained within this book may not be reproduced, duplicated or transmitted without direct written permission from the author or the publisher.

Under no circumstances will any blame or legal responsibility be held against the publisher, or author, for any damages, reparation, or monetary loss due to the information contained within this book, either directly or indirectly.

<u>Legal Notice:</u>

This book is copyright protected. It is only for personal use. You cannot amend, distribute, sell, use, quote or paraphrase any part, or the content within this book, without the consent of the author or publisher.

<u>Disclaimer Notice:</u>

Please note the information contained within this document is for educational and entertainment purposes only. All effort has been executed to present accurate, up to date, reliable, complete information. No warranties of any kind are declared or implied. Readers acknowledge that the author is not engaged in the rendering of legal, financial, medical or professional advice. The content within this book has been derived from various sources. Please consult a licensed professional before attempting any techniques outlined in this book.

By reading this document, the reader agrees that under no circumstances is the author responsible for any losses, direct or indirect, that are incurred as a result of the use of the information contained within this document, including, but not limited to, errors, omissions, or inaccuracies.

ISBN: 978-9953-576-63-3

Dedication

With heartfelt gratitude, I dedicate this debut novel to my cherished family, whose unwavering love and encouragement have been my guiding light. To my precious son, whose love fills my days with joy, and to my beloved parents, siblings, and cousins, whose endless support has fueled my journey. To all my dear friends who have become like family, you know who you are and to every single person who was there for me all through it—your presence in my life has been a source of strength and inspiration.

As I embark on this entertainment adventure, I am deeply grateful for your continuous and unconditional support. Your belief in me has been a constant source of motivation, pushing me forward even in moments of doubt.

I am confident that you will continue to be my greatest champions, spreading the word about my book with enthusiasm and pride. Together, we share in the journey ahead, and I am honored to have you by my side as ambassadors of my work.

Jaafar.

Table of Contents

Ch. 1 : Diplomatic Connections 9
Ch. 2 : Seeking a Good Night 31
Ch. 3 : A Life in Dreams 53
Ch. 4 : Juggling Relationships 79
Ch. 5 : Chasing Art 103
Ch. 6 : Lucid Dreaming 129
Ch. 7 : Bonjour Paris 139
Ch. 8 : A New Crush? 153
Ch. 9 : A Tourist in Town 169
Ch. 10: Mixing Business with Pleasure 185
Ch. 11: Conflicting Emotions 203
Ch. 12: Not Again! 215
Ch. 13: A New Adventure 229
Ch. 14: Sleepwalking 247
Ch. 15: A Sandy Day 265
Ch. 16: What Would I Do Without You? 279
Ch. 17: Reality Kicks In 297
Ch. 18: Was It Just a Lesson? 313
Ch. 19: When Destiny Strikes 325
One Year Later 341

Ch. 1

"Diplomatic Connections"

The sound of Sam's sigh masked the dull hum of the crowds gathered outside. He stared out the tinted window of his Cadillac, admiring the elegant designs of the dresses and tuxedos passing by. People happily skipped up the palace steps of the Istana, the clacking of high heels echoed into the quiet interior of the car. He wanted to join the joyous event—it was Singapore's National Day, after all—but he felt sunken into the leather backseat. A strange sensation twisted in the hollow of his chest—the kind that came to him on lonely evenings when he couldn't seem to get comfortable in bed. It was a nameless unease—neither anxious nor sorrowful. Just a dull feeling that washed over him and eventually, with time, dissolved.

As an ambassador for the United States, Sam Cooper carried an immense sense of pride in his job. The successful political outcomes achieved through his efforts stood as a significant source of fulfillment and dignity. His peers often praised him for his levelheaded approach to resolving conflicts and his ability to deliver charismatic, impactful speeches. Over time, he embraced responsibilities he hadn't imagined himself capable of handling, discovering new strengths within himself and refining his expertise. What he cherished most was the constant evolution—the reassurance that he wasn't stagnating but continually growing in his career.

And yet, sitting in the car, bracing himself for another glamorous event and decadent cocktail dinner, Sam felt as if the world outside were an illusion. Déjà vu settled over him like a shadow haunting his thoughts—an endless repetition of events, each one blending into the next. Somehow, in that moment, the cycle felt like a burden. Much like the weight on his shoulders from the demands of his work, he felt undeniably weighed down. He was a man at sea—lost without knowing quite why.

"Are you alright, Your Excellency?" his driver asked, glancing at him through the rear-view mirror. The older man's eyebrows furrowed in his reflection, and the deep wrinkle of worry that formed into his skin was illuminated by the spotlights filtering in through the windows.

"I'm fine," Sam assured him and flashed a perfectly bright smile that melted the driver's unease.

The only way to convince both of the men in the black car that this was the truth—that Sam Cooper really was fine—was for him to exit the car. Sam swiftly opened the door without letting himself dwell much longer.

The noise of the event swelled around him. It was like surfacing from the ocean, the water draining from his ears, revealing the depth of the sounds of life. Sam straightened his impeccably steamed and tailored suit, making sure his bow tie was perfectly aligned. His usual confidence flooded back as the party seemed to pause for a few seconds, marveling at him. Sam was used to this kind of attention—he came into his looks early as a teenager and had experienced compliments on a daily basis ever since. He tried to not let it get to his head, but on a night like this, it was good to be reminded of his naturally engaging aura. With his dark hair, expertly pushed-back, and his full lips curled into that award-winning smile, he was ready to immerse himself into the crowd.

His heart rushed against his rib cage as he exchanged cheerful greetings with familiar faces, even if the specific names were escaping him at the moment, given the masses of people he meets on a daily basis.

Sam's bodyguard, Jack Smith, ghosted behind his every step. Quiet and reserved, the man mostly kept to the shadows at Sam's request. It still felt uncomfortable to Sam, having an agent dressed in all-black follow him around, though he'd grown used to it since his promotion to Ambassador.

As if on autopilot, Sam worked his way up the daunting palace steps lined with a luxurious red carpet and through the cavernous building, making a charismatic entrance reminiscent of James Bond's grand arrival at casinos. Voices carried through the corridors as people gathered around trays of champagne flutes, and Sam plucked a glass for himself off a waiter, who smiled at him timidly. Bubbles danced on his tongue as he moved in to greet Jun Cee, the Minister of Trade, a figure he had been dealing with more frequently lately.

Jun lit up upon Sam's approach.

"My favorite diplomat," he announced, his expression enthusiastic as he adjusted his glasses on his puffy face. He held his arms open as if to hug Sam at first, but as was proper etiquette, he brought his right hand down for a firm handshake instead.

"Not so loud, Jun." Sam grinned. "Special treatment doesn't work if everybody knows about it."

"Right, right. We'll keep it a secret."

"How else do you expect to expand your exports?"

"Always on the job, aren't ya?" Jun teased, taking a gulp of champagne.

"Politics never sleeps, so neither can I, it seems."

"Well, I'm sure the United States and Singapore will stay friends for at least one more night. You can relax a bit." Jun got closer to Sam, motioning for him to bring his ear in as if to share a private message. "I heard they have mini hot dogs wrapped in pastry floating around," he whispered.

"Really?" Sam asked in mock surprise.

"Ooh, but don't tell my wife—I might have a couple. She's worried about my cholesterol."

"I'm more worried about the aftertaste caused by washing hot dogs down with champagne."

"See? Another example of your rigidness. Let loose, Sam, I beg of you."

"Unfortunately," Sam muttered as he eyed the Prime Minister making his entrance, "duty calls."

Jun let out a rough sigh and sternly patted him on the back, leaving to retrieve the forbidden delights being served by the waiters.

Sam took the opportunity to stroll over to President Tan, who was standing under a chandelier in the middle of the grand entrance hall and accompanied by Prime Minister Chua and the Minister of Foreign Affairs, Mr. Lim. Though he frequently consorted with the group, he was nervous as he approached them tonight. He was not feeling at the top of his game with his mind so foggy.

He wiped off the excess moisture from his palms on his pants. He hoped he hadn't left a stain. Perhaps Jun was right, and he needed to relax.

After this, Sam promised himself.

"President Tan," Sam heard himself announce as he stood before the broad-shouldered man. "Prime Minister Chua." He concluded his greeting with a bow to Minister Lim, the man whom Sam held great admiration for.

A photographer came around, politely asking if he could snap a photo of the president and his companions.

President Tan smiled, happily giving his consent to the photographer as he pulled Sam in for a quick picture. He released his hold on the diplomat's solid arm as soon as the flash dissolved and wandered off into the crowd.

"Our countries have celebrated a union for... how many years now?" the Prime Minister asked with a humorous tone.

"Is that a trick question?" Sam responded with a wink. The ease with which this important man was conversing with Sam made his nerves settle a little.

"No, I never play games," The President dismissed the idea with a good-natured shake of his head.

"Well, Mr. President, that isn't the message I got last time you beat me so spectacularly in golf," Sam teased. He felt the tension in his joints relent completely as laughter erupted from the men.

They had likely been feasting all day—parades, food festivals, and endless drinks filling their plates and cups.

Earlier that day, Sam had found himself on the sidelines of those celebrations while the marching bands stomped by, his eyes glued to the sky as planes circled the stadium where the parade was held and flags waved below their pristine bellies. He had been reminded of the complete honor it was to be stationed here in Singapore—despite sometimes missing the comforts of his home in the States.

A delicious, airy slice of sugee cake could sometimes quell his craving for his grandmother's homemade pound cake. It was those small similarities, despite being a world apart, that could make it all a little easier.

Sam held out his champagne flute to clink against the President's and said smoothly, "I look forward to another year of independence for your country."

"And to another year of partnership with yours, Mr. Cooper," the Prime Minister added, raising his glass with a drooping smile as he joined in the cheers.

"Well," Mr. Lim interjected, "if *DC* continues their wonderful hosting, I will personally see to it that we always remain friendly!"

"The spoils of America never get old, do they?" Sam asked knowingly.

"No, but the waistbands of my pants are tired of my travels."

The hosts were approached by the Chief of Protocol, who was wearing all black.

"You must continue making your rounds, Your Excellencies," the Chief requested firmly, gesturing for them to mingle with the other guests.

While the others excused themselves and continued their tour, the Prime Minister smiled warmly, shaking Sam's hand and pausing for yet another photo Sam barely noticed being taken.

Sam swiveled in place, scanning the crowd to see who next to cozy up with, only to spot—as if by magic—the very person he had subconsciously been hoping to find walk into the room.

Dressed in a powder-blue gown with sheer tufts of fabric draped around her slim waist, the remarkably beautiful woman instantly met his eye and smiled at him from afar.

He stood rooted in place as she floated over to him. The closer she drew, the more he could smell the aroma of her rose perfume. It immediately put him under her spell. He fought the urge to dip his head down and press his lips to her sleek neck—exposed since her wavy brown hair was pulled into a glossy bun. She usually opted to wear her hair down.

"Hello, you," Kate Moore, the U.K. Ambassador to Singapore, hummed softly as Sam took her delicate hand in his and brought it up to his lips, where he placed a loving kiss upon her knuckles. "Have you had too much to drink today, or is the castle making you feel romantic, Mr. Cooper?"

"Why shouldn't it?" he asked gently. He wished he felt anything like a heroic prince while standing in front of this woman who was the picture of a modern princess. Instead, the faintly sarcastic edge to her voice made that nameless unease deepen in the pit of his stomach.

He had been seeing Kate for nearly a year already, but it still felt like there was a layer of diplomatic frost keeping them at a distance from each other. Like they were simply co-workers who occasionally indulged in some flirting.

Kate shrugged her shoulders but couldn't come up with a defiant response to his question.

Deciding not to pay too much attention to the cool distance in her demeanor, Sam held out his arm for her to take. There would be no arguing or mismatched intentions tonight, he promised to himself. Even if it's just for tonight.

Wordlessly, she grabbed hold of him, and Sam weaved his way through the densely packed rooms of their associates until they reached an exit. With the fresh air descending upon them like a much-needed wave of relief, both of their shoulders noticeably relaxed. Kate was always a little easier to talk to when they weren't surrounded by people whom she believed had their ears tuned in on their conversation. She had once sharply chastised Sam for mentioning her daughter in a business setting.

"It is *deeply* unprofessional, Sam. I already have to fight for people to see me as a serious colleague and not simply some sad single mother." Sam still remembered the tight-lipped cheek kiss she had given him in greeting that day after he made his sincere apology.

The memory made the back of his neck prickle with sweat. He did not want a repeat of something like that again tonight.

Slowly and in companionable silence, the couple approached the gardens, where hedges dotted with flowers made winding pathways through the greenery. Kate picked up the hem of her flowing blue dress as they strolled along cobblestones and commented on the extravagant fountains that seemed to populate every few steps. The sound of running water was a comfort, becoming the soundtrack to their conversation.

"So," Kate started with a short, terse exhale of breath, "can I ask you how your day was?"

"No. That would involve discussing work." Sam smirked and squeezed Kate's waist playfully. They had made that rule months ago, but it rarely ever held up for very long.

Kate rolled her eyes and twisted out of his grip. Her eyes were glittering in the gentle light of the quarter moon hanging in the cloudless sky. "Please, if even the Prime Minister got a half day, I'm sure you did, too."

Sam chuckled, cocking his head to the side in resignation. "It *was* nice to get a bit of a breather... Did you and Sara enjoy your day together?"

Kate leans a hip against one of the gently bubbling fountains. Her mouth turns up into a gentle smile at the mention of her young daughter. "Of course. She was not very happy about needing to stay with the nanny tonight—she begged to come be a princess with me." A silent beat passed between them as Sam joined Kate, their shoulders pressing together while he waited for her to decide whether to share the words he could see she was holding back.

Finally, clipping her words short like she wanted to be rid of them as soon as possible, she said, "She asked when she could hang out with you and Chalk again."

Warmth spread unintentionally across Sam's face. Kate had only introduced Sara to Sam and his stark-white Swiss Shepherd dog, Chalk, around a month ago, so Sam was involuntarily flattered by the little girl's approval of him. Especially because of the complications her biological father posed in her life.

He grinned as he replied, "Chalk would be absolutely flattered to see her anytime. He's always ready for some playtime whenever she needs him."

"Well, don't let it go to his head. He's already her favorite—might start thinking he's more popular than the rest of us."

"Remind me what your favorite color is again?" Sam asked, changing the subject. He continued walking backward down the path of the lush garden, his eyes still trained on Kate.

"You already know that," she giggled dismissively, her dress billowing as she followed him.

"Do I?"

"*Yes.*"

"Blue," Sam exhaled as he stopped suddenly, making Kate bump into his chest.

Kate mockingly gasped, looking down at her powder blue dress. "Cheat."

"I thought you said I knew the answer?" Sam smiled, his hand gently brushing down her elegant neck. The touch made Kate hum in pleasure as she grabbed onto the lapels of his shirt. He looked down into her eyes. "It's good that blue is your favorite color, though. It suits you."

"Charmer," Kate smirked. She pulled away from him, refusing to let him get too much of the upper hand. "Since you like acting like you have all the answers—what is my favorite food? Specifically, my favorite *breakfast* food?"

"What—are we on a first date or something?" Sam's mind reels with possible answers. He and Kate rarely really spent any breakfasts together.

Kate wags a finger at him accusingly. "You started it."

"Would it be too on the nose if I said an English breakfast?" Sam winced out his answer.

"*And* here we go with the schoolyard banter," Kate bites out with a firm shake of her head. "Sometimes, I swear you can be serious about *anything* and everything except for me."

Sam laughed it off, hoping to keep the conversation as lighthearted as possible despite her irritability. "Oh, come on, Kate. I'm way serious about you."

This didn't seem to be the correct answer either, as she made a faintly gagging sound at the back of her throat. She seemed resolute in her goal of dismissing his sincerity tonight.

Desperate to shake off the ice that had formed between them, Sam drew their bodies closer again, inhaling the scent of Kate as she looked up at him.

He loved the way her hips felt in his hands—the curves followed the depressions of his palms. Slowly, he encircled her waist and pressed his hand to her back.

She fit into him like a puzzle piece, and yet, somewhere, they had become disjointed.

The way Kate stared at him now, with lust in her eyes and gloss on her lips, was a rarity these days. This was how he wanted her, but something always seemed to be standing in their way.

His job kept him preoccupied most days, and Kate, as a diplomat herself, wasn't always easy to reach. Then there was the issue of their chemistry—it ebbed and flowed but never found a steady stream.

His heart gave a pained lurch at the thought that it might eventually decline completely. But he shut his eyes firmly, leaned in to press his cheek against the side of Kate's head, hoping the feel of her would distract him enough from his concerns.

There was always more time to talk about what they lacked, but tonight was coming together perfectly. He didn't need to spoil it.

"Am I going home with you, Sam?" Kate asked innocently.

"Always."

***

Later that night, after the presidential palace event had drawn to a close, Sam handed Kate a glass of chilled white wine. She accepted it gratefully, sitting on the floor and drawing her legs closer as her fingers idly brushed the soft fabric of *the carpet.* Sam joined her on the ground, leaning back against the leather sofa and stretching his legs out comfortably. In the corner of *his living room*, Chalk was peacefully napping on his doggy bed. Sam couldn't help but think, not for the first time, that his dog had a better sleep schedule than he did.

His feet hidden under the dark wood coffee table, a piece he'd collected from a local antique shop in Singapore. His mother had nurtured his appreciation for vintage pieces from a young age. Absentmindedly, he ran his hand over the smooth surface, the memory of weekend trips with her to antique stores back in the States flooding back to him. He glanced at the clock and mused that it must be about midday back home by now.

Sam's homesick reverie was interrupted by the soft sound of Kate whispering, "I feel like we've just come home from the prom." Her expression was thoughtful as she took another sip of her wine. "And I've been snuck into your room, where you're nervously going to kiss me for all of ten seconds while we listen for your mother downstairs." Kate had changed out of her lavish dress and hung it in the bathroom, insisting that Sam leave it there the next time he showered so the steam could erase any wrinkles. Now, she was wrapped up in Sam's brown terry cloth robe, her legs bare against the carpet.

"So *you* break the kiss when you hear her coming upstairs, worried about how you're gonna get home without your dress. You can't climb out my window like this." Sam gestured to her cozy outfit, ghosting his fingertips over her bare feet.

"Exactly," she laughed. "This might call for a sleepover."

"But what I've failed to tell you is that my mother does the laundry on Saturdays, and so tomorrow, bright and early, she'll be digging through the clothes on the floor of this very room."

"We'll be caught. How scandalous..." Kate purred.

"I feel like you're reliving something." Sam raised a questioning eyebrow. He watched as Kate's face turned. He didn't recognize the expression.

"Prom isn't a thing in Britain, really," Kate admitted. "Actually, I've heard they've finally let the kids have 'em, but when I was growing up, it was more of a formal gathering or a disco party. Isn't that awful? A *disco*."

"I mean..." Sam shrugged. "What's the difference?"

"The *movies*. That's the difference. Tell me the last time you saw a British comedy tackle the prom; I'll wait." Kate imitated Sam's seating position, stretching her legs under the coffee table and wiggling her feet cheerfully. Kate watched Sam with a sly grin and a raised eyebrow, one arm folded across her chest while the other loosely held her glass of wine.

"You're going to spill on the carpet," Sam said lightly as he shifted his gaze away from hers. For some reason, the attention made him uneasy—he wasn't used to her giving him more than the occasional glance while they were speaking. She only ever stared at him this hard when she was feeling especially eager to be satisfied by him.

He wanted to act on it blindly, as he always had, to accept it for what it was. But the longer it went on, the more he felt his feelings were holding him back. Perhaps it was the fear of their fragile connection evaporating with the next sunrise that still had him in its relentless grip.

"Oh, Sam," she breathed in an attempt to ease the blow of his rejection of her attention. She carefully put her wine glass on a coaster to quiet his concerns. "Still feeling tense from the reception?" She was all too familiar with the pressure that came along with these diplomatic exchanges. Where every laugh had the power to forge a valuable connection or jeopardize a trade or a political agreement entirely. You constantly had to maintain flawless composure in a crowd.

"Yeah," he agreed hesitantly, "It can be difficult to snap out of the tension of it all, you know?"

"Well, we should at least try." Kate was smiling again, pulling at the hem of Sam's loose collar.

She kissed him lightly on his dimpled cheek, her breath sweet and making his thoughts swim. He softened, melting into her touch as she leaned in again to kiss him on the lips. Giving in to the wordless pleading of her mouth, Sam gently cupped her face.

"You—" he began, intending to tell her just how stunning he found her.

But she shushed him quickly, wrapping her arms around his neck. "No more words tonight, Sam."

Desire flared between the couple. Forgetting everything around them, Sam picked Kate up off the carpet, eliciting a pleased giggle from her, and carried her to the bedroom. From his spot on the floor, Chalk raised his head, ears perked, and followed their steps with his watchful eyes.

***

It was nearly four in the morning, and Kate was bustling around in Sam's grayscale bedroom. She gathered her things from the floor and scanned his closet for something to wear. Sam watched, amused, as she tried on a few pairs of jeans in a huff, worrying over the poor fit.

"It's too late for anyone to see you," Sam said while the dark sky stretched endlessly above them, dotted with faint stars.

"Sara might be awake," Kate replied, her voice tight with anxiety. Sam held back a strained sigh.

Just a few hours ago, her voice had been soft with gentle praise and begging.

"Impossible." He waved a hand in casual dismissal. "What kid is gonna be up at this hour?"

Kate shot a glare at Sam over her bare shoulder. "You know, she gets very worried when I'm not home, Sam." She paused for a moment as she stood in the closet, her back to Sam. He could see her arms falling helplessly at her side. "You've seen it in action."

"Not even one more hour?" Sam hated how needy the question came across, but he tried his best to keep his tone of voice casual. "You'll be home in time for breakfast. That's what matters, right? Plus, you always say how good the nanny is with Sara."

"She can probably sense that I'm missing."

Sam desperately wanted to plead for her to return to his arms, but he held his tongue.

He knew she would respond with some variation of refusal, citing his lack of children as a sign he did not and could not know what he was talking about. She had made it very clear to him before that she didn't take advice from bachelors.

Sam had thought about what it would be like to be Sara's stepdad every now and then, but the idea made every muscle in his back tense with worry. Sara was a good kid—that wasn't the issue, but Kate's perpetual stress over her made him worry about how the responsibility of having a child would impact *him*. Would he also be sick with concern over the seven-year-old every day? He could barely handle the panic that came along with the responsibility of looking after Chalk when he was a puppy...

On top of that, would he be able to reduce Kate's stress at all if they were co-parenting? Would she trust him and his apparent lack of experience enough to believe he would be a competent stepdad?

Maybe all he had to do was prove himself to her. The intimidating challenge made the entire night feel heavier.

After throwing on a plain white T-shirt and belting the jeans tightly so they gathered around her waist in an attractively messy way, she called for her car.

Waiting at the foot of Sam's bed, she extended a hand to his thigh and gave him a mournful glance. They didn't say anything—there was nothing more to say. Kate had made herself perfectly clear. Together, they watched the serene city lights of Singapore shimmering like scattered stars against the dark sky. The world outside felt far away, leaving them cocooned in a quiet, unspoken stillness.

When her phone buzzed, she jumped up and planted a kiss on the corner of Sam's courteous smile. She threw one last look toward him before dashing out the door and simply said, "Have a good night, Sam, or whatever is left of it."

Alone in his room, he was a little relieved. It made his stomach twist with guilt, but Kate's anxiety was infectious.

He reached out and felt the coldness of the second pillow on his huge bed. Not for the first time, he wished that there was someone who could permanently fill that position next to him every night. He wasn't too sure Kate had the desire for something like that.

He didn't know what he had to do to make Kate understand the void in his bedroom—to make her stay and fill it.

The emptiness in his bed woke him up routinely throughout the next hour as he restlessly tried falling asleep again. Luckily, it was the weekend, and he could enjoy sleeping in a little longer than usual.

At some point, Chalk sidled into his room and lay down at the side of Sam's bed with a contented sigh. Sam let his hand drop over the edge to pat Chalk's soft fur lovingly. Thankfully, sleep came quickly after that.

***

Sam opened his eyes to a misty grey expanse. It stretched out all around him—mysterious yet strangely familiar. Comforting. Like the sensation of briefly thinking that you're waking up in your childhood bedroom, only to gradually remember that you fell asleep in a completely different place, in an entirely different country.

He blinked against the blurred vastness, trying to gain his bearings. In front of him was a door, standing loose a few feet ahead of him in the mist. Had it always been there? He tilted his head at it curiously.

A faint golden light penetrated around the edges of the doorway. It was inviting in a way that seemed impossible to ignore, and Sam put his hand on the gilded doorknob. What was that noise coming from the other side of the smooth, dark wood door? A persistent beeping—almost like the alarm clock that usually roused him awake on a weekday.

He needed to wake up, he thought. Without wasting another second, he turned the knob, swung the door open, and stepped into the warm light that enveloped him.

Ch. 2

"Seeking a Good Night"

Sam woke up irritated. The blare of his alarm clock had infiltrated his dreams, persistently yelling at him for the last half hour. In his half-asleep state, he kept hitting the snooze button, trying to return to the peace and quiet of his sleep.

That wasn't like him, though. He was the kind of guy whose eyelids flew open seconds before the first alarm, and who got up immediately after the initial beep.

The deep orange of sunrise was starting to turn into the bright light of early morning. The West Coast breeze was ruffling the palm trees in the backyard of his little townhouse. It gave the morning a dreamlike quality.

He sat up in bed and rubbed his neck as he glanced at the time. Immediately, he jumped into action. His morning was already off to a rough start. At this rate, he was barely going to make it in time for his first consultation, and being late for work is extremely bad etiquette for a doctor.

He took a brief cold shower in an attempt to shock himself awake and gulped down a glass of orange juice as he searched his townhouse high and low for a clean pair of work trousers.

He wished he could stay and admire the untamed, inspiring beauty of nature just outside the window, instead of wasting yet another morning stuck in his car and then the clinic. But he didn't have much of a choice.

Throwing his wallet in his leather messenger bag, he raced out the door to his SUV and began the short commute to work.

Traffic was surprisingly light for Los Angeles. His being a few minutes late had luckily resulted in him missing the worst of the rush hour.

Though Sam was situated in a suburb away from all the activity, the entire area had become so populated that it was a useless effort to try and avoid other people. He rarely had a roadway to himself, except for this morning, which was fortunately when he needed it the most.

Despite his luck, he was still ten minutes late for his first appointment of the day. He quickly greeted his assistant, Maria, who informed him that his visitors were already waiting inside.

Wiping the sweat from his forehead, he stepped in to meet his patient, Kareem Asfahani. The retiree had been under Sam's care for a few months, struggling with persistent health issues. The kind old man might soon require surgery.

Strolling into the room, with his binder tucked under his arm, Sam planted himself in his rolling chair before addressing the elderly man before him.

"My apologies for being late, sir—" He held still at the sight of her.

In his hurry, he hadn't noticed the beautiful woman sitting beside his patient. Her deep-brown, windswept hair shone even under the harsh fluorescent lights, and her equally dark eyes peered out at him through thick lashes. She smiled in greeting, a wonderful sight despite the apparent worry on her golden complexion. She had to be directly related to Kareem—the family resemblance was clear as day.

"I've been horribly rude," Sam excused, rising to carefully shake the woman's hand. "I'm Dr. Sam Cooper; it is a pleasure to meet you."

Her grip is gentle in his as she laughs lightly. "No worries, I can imagine you're a busy man."

Noticing Sam's hesitance, Kareem interjected, "I brought my daughter, Shiva, with me today. I hope that's alright."

"O—of course," Sam stammered, trying to regain his cool under Shiva's amused glance. He must have looked terribly awkward.

"My father doesn't always remember what to ask," Shiva added. They laughed carefully despite the confirmation that Kareem had a history of innocent memory lapses.

"Yes... Sometimes, it can feel overwhelming to keep track of everything," Kareem admitted. He crumpled a little, the wrinkles on his face deepening as his skin pulled into a frown. Shiva rested a hand on his shoulder, squeezing it reassuringly.

"But my father has told me wonderful things about you, Doctor. I know you've been as considerate as possible with him."

"I don't make it easy," Kareem chuckled again.

"Oh, please," Sam said finally. "You're a very cooperative patient, and I'm just doing my job—nothing special."

"I beg to differ," Shiva responded. "Anyway, my father's been complaining about joint pain, and I wondered if it could be a side effect of the meds or his condition..."

"It's likely just due to physical weakness during this challenging time," Sam reassured both of them.

"And what about his dry mouth? What could be causing that?"

"That would be the medication," Sam explained. "Always my least favorite part of the healing process."

"But it's not, you know, an early warning sign of a heart attack?"

"What makes you say that?"

"Just... his heart could be beating so fast, because of anything, really. Anxiety, illness, and so on. And I know, at least for me, that always gives me a dry mouth. But it can't be a good thing for a man his age to experience that."

Sam felt a rush of empathy towards Shiva. She had clearly worried about this a lot.

He shifted his gaze away from her and turned back to Kareem. "Are you getting outside for a walk each day?"

"Of course, and Shiva helps me."

"Well, then that's perfect. To be safe, we can check your blood pressure, Mr Asfahani," Sam remarked, roving his head to look at Shiva again. "That's easy to keep track of. But with regular physical activity and a good diet, I'm confident he'll be fine."

He paused once more as he watched while Shiva absorbed his words, her stunning face finally softening in relief.

He wondered what it was like to be cared for in such a way. If Sam had been her husband, would she be as worried about him? Monitoring his caffeine intake and counting his vitamins. Preparing home-cooked meals and encouraging him to get fresh air.

He had never had a girlfriend who worried much about his well-being. Whenever he felt ill—which happened occasionally in his line of work—they often left, viewing sickness as an unacceptable weakness in someone whose job was to prevent it in others.

Independence was a privilege, but sometimes, Sam grew tired of it. He just wanted to be cared for, and he'd return the favor, of course. In his imagination he could see Shiva's appreciative expression as he nestled her under the blankets on the couch, placing a box of tissues and a bowl of soup on the coffee table before her. They'd take turns sharing the same illness, nursing each other back to health without missing a beat, simply too caught up in each other's company to let a silly cold keep them apart.

"There are a few more tests we need to send you out for, Mr Asfahani," Sam continued, his voice steady and careful in his compassion. "I'll have my receptionist book them on the same day so you don't have to go running around the city more than once. We need to reduce the amount of stress you experience as well."

"Thank you, Doctor," Kareem replied.

Sam walked them to the front desk, his hand resting softly on the old man's shoulder as he guided him out of the consultation room. Sam had seen a few too many elderly men buckle without warning before, and a sudden fall like that could lead to many complications.

Shiva kept stealing glances at him and then turning her head away, blushing whenever she got caught. She was quiet while they checked out, standing by the counter and carefully noting each appointment in her planner—its location, time, and purpose.

"Are you in the healthcare industry yourself, Mrs..." Sam lingered as he realized he had no clue what her current surname was... Then again, no wedding ring adorned her fingers.

"Oh no, I'm not a Mrs. Anything. Just Shiva is fine." She grinned. It was impossible not to notice the hint of embarrassment flashing in her eyes, however. "And no, I'm not in the healthcare business—although I have done a lot of research lately to help myself take care of my father better. No, actually, I run an art gallery."

She shot Sam a polite smile before continuing to scribble the final details in her planner.

Sam watched her pen strokes, silently marveling at her refined script. Cursive—the flowing, interconnected style of handwriting—had always been romantic to him. There was something distinctly artistic about the way she carried herself. Sam could easily imagine her roaming through her art gallery, passionately explaining the meaning behind each piece with genuine enthusiasm.

"You should come by my gallery sometime," Shiva offered sweetly, biting her bottom lip. Was Sam hallucinating, or did her eyes trail down his form with a hint of admiration?

Was she... Could that have been a subtle sign of something more—like interest? Sam hadn't had time for anything close to romance in years, not since he started practicing after medical school.

Yet the gorgeous woman's attention left him feeling oddly unsteady on his feet.

With the kind of grace you'd expect from a buffalo, he muttered, "Yes, of course. I'll do that."

As the patient and his daughter left, waving goodbye with a final appreciative "Thank you, Doctor" from Shiva's full mouth, Mike—an obstetrician at the same clinic and Sam's best friend—emerged from his consulting room.

He laughed when he regarded Sam's charmed expression, staring out after Shiva. "Lookin' a little desperate there, buddy."

Sam shook his head, snapping out of it. "I'm not," he protested.

"She's beautiful, don't get me wrong—"

"You know her?" Sam asked, excitement sparking within him.

"Nah, I just saw her in the waiting room earlier. Beautiful, no doubt, but that's all I can tell you."

"I wonder how someone like *her* could be single," Sam murmured, more to himself than anything.

Mike laughed as he grabbed Sam by the shoulder and gently dragged him back and forth. "You got a crush, man."

"That's... childish." Sam couldn't bring himself to deny it, though. Was it really such a crazy thing to fall for a woman instantly? Last time he felt this excited and nervous at the mere idea of holding a woman's hand, he was about fifteen and *deeply* in love with his lab partner, Diane.

"It's okay, Sam. I had a crush on Julia before she became my fiancée. Happens to the best of us."

Sam weakly protested, turning to prepare for his next consultation. He couldn't risk falling behind any more today.

When Sam was finally done for the evening, back home in his comfortable clothes and happy to be rid of the clinical scrubs he wore at work, he dropped onto the couch in front of the TV.

Sinking into the cushions as he stuffed a series of pillows behind his head, he sighed gratefully.

All the lights were off in his house, yet the yellow walls were still illuminated by the glow of the television. His friends often criticized him for never changing the color, but Sam liked the memories it recalled. His grandmother had left him the house in her will, and though she made no special requests to maintain its original look, he liked that it remained a symbol of his family. In his mind, he pictured Sunday mornings in the kitchen with her and Christmas eves spent in the living room surrounded by his cousins.

Flipping through the channels, Sam dug his fingers into a bowl of popcorn and allowed his streaming services to pick something for him. As if reading his mind and the events of his day, a romantic comedy was recommended.

Viewers like you gave this movie a thumbs up.

Sam clicked on it without hesitation, and as his speakers amplified the music of violins, his mind drifted to thoughts of Shiva. He wondered what her favorite movie was, her favorite artist... Why is it that when you are attracted to someone, you suddenly want to know every minor detail about them? Even the silly things...

While the movie played, Sam caught himself imagining the conversations he would have with Shiva if they ever met again. He could practically hear her quiet voice in his ear as his eyelids became heavy.

Sleep wrapped Sam in a comforting hug as the couch cushions molded to his body.

The entire day felt like a hazy dream.

The perfect picture of Shiva's warm, chestnut eyes filled his mind. Maybe she could be the woman for him...

***

Sam blinked his tired eyes heavily. Despite finally falling asleep after Kate left, his few hours of sleep did not feel very restful. He had the most vivid dream ever, and to make matters worse, a mild hangover hammered in his head.

His fork scraped against the plate as he dug into the pile of breakfast sausages and pancakes before him.

Tiffany Marshal, his personal assistant, had sent out for an all-American breakfast that would put his mind and stomach at ease when she phoned earlier to let him know he could, in fact, need to come into the office later today. Sam accepted the order with little complaint. At least he now had something to keep his mind preoccupied. Perhaps focusing on work would help him shake off his confusion this morning.

He had promptly devoured the food—naturally tossing a part of the syrup-soaked sausage into the air for Chalk to snap up. The dog gave a bark of thanks that made Sam grin for the first time that day.

With his mind and body feeling a little better, he decided to venture onto his phone and browse the pictures sent to him from the previous night while he finished his coffee. Despite the lingering unease he had felt the entire night, he was thankful to see himself smiling in practically every shot. To his surprise, a few photos had been captured of him and Kate.

He thought he had stolen her away from the cameras, but someone must have caught sight of them as they walked the gardens. He zoomed in on the candid photos, making note of their expressions—they both looked happy.

Guilt wrapped tightly around Sam upon recollecting the disappointment he felt every time Kate left him. Did he really expect her to prioritize a morning with him over her own daughter?

His selfish desires puzzled him. He thought he had outgrown such childish impulses as a teenager and was ready to be a mature partner in the dating world. Yet he couldn't shake the feeling of abandonment whenever he spent another night alone.

The slight resentment that came with those thoughts made his coffee taste a little more bitter than usual. Without meaning to, his mind drifted back to his ex-girlfriend Karen, from his days at Stanford.

Sam had been ready to go all the way with her—a fancy white wedding, attending the kids' baseball games, growing old together. But Karen had found such dreams of domestic bliss utterly repulsive. Why would she settle down so early when she had her whole life ahead of her?

She had broken up with him at a party, and by the end of the night, Sam had already seen her cozying up to some new guy—a complete loser.

Unsurprisingly, the experience left him hesitant to jump into another relationship for a long time.

Although a few casual dinner dates with perfectly nice women had helped him pass the time throughout the years, Sam hadn't pursued anything long-term until he met Kate after moving to Singapore. Even then, he and Kate weren't exactly serious. They had both agreed to keep things informal, somehow. But it certainly wasn't easy to do, especially with someone as remarkable as Kate.

Fighting off the unpleasant feelings, Sam opted to text Kate, inviting her to a late lunch that afternoon. He set his phone down for only a few seconds before receiving her reply: *I would love to.*

Feeling more settled after finishing the last bites of his hearty breakfast, Sam left his dishes in the sink, knowing they would magically disappear when the Embassy's maid, came by later to make his already tidy residence even tidier. Sometimes, he wished the dishes would still be there when he got back as a reminder that somebody lived in this place.

Cleanliness was one thing, but his home often felt empty. There was never a trace of dirt on the polished concrete floors, and his clothes seemed to reappear in his closet as if by magic. He'd blink, and everything was reset—items stored neatly in drawers, his bed made with hotel-like precision, and the walls staring back at him, lifeless in their vacant spaces.

The only thing that brought him comfort was the floor-to-ceiling windows that exposed the Singapore skyline. Between glorious patches of water stood skyscrapers that housed thousands upon thousands of people. He lived among them as one of them—just because his house was lonely didn't mean he was alone. That was what he tried to tell himself, at least. It wasn't always a successful mantra.

***

That persistent sense of loneliness troubled him as he carried out his diplomatic duties of the day. It was the same formless feeling that had struck him in the car just before he entered last night's event, Sam realized with a painful ache. Sure, it had dissolved a little when Kate was with him, but it seemed to double in intensity from the moment she left.

So much so that it even haunted Sam's strange dreams of being a doctor in Hollywood... In real life, he had only been to Los Angeles twice at a younger age. Perhaps he had a stronger imagination than he ever realized, given how realistic his dream was. Especially with how vividly he could still recall that woman's breathtaking face.

"What was her name again?"

He shook off the useless memories of the dream as he walked the elegant halls of the embassy, suddenly aware that the colonial décor was in juxtaposition with the cold, institutional exterior of the building. Heavy curtains draped every window, and the desks were molded after vintage furniture.

Sometimes, the strangeness of the typically American designs made him forget where he was. Part of him was still at home, on soil that had comprised his DNA and fashioned him into the man he was today. His father, Jeffrey Cooper, was a district court federal judge for all of his life before he passed away in Sam's senior year of high school. His dad had taught him the value of integrity—to do what is right even when those around you challenge it.

"The best way to know the difference between right and wrong is to educate yourself, Sammy," his father had always told him with a firm pat on the back. "Learn the truth about the world around you, and it will become easier to find yourself, no matter where you are."

It took Sam a while to fully understand the importance of this sentiment. It wasn't until he realized he would have to adapt to his new, busy lifestyle in a new country that it really struck him. There is always more to learn about yourself and more to redefine when you find yourself somewhere new. And yes, Sam loved being a traveler, but sometimes his solitude left him without a lifeline.

He hoped that seeing Kate later today would anchor him again.

Sam shook hands with visitors but didn't notice the sensation of their skin on his. He answered phone calls with diplomats stationed in other countries, but couldn't make sense of the words leaving his mouth. What were once the motions of his daily routine seemed foreign, and although Tiffany affirmed what he knew to be true without having to confide in her—that he was still doing his job accurately and with dignity—he still did not feel the usual satisfaction that his career gave him, no matter how hard he smiled and pretended to.

***

Sam sat at a table near the window, idly adjusting his place setting as he waited for Kate. She was already a few minutes late, but he tried not to let it bother him. After all, he knew how hectic the life of an ambassador could be.

The waitress checked on him numerous times, filling his glass of water and attempting to take his order, which he declined politely. The sun was hitting the tablecloth with its warm glow, while Sam allowed the heat to calm him. He observed the buildings surrounding him, making up stories about the people behind the windows he couldn't see into. They were blacked out by shadows.

His phone buzzed on the table.

"Hello?" he said with a casual cadence, even though he knew he was about to be let down yet again.

"Hi, Sam," Kate replied, mournful.

"Something came up?" he asked knowingly.

"Yeah... it's Sara. She's not feeling too good today, and, well... I'm needed at home." Kate rarely shared details about her troubles with Sara. To Sam, it always seemed like she assumed he wouldn't care enough to listen—that he'd be just as indifferent and dismissive about mother-daughter issues as her ex-husband.

It stung that she seemed to think of him this way, hiding such an integral part of her life, but he couldn't force her to indulge him. By now, he'd learned that the more he tried prompting information about Sara from her, the more she withdrew into herself.

Sam guessed she simply didn't think it was his place to know more about her affairs at home. Besides, the occasional date and the invitation to his bedroom hardly afforded him full access to her life.

"I understand." He played with his fork, gently mashing it into the tablecloth. He tried not to think about how he was using the voice he usually reserved for business meetings. "I wish you both the best."

"Thanks, Sam. I appreciate you. *Really* appreciate you." Kate's relieved sigh echoed over the phone.

"No need to thank me, Kate," he dismissed her relief as casually as possible. Maybe it will make Kate believe he truly doesn't mind. "See you soon, yeah?"

Kate gave a rushed farewell before Sam hung up and placed his phone in his pocket, not wanting to be disturbed for the rest of his meal.

He flagged down the eager waitress and asked her to take away the second menu.

"Only one will be dining today," he said kindly.

He tried his best not to let the waitress's pitying expression get to him. It was clear she felt bad that his date had failed him, but Sam ordered and ate his food without revealing how upset he truly was. One more meal alone surely wouldn't kill him. He downed his glass of wine and tried his best to convince himself that the sentiment was true.

***

Sam stretched out on the couch with Chalk jumping up to join him at his socked feet. He had just prepared to watch a new movie when his phone rang.

He sighed, knowing it was Kate following up about their earlier conversation. Sam just hoped that she wouldn't ask him if he at least still had an enjoyable lunch. Somehow, that would make things ache even more if he was forced to lie and say that he did.

She had a bad habit of never letting their minor road bumps go, and while Sam knew it was her nature to make up, he just wanted to forget about today's events and lose himself in his sleep. It didn't help harping on over the same issues. He picked up anyway.

"Hey," Kate said all too casually.

"Hey there," he replied in a flat tone.

"So, I just wanted to apologize to you about lunch."

"You don't need to, Kate." They had probably had this exact same exchange of words about a dozen times before. Sam felt like he was so practiced in it that he might as well be a prerecorded voice actor reciting the same lines over the phone.

"But I do." Was he imagining things, or did he detect a faint trace of breathiness in Kate's voice? Was she getting emotional? Chalk raised his head in alarm as Sam sat up straighter, paying careful attention to her words. "I feel like I'm always rushing to get away from you..."

Her admitting something like that felt a bit like a twist to the knife. "You have a daughter, Kate, and I knew that before we started this whole thing. It's not like I don't understand..."

"I know, and that's not even what I'm apologizing for—"

"Then what is it?" he asked carefully. Part of him wished they were having this conversation in person. He would have much preferred being able to look into her eyes while she was telling him all of this.

She sighed. "I don't know. I think I'd like us to spend more time together; it just never feels like... the right time, if that makes any sense. Our lives are both so hectic, Sam."

"Yeah... Kind of shit to be a diplomat dating a diplomat. We didn't think that through, huh?" His chuckle dried out as Kate didn't laugh along at his weak attempt at lightening the mood.

The urgency of his heartbeat was preventing him from getting comfortable on the couch again. Chalk gave a concerned whine, which Sam quickly attempted to ease with a rub between the dog's fluffy ears.

Whenever he had these conversations with Kate, he always worried they would end with the dissolution of their relationship. He didn't know why he was holding on so tightly, but the thought of her leaving his life felt more unbearable than the distance that already existed between them.

The thought of having no one, of starting completely new with someone who lacked Kate's insight into the life of a diplomat... loomed over him, rising like Singapore's tallest skyscraper.

"We're about to enter another season of travel, too," Kate continued. "So, who knows how often we'll see each other."

"Yeah..." His chest tightened unpleasantly. She was going to say the words any second now. What could he possibly say to make her stay? Would anything he had to say be enough to actually change her mind?

What would be the point of forcing something between them if it simply did not work as smoothly as they had both hoped? If Kate didn't feel up for dealing with the added stress to her life anymore?

Sam had never intended to be yet another worry for her. He had sincerely believed he could be okay with the whole casual thing, but it was becoming more and more obvious that it simply was not him.

And she was saying it. The worst was coming true. "I just... I'm worried we don't have what it takes to make it, you know, work long-term."

"Are you saying we should—"

"Stop seeing each other? No—no, no."

Sam settled back against the pillows in relief. Chalk rested his head on Sam's leg, enjoying the steady flow of pets he was receiving.

He let Kate continue. "I just feel like we're friends more than lovers sometimes, Sam, and I wonder how all this business is going to add to that. We need to figure out a way to find our rhythm again, or else we'll really be..." She cut herself off from completing her sentence.

But Sam felt too on edge to keep dancing around it. "Or else we'll really be breaking up."

"I really love our time together, Sam—you know that. It's amazing to know I can come to you after a long day, and we can just make it all go away for a few hours..." Her tone was heavy with unspoken meaning, and the memory of doing exactly the same thing during their time together the previous night made Sam clench his jaw.

He wished they could stop the conversation there and focus entirely on the parts of their arrangement that were working so well. But Kate, as he already knew, had more to say.

"We've been struggling for a while, and... I don't want us to drag this out just *because*, but I also don't know what to do to fix everything that's making it harder than it needs to be."

"I don't know what to do, either, Kate. I'm really sorry things have gotten this complicated in the first place..." He exhaled slowly, feeling nothing and everything all at once. The remote was in his hand again, the screen flashing as he flipped through channels while his mind grew numb.

Kate breathed into the receiver, but neither of them had anything further to contribute. They couldn't even talk their way into a better relationship, for every promise they made would be one they eventually gave up on, and they both knew it.

"What are you doing?" she asked after a while.

Sam shrugged. "Watching TV."

"Anything good on?"

"No..." He put on a romantic comedy—he'd been feeling in the mood for one all day—and eventually, the distant sound of Kate's breathing was drowned out by the cheesy dialogue.

They hung up the call at some point after they both admitted to themselves that nothing they had to say was going to make this conversation suck any less than it did.

Sam curled a pillow under his bicep and allowed himself to be eased into the fuzzy comforts of sleep by the warmth of his dog at his feet and the predictable themes of the rom-com playing out in front of his eyes.

***

The door was there once again, in the grey expanse of his subconscious. But this time, it was open a crack.

Sam reached forward once again, curiosity getting the better of him.

What happened the previous time he stepped through this doorway?

All he could remember were flashes of caring chestnut eyes and delighted smiles. Was that it? Was he going to see her again?

He pulled the door open further and stepped through.

Ch. 3

"A Life in Dreams"

Sam sank into his rolling chair, exhausted, as he took a much-needed breather. His fingers felt rigid from constant exposure to disinfectant and hours in rubber gloves, while his eyes burned from the intense amount of concentration it took to perform surgery. He had been doing them back-to-back today, and he silently cursed himself for allowing his receptionist to book him such an absurd schedule.

Oh well, he thought. *People need help.*

Back in his office and opening up his email, Sam dug through the barrage of messages for notes on his patient Mr. Asfahani. There, buried under a slate of attachments, were his test results. Sam carefully studied the data, biting his lip as the graveness of Kareem's condition became apparent. He had to get him in urgently. He had truly hoped that the older gentleman's condition would not call for it, but he knew the benefits of completing the surgery far outweighed the risk of letting it go untreated. He quickly prepared the information to pass on to his receptionist.

There was a knock at his door. Mike popped his head into Sam's office. "You comin'?" he asked.

"Just give me a second," he replied, tossing the mask dangling from his ear into the garbage and gathering the results he printed off.

Mike followed him to the reception desk, where Sam instructed his secretary to call Kareem immediately and arrange for a bed as soon as possible.

His assistant Maria raised the receiver to her ear, ready to dial the number on his medical records. "On it, Doc. And if his daughter answers—may I share the information with her?"

Anxiety twisted in Sam's stomach. *Shiva.* Given her concern during Kareem's previous consultation, she would be beyond worried if she heard he would be needing surgery. He bit his lip as he considered Maria's question.

"Yes, but Maria, please make sure she's informed about everything. Her father sometimes struggles to remember details, so if she's available, it might be best to relay the message to her directly. Just—try not to alarm either of them too much," Sam said, striving to act cool as thoughts of Shiva swarmed his mind.

"Of course," she responded with a smile, narrowing her eyes at Sam slightly. "I know how to do my job, Doctor, I promise."

"You're the best." He grinned as the woman shook her head playfully.

Mike whistled in impatience at Sam, and they headed out the door for lunch.

***

Mike and Sam sat in the sterile cafeteria, eating takeout they'd ordered to avoid the tasteless food that was being served up to the rest of the staff. Sam often criticized the hospital for preparing such pitiful nourishment—people were sick and maybe dying; they deserved something better to lift their spirits. More often than not, the meals felt like a punishment, and he skipped them whenever possible.

Mike munched his burger while Sam picked at his fries, his thoughts elsewhere, as all the feelings he'd been suppressing finally surfaced. Everything he'd been pushing aside to focus on work came flooding back—a tsunami he didn't want to stop.

"What's got you tongue-tied, buddy?" Mike asked between bites of his greasy burger, the fat-soaked bread squishing in his grip. He licked the sauce off his fingers.

Sam paused. Though Mike was aware of his attraction to Shiva, he didn't know how much to reveal. Perhaps his feelings were best kept under wraps while he sorted through them. Then again, Mike was his closest friend, and behind all the teasing, he knew Mike had his best interests at heart. So he said, "I'm thinking about asking this lady out, but I'm not sure... how *ethical* it would be."

"Is this about that woman who came with her father? What was her name again? Sheba?"

"Shiva," Sam corrected. "But yeah..."

"That crush hasn't gone away yet, huh?" Mike teased, grabbing a few fries from Sam's pile after finishing his own. Sam didn't really mind, but he still shot a playful, warning glare at his friend.

"It's only been a *day*," Sam defended the intensity of his infatuation with the art gallery manager.

"Come on, man. She looks cute, and I haven't seen you go out on a date in months. Maybe even a year." Mike seemed horrified at the idea of going without a woman's touch for that long, wincing dramatically at Sam. To be honest, Sam wasn't thrilled about the situation either, but after his last relationship ended when the woman moved out of state, time had just slipped away from him. With his constantly busy schedule, he had barely noticed that a year had passed.

Mike watched him with a sense of brotherly admiration and said, "You *deserve* it. And you need it at this stage."

"I don't *deserve* a date with Shiva, Mike."

Mike rolled his eyes. "You know what I mean."

"It's just... She's going through a hard time, you know? Taking care of her dad and his condition, it's definitely rough, and I don't want her to feel cornered—like she has to say *yes* or risk me not treating her father."

"She's not gonna think that, Sam. You're really overthinking this. If she doesn't show interest, you just back off—simple as that. I'm sure she'll see that your intentions are good."

Sam contemplated Mike's advice, but he still wasn't certain. He understood the power he held over Shiva, especially in such a vulnerable moment, and he didn't want to gamble his chances with her by taking such a bold step at an inappropriate time.

He didn't want Mike to feel like he hadn't taken his word seriously just because Mike had a reputation for messing around with girls' feelings before he settled down with his fiancé, Julia.

"I'll consider it," was all Sam could say in reply, and Mike seemed happy enough with that response.

***

Sam sighed as he opened his locker, removing the cap from his matted, dark hair and grabbing a fresh set of scrubs from his bag.

He wasn't able to clock out for the evening just yet, but he still needed to clean himself off after Kareem's surgery.

It went spectacularly—there were no dangerous surprises or tense moments, his entire team was prepared and moved vigilantly, and they managed to keep the patient stable the entire time. At Kareem's age—touching the start of seventy—his body's response to being opened up and meddled with was always a potentially risky wager, but the old man had truly been taking care of himself between operations and treatments.

Sam was sure that this was in part Shiva's doing, and he wanted to thank her, to let her know what a wonderful job she had done in supporting her beloved father on his health journey so far.

After a quick shower and a small snack break at home, Sam returned to the hospital hallways and flagged down a group of nurses to find out where his patient was resting.

He didn't have to fight for their attention, though, as the moment they spotted him, the three women turned to face him with ready smiles. It was rare that they would be caught off guard by a doctor paying a visit to a patient in residence. But on top of that, Sam knew they had a reputation for being the clinic gossips and were always loitering around the reception area for intel on the doctors and patients.

"Afternoon, ladies." Sam grinned at them with a polite incline of his head. "I'm here to check up on Mr. Kareem Asfahani." Hoping he didn't seem too eager while asking, he glanced past the nurses down the hallway. "Has his daughter, Shiva, happened to come around for visiting hours? I was hoping to discuss some things with her."

"Oh, Doctor Cooper," the red-haired lady, Susan, said. "She was all in a panic."

"Rambling and pacing outside his room," confirmed Lelanee, who wore round glasses that magnified her bug eyes. "We couldn't get her to calm down."

"She was so sure *something* bad would happen during the surgery," chattered Susan.

"But we said—" interjected Caroline, a frizzy-headed woman with a busy lanyard around her neck, "and didn't we say this, girls?"

The group of nurses concurred the unspoken phrase with stern nods. "We said, 'Doctor Cooper is a magician on the operating table,' and we told her that her father couldn't be in better hands than yours."

"And, as always, we were right." Lelanee smiled cheerfully.

"She showed up with Mr. Asfahani and pretty much guided him to the doors of the operating room," said Susan.

"Where is she now?" Sam asked, and then quickly added, "So I can tell her the good news. Ease her mind once and for all." Sam hated that his calling for surgery was the reason behind Shiva's intense worry today, but he supposed that if you were someone who cared that deeply for your parent, it couldn't be avoided either way. He simply hoped that seeing her father's health improve after his recovery from the operation would make it all worth it to Shiva.

Lelanee consulted a clipboard. "Patient Kareem Asfahani and his daughter have been moved to room 301 for some relaxation and mild supervision, given her state of distress."

"Thank you, ladies."

Sam wasn't far from their room, and after a few moments in the hallway, he found his knuckles knocking against their door as a quiet forewarning of his entry.

The scene before him was standard for a post-operation setup—Kareem was fast asleep in his slightly raised bed, and Shiva was at his side, gripping his hand as she quietly wiped tears from her cheeks, raising her head at the sound of someone entering the room. Surgery always seemed to be harder on the loved ones of the ill—perhaps there was a level of acceptance in death that the patient reached, something that couldn't be felt or understood by those around them.

A bright bouquet of yellow tulips sat on the bedside table. It seemed to light up the room equally as much as the stunning woman.

Sam cleared his throat. "Miss Asfahani."

She looked up at him tearfully as Sam came to stand next to her. "Doctor, are you sure..." she began, but she did not even think to complete her question after Sam smiled at her with a careful nod. The tension seemed to bleed from her expression as she swallowed back her tears.

"Everything's fine," he stated in full confidence as he glanced over at the monitor displaying Kareem's heart rate. He kept his voice as low as possible so as not to disturb the peacefully sleeping patient. "There were no complications during the surgery, and we expect your father to make a full recovery in no time."

Shiva got up from the uncomfortable hospital chair to meet Sam where he stood, taking his hand in both of hers. Her palms were cold from the air conditioner's breeze blasting into the room.

"Thank you for being so kind to my father," said Shiva. "I know some people might think that I'm overreacting a little—but I can't tell you how grateful I am that the surgery went well." Her eyes swam with tears as she delicately blinked them away. "I just don't know what I would do without him."

Sam squeezed her fingers in the most professional way he could. He understood exactly what Shiva meant. He always felt like he had lost a part of himself when his father passed away. He never wished that feeling upon anyone.

"You love your father a lot. I respect that, and it shows in how well you've taken care of him. He's perfectly healthy in all other aspects, and after this surgery, I doubt he'll have many more troubles."

"Well, health isn't exactly guaranteed to us, especially not at his age," Shiva countered, glancing at her father with a frown.

"Having people to support you and care for you goes a long way in staying healthy, I can promise you that. Just keep doing what you're doing, Shiva."

She grinned at him for a long moment, tenderly clutching Sam's fingers. "You're such an attentive doctor. I'm so grateful he found you. Some of the doctors we've seen before... they didn't seem to have a heart as beautiful as yours."

Sam had always felt a rush of appreciation knowing his patients and their families had the best experience possible with him as their doctor. He was well aware that many of his peers had grown insensitive over the years, losing sight of the true purpose of their profession—to help people.

They tended to blame indifference and claimed that it was impossible to care for every single person who crossed the threshold into their consultation room. Perhaps it was because Sam didn't have a family or children of his own to worry about, but he still felt it was important to make a personal connection.

He rubbed the back of his neck with the hand Shiva wasn't currently holding in hers, sending faint sparks up his arm.

"Wow. Now, I've seen a few hearts myself, and I'm not too sure if I'd describe it as *beautiful*." He hoped a bit of humor would ease the heavy tension between them, but Shiva's warm gaze never left him.

"Believe me," she said. "I work with art. I'm around beautiful things all the time—I know what I'm talking about."

Sam gave a nod, as if he was giving in to her way of seeing things. He grinned widely. "Fine, then I will believe the professional on the matter."

She let out a small, nervous laugh before quickly wrapping her arms around Sam's waist, pulling him into a hug. "I hope that if I ever get sick, you'll take care of me too."

Warmth flooded through his body at her touch, and he fought the urge to hold her in return, to complete the embrace. She felt *right* pressed against his chest, close to his heartbeat. She felt like *home*.

"Of course," he said, his muscles relaxing in the circle of her arms despite himself.

When she finally pulled back, he flashed her a courteous smile.

He had to keep this professional—at least on hospital grounds and especially after an emotional day for

Shiva. He didn't want to push it. Not when the expression she was aiming at him was this unreadable mask, as if she didn't want to reveal the extent of everything she was feeling either. Her features glowed with a softness that sent Sam's pulse racing.

Sam hoped against all odds that the slight smile she offered him in return meant that the hug she just gave him made her feel exactly what he was feeling, as well.

He cleared his throat to break the tension and left shortly after, wishing Shiva and Kareem all the best on his road to recovery.

His arms still buzzed with the memory of her embrace as he made his way home for the day. His skin pulsed and radiated as if electrified by her touch. He imagined that it would be a while before he recovered from the feeling of her.

***

At the start of the week, walking out of a meeting at the embassy, Sam could not contain himself any longer.

He tapped Tiffany's elbow to get her attention and beckoned her into an empty hallway, where she gave him a quizzical yet excited look. Tiffany was in her late forties and still seeking out exciting adventures at every turn. She had been with Sam from the beginning, always claiming how much she admired his determination in the work field. She often mentioned that she found massive benefits from Sam's success, as it allowed her to tag along with him from country to country.

Tiffany was always the first to book an interesting cultural experience or an immersive dinner featuring the local cuisine of whatever place they traveled to. Sam appreciated her can-do attitude most of all. Her positive outlook and general enthusiasm made it difficult for him to yield to exhaustion.

She had never married or had children, but she had always said it was for the better—with her mind perpetually occupied by Sam's needs and schedule, she'd never remember an anniversary with her husband or a recital for her child. It quietly made Sam's stomach drop with guilt whenever she said something to that effect, afraid that he was holding her back in life. But she kept assuring him that working with him only ever made her flourish.

Now, as he ensured the coast was clear, Sam was confident Tiffany would have valuable insight to offer. Or, at the very least, an open ear to speak into.

"I feel weird, Tiff," he announced.

Her face drooped a little, switching immediately into Mother Hen Mode as she inspected his features for some sign of disease. "Okay, um, is it your stomach? Head? What kind of pills am I being sent out for?"

"Oh, no." Sam held up his hands, trying to ward off her worry. Bracing himself for how ridiculous this might sound, he took a deep breath. "I've been having dreams. *Real* dreams, like where I'm this surgeon hitting on my patient's daughter."

Tiffany seemed simultaneously intrigued and deeply confused. "And?"

"*And* they're elaborate. They continue, night after night, picking up right where I left off. I go to sleep as Sam Cooper, the one you're seeing before you, and wake up as the other Sam Cooper, the doctor who lives in California with a crush on this absolutely amazing and beautiful woman."

"I still don't see what the issue is." Tiffany shot him a knowing smile. "That sounds like a pretty entertaining dream to me."

"I mean, I'm not saying it's a problem per se, but it is strange, isn't it?" Sam was starting to worry that he sounded absolutely insane. He did his best to explain why he felt so unsettled.

"Everybody has all ten toes, and the world looks exactly as it should be. But the worst part is—and I know this sounds a little creepy—but this woman, Shiva? I can feel her touch. I can respond to it. It's on my skin, even now. It's like when I wake up here, in Singapore, my head is back in California. It feels *too real*."

Tiffany contemplated the information, and Sam could see her growing accustomed to the details. "So they're not surreal?"

"Right."

She pressed the back of the ballpoint pen in her hand against her mouth while thinking. "And they move along chronologically, as if you're actually living out each day?"

"Correct."

"And this woman—"

"Shiva."

"Right. Shiva never changes? She looks the same each time?"

"Yes."

Tiffany clucked her tongue. "While I love a good fantasy, Sam, you're probably just watching one too many soap operas. I know you have a weakness for them. Don't worry, that's still our little secret, but they must be bleeding into your dreams. Shiva's an actress whom you're admiring, and now you're imagining a world where you're together. Standard stuff, sir." She shrugged like it was the most simple thing to understand.

Sam was sure it seemed like the kind of story one could wrap their head around easily if you excuse it as just a random bunch of dreams, but he wished he could make someone understand just how real his dream world felt. It was as if his reality in Singapore was nothing more than a dream to the Sam Cooper in Los Angeles—like the doctor version of him was somehow just as real as the diplomat version of him.

Sometimes, when Sam woke from those dreams, he could swear he smelled the sharp scent of alcoholic disinfectant on his hands.

"But I've never seen Shiva before," Sam argued. "I've never seen *anyone* from these dreams in my actual life. Imagine—there, I have nurses, patients, and friends... I have an entire life, and a family history. And I remember it all as if I really live in that world. It's just too elaborate to be something I've completely made up out of nowhere. Or maybe I did, I don't know—but it's strange either way. To have this whole ordinary, detailed world that I keep returning to. What do you think it means?"

"I think it just means you have an overactive imagination, sir—and fortunately, that's not a medical condition," Tiffany said with a tight smile, seemingly holding back a giggle as she continued walking down the corridor.

"Maybe it is a mental condition." Sam ran his fingers through his hair and followed after her. "I can feel the weight of my life in California on my shoulders right now. I have things to do over there."

"Sounds like you need a vacation, Mr. Ambassador," Tiffany interjected.

"Yeah—yeah, maybe you're right."

"It's a good thing you're going out tonight," she said with a laugh, tipping her planner diary at him.

"I am?"

She gently smacked him on the arm with the very same diary, as if she could transfer the knowledge of his complicated schedule to him by force. "Your date with Kate, Sam. At the opera."

He checked his watch—it was later than he'd thought. "I have to get going soon, then."

"I've already sent your suit to the house."

"You're the best, Tiff."

"I know," she drawled, walking off to conclude the duties of her day.

***

The opera evening wasn't going as planned.

Sam and Kate sat awkwardly in their seats, the red cushions beneath them forcing a stiffness into their postures, making them appear tense—almost angry.

For some reason, that soured Sam's mood. He could see the strain in Kate's neck as she scanned the stage, holding the binoculars to her eyes with fake enthusiasm. He even caught her yawning a couple times.

Hoping to entertain her a little more than she seemed to be—though he wasn't particularly amused himself—Sam leaned over to whisper to her, "Do you think he has someone pinch him on the ass to get to a note that high, or does it just come naturally?"

Kate snorted, lowering her binoculars just enough to shoot a glare at Sam. Like the picture of a stuffy librarian, she shushed him.

He sat back in his chair, feeling a little astonished. Usually, they were able to pass around teasing jokes about the dramatic entertainers all night.

It was their *thing*.

But Kate seemed to have no interest in shared whispers this evening.

She looked splendid in an elegant yellow dress that cascaded in soft ruffles at her feet. Beside her, Sam stood in a flawlessly tailored three-piece tuxedo.

Together, they matched the grandeur of the Gothic decor and vaulted ceilings. Kate's old-world beauty shone even brighter in such an extravagant setting.

Sam wished that they felt as good as they must have looked together.

At the intermission, he excused himself to get some fresh air and grab glasses of wine for both of them. His mind felt persistently foggy, and it bothered him deeply, as if he were wandering through a misty expanse, with everything around him playing out at a distance.

He took a mouthful of red wine into his mouth, allowing the bitterness of oak and fermented grapes to fill his senses. It grounded him.

When he returned to their lavish seats, Kate looked exactly as he'd left her. The sight of her made his heart ache. Perhaps he was being too harsh on her due to his recent disconnect from reality, his muddled mind making it hard to notice anything but the negative aspects of her behavior towards him.

Or maybe she had simply lost interest. The possibility echoed clearly in his mind once again, unsettling him. Would he really blame her if she had?

He couldn't shake the slight agitation as the music returned, and the silence between Sam and Kate grew louder than the shrill of the operatic singers.

Kate politely applauded between pieces, while Sam indulged in a few more glasses of wine before the show concluded. His mind buzzed pleasantly, and as the opera unfolded, he allowed himself to be drawn into the story. The more he immersed himself in the performance, the more he found himself genuinely enjoying it.

As the lights illuminated the audience at the end of the extravagant show and its stunning performance, Sam turned to Kate and asked, "Would you like to come home with me?"

She gave him a knowing look, her eyes becoming dark with flirtation. The first sign of life—of the Kate he knew and liked. It sent his pulse racing in excitement.

But her pleased expression didn't last very long. She shook her head wordlessly, and Sam surrendered. There was nothing to argue over, and Sam didn't need her to provide an explanation for her *no*. No explanation even existed that would compel him to pressure her into changing her mind.

Despite swearing that they needed to do something to make their relationship better soon, Kate had made no mood to repair their bond. At least not for tonight.

With a sickly sense of disconnect, Sam realized that he wasn't bothered by the rejection at all, in fact.

All he could think about was that when he finally fell asleep in a few hours, it would mark the return of the world with Shiva in it, offering him another chance to savor the pleasure of her caring presence.

***

Sam stood alone in the empty hospital room.

The sheets were pulled tight over the thin mattress, and the blinds were wide open, allowing the sun to flood the room with heat. The floor had been mopped and waxed. The machines were silent, unattached to a patient.

The place seemed dull and lifeless without the presence of the cheerful bouquet of yellow tulips. Sam wondered about the possibility of placing flowers in every patient's room ahead of time. It was bound to lift anyone's spirits.

He had returned to the hospital bright and early, having jumped out of bed before his alarm in order to rush over to Kareem's bedside before his first appointment of the day, only to discover that the patient had been safely discharged the previous night.

"Such a shame they left already," announced Susan, who had sneaked up behind Sam.

In his malaise, he didn't react to her sudden appearance. With a mix of surprise and disappointment, he asked.

"Oh, his daughter did. She probably didn't like sleeping in a chair all night—but who would?" She released a laugh at her own joke. "He was good to go, though. Just as you said—healthy and able."

"So, Shiva packed up and left..." Sam murmured, lost in thought.

Susan watched him curiously. He quickly readjusted his features into something more professional.

He didn't need to give Susan any incentive to spread any overreacted stories about his interest in his patient's daughter.

"I'll be back later to check on my other patients," he said and promptly left the vacant room.

He still had no idea what Shiva's art gallery was called. Once again, he hadn't gotten a chance to ask. She had left before he could...

He didn't know why he felt abandoned at the thought that Shiva left after their conversation the previous night. It wasn't like Shiva had known him beyond a medical setting, and he had done what he had to in order to take care of his patient with better results than he could have dreamed.

Perhaps it was Sam's fault for getting so ahead of himself in imagining that the undeniable chemistry he felt for her was reciprocated.

He finally saw an opportunity to complete his home, to create new familial memories in such a beloved place. The charming yellow walls of his family house were begging to echo with the sounds of laughter and singing and buzzing conversation during a delicious family dinner once again.

Sam had been captivated by Shiva's beauty and had started filling in all the gaps with his boyish fantasies—of course he was disappointed when they didn't materialize, but he had no one to blame other than himself.

No one had forced him to obsess over Shiva or to hold onto the hope that she might be the answer to his loneliness.

His time would come eventually, he reminded himself as he strode into his consultation room. It *had* to come.

But... Why couldn't it be now?

Suddenly, Sam was behind his dark wood desk, his fingers flying across the keyboard of his computer.

His screen glowed bright in his sparkling blue eyes, as he typed Shiva's name into the Google search bar without a second thought. Several websites popped up in response, all of which belonged to the exquisite woman.

He looked at her Instagram page first, opening up pictures of birthday parties, road trips, and dinners with friends, where Shiva held a glass of wine to her lips and smiled playfully. He watched her through the seasons, enjoying holidays with her family and fleeing to the southern parts of Florida during the mild winter months. California never truly got cold, but Shiva seemed to thrive in its perpetual warmth. Her captions often mused about beaches, campfires, and poetry, reflecting her love for art and nature in her posts.

She also shared links to an art gallery, inviting her followers to explore her world of creativity.

Sam clicked the link, navigated to the page, and explored her workplace—a chic downtown gallery where her employees seemed more like friends, and they regularly hosted events for donors and emerging talents.

He marked down the location, his heart fluttering as he wrote her information into his notebook. Was he a stalker? Or was he putting himself on the correct path toward a destiny they both deserved?

Before he made any final steps, he decided to search through her other profiles for details of her love life. She had said that she was single, so a trip to her gallery would be harmless at worst.

He could ask about her work, assess her interest in a date, and if she turned him down, she'd never have to worry about seeing him again. He wasn't the type to argue with rejection.

If she had a boyfriend—although she didn't seem like she did—he would excuse himself and end his inquiry right then and there. Sam had never been the type to pursue a taken woman, regardless of whether she was happy in her relationship or not. He wasn't interested in diving into such messy situations, only to end up hurt the same way one day. The turbulent emotional games of his youth were long behind him—he was serious about finding real love.

Her Facebook page lit up the screen, and though it hadn't been modified in a while—her profile picture had a filter on it that resonated with her college years—her location seemed to be accurate. He carefully went over the rest of her personal details:

Studied at UCLA

Lives in Los Angeles

From Newport Beach

Single

Sam jumped out of his chair, exiting the webpage and grabbing his notebook with all the relevant information scribbled within.

He found Mike chatting with a nurse in the hallway and signaled that they needed to speak in private. Mike excused himself, while Sam guided him to the corner to show him the information he had just found.

"I got the address of her art gallery. She had told me to come by sometime," Sam proclaimed proudly.

"Who? Shiva's?"

"Shiva, yeah. I found her workplace. She runs an art gallery downtown. I'm thinking about going right now." His head and heart were spinning, his words rushing out like runners on a racetrack.

He couldn't believe he was admitting this. "I'm just," he continued, "still unsure of the—"

"Ethics," they said simultaneously.

"Calm down, Sam," urged Mike, punching his friend's arm playfully. "There's nothing wrong with asking a girl out. That's all you're doing. Aren't we all adults?"

"But I had to, you know, *google* her name to even find this."

"So? This is the twenty-first century. As long as you don't track down her parents, cousins, extended family, whatever, and start asking them for private details or pretending like you're already cool with her, you're not in the wrong. And if you're so worried about it, just fess up the first opportunity you get. If you're honest, she'll appreciate it."

"You sure?"

"I promise, dude. I wouldn't send you to the wolves like that." Mike nodded in assurance, his expression clear with the same professional earnestness that he usually only reserved for patients.

"I know."

"When have I ever let you down?" Mike and Sam shared a look. "*Recently*. I meant recently."

Chuckling at his friend's response, Sam paused, turning his attention to the notebook in his hands, which now felt like both a treasure and a burden.

He couldn't possibly give up an opportunity like this.

Mike grinned. "Go get her, Sam!"

Ch. 4

"Juggling Relationships"

The doorbell rang at Sam's residence. His heart jumped underneath his button-down shirt, and suddenly, he regretted how formal he appeared. Though it was a regular working day and Kate would know he was still in his business attire, he somehow thought the outfit was too much. Like she wouldn't be able to relax if he was in his stiffly ironed shirt adorned with sterling silver cuff links. He tried letting out the buttons, but it didn't seem to do anything other than make him look disheveled.

Frustrated, he answered the door, which Kate was now impatiently knocking on.

"Hello, you," they said simultaneously, both of them in states of mild disorder.

Kate was struggling to hold a large pot of flowers, which she promptly handed to Sam as she crossed the threshold.

"For you," she said, out of breath and sighing as if she was relieved to finally be rid of them.

He gave her a cautious smile and set the pot down on the kitchen counter. His maid would likely find a better spot for it. He trusted her instincts more than his own when it came to arranging a home.

"Thanks a lot, Kate," he said softly, his cheeks a little pinker than he would like to admit. Did the flowers mean she wasn't harboring a hidden wish to be leaving him? Or was he reading too much into a simple, thoughtful gesture between people who occasionally shared a bed? "What did I do to be spoiled like this?"

Kate shrugged, patting Chalk dismissively on his head as he came up to greet her—always the politest dog his owner had ever seen. She eyed Sam's barren mansion. "Just something to liven the place up a bit. I thought it would go nicely with your curtains."

Sam's glance moved from his grey curtains to the butter-yellow carnations on the table. He scratched the back of his head, wondering if he knew even less about homemaking than he had originally thought.

In the blink of an eye, the carnations were gone, replaced by tulips. A faint scent of coconut sunscreen drifted through the air, mingling with hints of vanilla and cocoa—the unmistakable fragrance of *Shiva*.

The sensation hit him so hard that he instinctively took a cautious step back, rubbing his eyes with his thumb and forefinger, as if trying to make sense of what he had just seen. Was it his imagination, or was she somehow finding a way to linger in his mind, unexpected and inescapable?

"Are you okay?" Kate's concerned voice swam through the echoing sounds pulsing through his head.

He gripped the edge of the kitchen counter to steady himself, huffing out, "Oh, yeah, no—I'm fine. Just... a headache. Don't worry about it."

Narrowing her observant gaze on him, Kate waited until Sam straightened his broad shoulders and smiled until she nodded in approval.

Sam suddenly felt deeply awkward with Kate standing before him. His limbs felt heavy with exhaustion—like he hadn't slept in days.

He had been preparing for a relaxing night at home, hoping to be ready for bed by nine, when he got a call from Kate informing him that she would be stopping by.

He planned to sit on the couch with Chalk curled up at his feet, waiting until sleep finally overtook him.

Given his weariness lately, he knew sleep would come quickly as long as he shut all the curtains tightly, ensuring that not even an ounce of light from the glittering city around him could bleed through the cracks.

He wanted total darkness and serenity.

He wanted to find Shiva at the art gallery.

That probably wasn't helping his nerves, either.

He had to get it together and be present for Kate. He owed them both that.

He couldn't let himself get lost in a fantasy, because that's all it was—just a made-up illusion, a figment of his imagination with no basis in reality.

Perhaps he had based Shiva off women he had known. He could certainly see small resemblances between her and Kate.

He desired Kate and enjoyed their nights together, when their lips met in nothing but kisses instead of arguments. He didn't need to make it more complicated than that, even as his feelings for her began to grow over time, especially as she opened up more about her personal life.

Kate's chocolate-brown hair was down across her back, the silky strands bouncing as she circled the living room, pretending to admire the furniture she had seen a million times before.

As he blinked again, he saw Shiva in Kate's place when she turned her back to him, when her face wasn't in view and his mind could drift. Could yearn. He pressed his palm against his sternum, trying his best to focus on the here and now without getting distracted by the powerful memory of Shiva's perfume while she hugged him tenderly.

Sam tried his best to recall a time when Kate had ever held onto him with such affection. Not even after their greatest days together...

He nearly jumped as she spoke, breaking him out of his swimming thoughts. "Alright, and maybe the flowers are also an apology. For the restaurant the other day, and then the opera..." She was referring to the second time she pushed Sam away by rejecting his invitation to come home with him. Was she really just trying to butter him up?

"Kate, we really don't need to keep hammering on about all of that. It's fine. I've seriously almost forgotten about it anyway."

This was clearly not the correct response, however.

Kate spun around, glaring daggers. "See, that's the problem with you, Sam. Why is it so easy for you to forget about me?"

His jaw fell open in a nearly comical gape. "What— No. No, that's not what I meant at all. Of course, I won't forget about *you*, Kate. It's just... I dunno! What's the point in holding on to that type of stuff? Life happens."

Needing something to do that would get him out of the icy eye line of Kate's glare, he turned and grabbed a bottle of wine from the fridge.

Silence filled the house as he popped the bottle open, poured two glasses, and carried them to the living room. It had become their tradition— or perhaps just a force of habit. She walked in, settled on the couch, and he handed her a glass of her favorite chardonnay.

"Do you even *care* to ask how my day went?" she asked as she gripped the glass from Sam's hand, pointedly avoiding touching her fingers to his like she usually did.

Sam winced. "Shit, sorry. You're right." He took a deep breath, filling his lungs and readying himself to ask the question before hesitating. "But... What about our *No Work Discussions* rule?"

"To hell with the rules, Sam!" Kate snapped, throwing her free hand up in frustration. The wine in her glass swirled much too close to the edge of her glass.

Irritation prickled its way up Sam's spine. He clenched his jaw.

"Alright," he replied, deciding to take a genuine interest in whatever had Kate so on edge today. Maybe it could even help them get to the core of their disjointed interactions lately. "How was your day, Kate?"

"My day's been hectic," Kate began, perching herself on the armrest of Sam's couch. "I've been in meetings all morning with the Minister of Defense, trying to pitch the idea of an upgraded naval fleet supported by the U.K."

"That hasn't happened yet?"

"Nope."

"But they're Commonwealth." Sam settled into the armchair across from Kate, taking a sip from his wineglass.

"I know! And we already have such a large presence here it's a bit ridiculous it's not a two-way street. The U.K. already has so much money you'd think they'd give just a bit to help the countries that rely on them. I mean, that's what I think at least. If we're trying to keep people happy, equality—even if it's just an illusion—is the right way to go."

Raising his thick eyebrow slightly, Sam asked, "So, you don't *really* want Singapore to have as good of a navy as Britain?"

"It wouldn't be *as* good, no, but that's not even what I'm trying to accomplish," Kate huffed in annoyance. "It's just a bit of a financial boost from the U.K. to go toward an upgrade the Singaporean navy genuinely needs. And besides, doesn't everyone think their country should be so mighty that it stands alone in a sea of competition? Shouldn't it hold complete power over its nation and people?"

"Sounds a bit... problematic."

Kate laughed into her glass as Sam shifted uncomfortably in his seat. Maybe he was being reminded of why he happily agreed to the *No Work Discussion* rule in the first place. This always revealed a different side of her that he was never very happy to see.

"Don't call me a fascist or anything, Sam. I know you Americans would prefer world domination over united nations."

"*Bollocks,*" Sam muttered, pretending to cough into his fist.

"Don't mock me, either." Her eyes narrowed dramatically.

"But we *are* a part of the U.N.," Sam replied with confidence.

"For now. It's probably all a trick."

"Just like your aid with the Singaporean navy." Sam tipped his glass towards her.

Kate smirked, running the tip of her tongue over her sharp teeth. "Touché." She was starting to get annoyed with him; Sam could tell in the way her shoulders stiffened.

She took a large sip of wine, then said, "There's also the matter of James." She practically spat out the name of her ex-husband.

The sound of it made Sam's hand curl into a fist on his lap. He knew a little of how unreliable the guy was, how he made extravagant promises to little Sara but never followed up on it. Needless to say, he wasn't the biggest fan of him either.

He let her continue. "He's coming down later this week to pick up Sara and take her on some guilt-ridden trip to Japan."

"You think he's plotting something?" Sam asked, studying her tense expression for any hint of fear for her daughter's safety. Would it be overstepping completely if Sam stepped in? He nearly cursed himself for the thought.

Kate would lose it if he ever suggested anything as intense as that.

"He *is* plotting something. There is no doubt about it. Either he's got a favor to ask, or he's lonely. Both of which will mean he's infiltrating my life in some way, and so he needs to get Sara all worked up."

Kate got up and started pacing across the living room. Chalk watched her every move with concern in his eyes. Still, his tail wagged subtly at her presence. She went on with her rant, venting her frustrations without pause. "He wants to try getting Sara on his side for once, because he needs to show me what a good father he's decided to become. I don't know why he thinks he has to prove something to me. He's not *mine* to care about anymore."

"Maybe he has regrets," Sam stated mildly. He didn't feel like he was addressing James, though. Not while part of him was wondering if Shiva would be just as protective of any children—if, in his dreams, he ever settled down with her.

Kate rolled her eyes. "Everyone's always got an excuse for James. He knew what he was getting into, alright? From the day he met me, he hated that I worked. And not only did I work, but I was good at my job, I was needed, I was flown places—and now I'm here, doing placements as an ambassador.

He could have shared this experience with me, but instead, he chose to shame me for 'leaving our daughter' high and dry to pursue my career."

Kate was intelligent—Sam had known that from the moment they met. It was part of what made her so irritating to him in the first place. And since they worked in the same field, her opinions on matters always caught his attention, no matter how sarcastically she chose to present them.

But it always came with the added difficulty that it rarely felt to Sam like he was ever stepping away from work when he was with Kate. Like he somehow still had to be sure to carry himself with the grace of a diplomat around her, for fear that it might embitter the bond between the two countries they represent.

Sam thought about how Shiva didn't have the same knowledge of healthcare or politics—beyond what she had dedicated herself to researching in order to better help her father—but maybe it was a good thing.

As a doctor, Sam could be the one teaching her something, or better yet, he could remove himself from work entirely and give over to immersing himself in learning more about the art world from Shiva.

He could leave his work on his desk and let it go at the door, embracing Shiva with a fresh spirit after every heavy workday.

Maybe that was what these insane dreams about Shiva were trying to tell him. Perhaps his problem was that his life had become so consumed by the same world, the same people, and the same political tensions that he was now burned out.

Kate was also busy all the time because of her intellect. Behind her jokes about the situation between Singapore and Britain, he knew she was the only person who could manage such a complex issue. It wasn't as simple as she had put it, and he admired her ability to find the light in such dense matters. There were few people who were as excellent in their jobs as Sam knew Kate was.

Sam filtered back into the conversation Kate was still having. Dimly, he realized his glass was empty. He really needed a refill—to soften the edges of his anxiety, which sent his mind spinning a mile a minute with thoughts.

"I mean, *look* at her," Kate grunted, referring to her daughter. "Sara is happy and thriving, and she's going to have so many experiences the other kids her age won't. She'll grow up to be this well-rounded adult who's worldly, speaks and understands different languages, and comfortable with the foods and norms of various cultures. You know how much of a rarity that is?"

Sam just nodded along a little dumbly.

Seemingly encouraged by the gesture, Kate spouted on, "If I had kept her in London, she'd probably be addicted to fish and chips and never want anything else. And you know what the worst part is?"

Trying to muffle a smile at the thought of a little British girl demanding fish and chips for breakfast, lunch, and dinner, Sam asked from behind his fingers pressed against his mouth, "What is it?"

"When I got pregnant, James filled my head with all these grand stories of us being a traveling family. He stopped hounding me about my job and seemed to fully embrace it—at least until my maternity leave ended, and reality kicked in."

She jabbed her finger in the air, as if imagining it pressing against James' toned chest. "Then he was, you know, actually responsible for helping me raise a child. Suddenly, he became acutely aware of just how horrible it was to parent solo whenever I was gone. I went back to work, and all those fantasies about this incredible life together just flew out the window. Because the truth is, he didn't mean any of it. He didn't want me; he never did. If he had, he would have either left me alone or sucked it up. I love my job, and I'm not giving it up for *anyone*."

In all the months that Sam had been seeing Kate, she had never admitted any of this to him. The corners of his mouth tugged downward as he looked at her. "I'm really sorry about that, Kate. That... It must have sucked."

Kate barked out a laugh, shaking her head sharply and falling onto the couch, "*Must* it have, mm?"

Sam angled his head to the side, wordlessly pleading with her to go easy on him. "You know what I mean." He couldn't put Kate through the wringer again. Hadn't he, too, been complaining about her schedule and lack of availability?

For all their issues, he couldn't deny that he had intentionally stepped into her life. Meeting her daughter wasn't a mere coincidence; deep down, he had been contemplating it—experimenting with the idea of immersing himself into Kate's world and exploring the possibility of building a new family together.

They could alter course—he could boldly tell her he wanted more affection—that he wanted to go all in despite Kate's reservations about seriously dating again—or they could make a plan to detach their lives for the time being while they figured stuff out.

The odds of which option Kate was more likely to choose made Sam bite his lip.

"You're awfully quiet," Kate mused. He could see the regret painted across her features. "I'm sorry if talking about James upsets you. I know it's probably not easy dating someone with so much baggage. But he's Sara's father, you know? And I can't punish him or her for trying to have a relationship. As much as I may despise him, I have to keep things civil. I can't imagine that's what anyone wants to hear, though."

"It's not that," Sam assured her. "I know what I signed up for."

"That's what they all say, isn't it?" she said with a small laugh.

She then shifted closer to him, reaching over and grabbing his free hand in hers while maintaining eye contact. "What would be your breaking point, Sam?"

"Huh?" He was taken aback.

"Exes? Cancer? A second child with a different man?"

"I'm confused..."

"Oh, come on. You can't pretend like you don't have your limits. Something will drive you away, eventually."

"I don't think like that, Kate."

She let go of his hand, seeming disappointed at his unwillingness to play along. "We all have our deal-breakers."

Possibilities swam through his mind. The loudest pounded through his mind, but he refused to speak it out loud in case it could upset Kate. Instead, he countered with, "Then what's yours?"

She seemed to shrink away from the question. "Changing the garbage but not replacing the bag."

"So, I should have scared you away a long time ago," Sam joked.

He could tell there was a genuine answer roaming around in her mind, but she couldn't decide whether or not to express it.

Neither of them felt like they could risk being vulnerable enough with each other to express it. Sam ran his hand through his hair in frustration, just as he was about to be honest—to offer up what his true deal breaker was—when Kate's phone rang.

He held back a sigh. Kate excused herself from the couch and strolled out onto the windy balcony, which was connected to Sam's living room.

He rose, refilling his wine glass. Staring at it for a second, he downed the contents with a few gulps. His hand smelled like the achingly sweet floral hand lotion Kate used when he wiped his mouth with his knuckles.

Hatred crashed over him as he wished for the scent of vanilla and sun-kissed skin instead.

His eyelids were becoming heavy as the alcohol warmed him up from the inside. Maybe it wouldn't be such a bad thing if Kate left. He didn't like being tipsy around her—he always found himself fighting internally to keep himself back from saying three sacred words to her. He always hesitated because when he got his sobriety back, he was never sure if he really did love her or if it was just the alcohol making him want to say the things he *wished* were true.

Maybe he would have a clearer picture of how he really felt about her if he imagined her response to those words. Would he be heartbroken if Kate told him that she didn't love him at all?

"I have to go," Kate proclaimed from the hallway. She was already pulling on her shoes, her phone still in her hand.

"Sara?" Sam asked. He couldn't get himself to move from his position behind the kitchen counter to see her off.

"Yeah." She merely passed him to get to the front door and didn't stop to kiss his cheek goodbye like she usually did. He heard the door unlock. "I'll make it up to you, Sam."

"It's fine, Kate. I understand." The words tasted like cardboard on his tongue.

"Sam?" She wasn't going to leave until he looked at her.

His shoulders tensed as he turned around. He just wanted the inevitable to be over. "Yeah?" He attempted to cover his pained expression, but he wasn't sure he was successful.

"I truly am sorry." She looked it, her usually severe features softened in the shadows falling across her face. She really was an amazing woman.

"I know." Sam gathered all the strength that was left in his body to tease his facial muscles into a small smile.

Kate sighed and was gone.

With his place absent of another human's voice once again, Sam sat on the couch for a while. Overwhelming sensations coursed through his body, a host of conflicting emotions he couldn't address or pinpoint. It made his head spin more than the wine did.

Every time his eyes closed for that brief millisecond of a blink, he saw his comfortable little family home in Los Angeles with its cheerful yellow walls instead of the colorless, impersonal home he lived in now in Singapore.

He poured himself another glass of wine, finishing the bottle he had opened for Kate. Maybe he really was starting to lose his mind.

He ordered a hot bowl of Katong laksa as takeout from his favorite restaurant near his home. He savored the creamy coconut milk-based broth, loving the refreshing kick of lemongrass and chili as he slurped up the noodles. Food like this warmed him, body and soul. It settled his nerves slightly.

Preparing himself for bed promptly after a warm shower, he situated himself on the couch in front of the TV, playing yet another romantic comedy. The world blacked out around him.

He was in a deprivation tank of his own creation, and he was certain his mind would eventually wander back to Shiva.

His dreams would create the soft curves of her shoulders and waist, the delicate lines of her smile. It would detail every perfect piece of her with warmth and love. It would make him feel secure.

He sighed happily as sleep washed over him.

***

Once again, the door. The wood was polished to a wonderful sheen, and the golden doorknob featured intricate floral details.

Sam could hear the noises of L.A. traffic rushing by. He could see the rays of the coastal sunshine through the open door.

He stepped closer in excitement, then broke into a full-on sprint. Mist curled around his feet, propelling him forward.

Toward Shiva and the promise she held.

Sam burst through the door with zero reservations.

***

It was late afternoon when Sam arrived at Shiva's art gallery.

It had been a slow morning at the clinic, and after reviewing his schedule for the day, he was delighted to see no upcoming appointments or surgeries. That meant he could take off early, and his staff were happy to accommodate him—he'd been pulling doubles and working overtime often enough.

He needed a little break.

The easy workday meant his cheerful attitude remained intact as he drove over to the gallery. Even with the traffic, Sam's spirits held high. He sang along to the radio, rolled down his windows to let the warm breeze flow through the space, and kept one eye on the time.

He had plenty of it; he was in no rush.

Unsurprisingly, the gallery was nestled atop a hill in a trendy part of town. Large windows showcased the magic inside, and Sam eagerly bounded up the long column of steps, a general admission ticket in hand. He had purchased it ahead of time, wanting nothing to disrupt his arrival and occupy his thoughts once he arrived.

He attempted to slow his pace as he entered the hallway, not wanting to seem out of place among the tourists and artists milling around and socializing casually.

When a quick glance through the space didn't reveal Shiva, he decided to make his way through the gallery, eyeing each piece slowly and allowing himself to be drawn into deep contemplation.

He didn't want to seem like he merely came to the gallery to see her with no interest in the art at all, but he also didn't want to pretend he came only for the art, either. Starting a relationship with Shiva on dishonesty was not his intention, but he didn't want to alarm her by approaching her too directly in her place of work, either.

He was overthinking it. He needed to relax.

Stopping in front of a huge canvas at about the sixth painting he inspected, he felt his jaw fall open slightly. The painting was some abstract expression of a man's face.

The paint was layered onto the fabric in thick, sweeping strokes of blue and purple—oil paint, or so Sam believed. With a quick glance at the information card posted next to it on the wall, he confirmed his suspicion.

The face was simple in its design, yet Sam couldn't help but feel a strange familiarity—like his own muscles remembered making that exact expression before.

It wasn't exactly sadness—more like a deep sense of letting go, tangled with desperate hope and an internal scream for something *more*. He had never imagined a painting could stir such intense emotions in him, but its raw humanity left him deeply moved.

How could someone possibly be that talented—able to capture such complex emotions on an empty white canvas with nothing but the magic of their hands and a few tubes of paint?

After a half hour roaming through the cavernous corridors, accidentally bumping into other visitors and genuinely becoming immersed in the art, Sam craned his neck around the room without care for his conduct.

He wanted to find her. He wanted to talk to her about all the amazing things he was seeing around him. The beauty that she had so carefully curated.

Her words still echoed through him—that he had a beautiful heart, and she knew it because she worked with beautiful things every day.

Now, the true weight of that compliment hit him differently.

Just as he casts his gaze out through the space, he spotted her by the window. She was staring out at the city, which buzzed with life.

The modern architecture of the skyline stood in unusual contrast to the mountains that surrounded the area—nature was always on the sidelines.

Sam wondered if the brutalism of the landscape was what inspired Shiva. He could ask her that. It would be a good way to get to know her, by understanding where her love for art started.

He approached the woman, who continued to stand with her back turned to the gallery, her face distorted by the glass windowpane.

"Shiva?" Sam asked politely.

His pulse froze. He was wrong. The woman who was now smiling at him had a distinctive appearance, marked by unique hairstyle, natural waves, slender lips, and elevated cheekbones. She was pretty in the way a recent college graduate who hadn't lost her enthusiasm for life yet, but she certainly didn't harbor the same simple elegance as Shiva.

"Are you looking for Shiva?"

"Um—" Sam's brow furrowed, and the woman picked up on his confusion.

"I work here," she said with a laugh, pointing to the name tag pinned to the pocket of her blazer: *Andrea T.*

"Ah, I see." He felt his cheeks warm as embarrassment settled over him. This hadn't been the interaction he anticipated, and now, word would get back to Shiva that a stranger was asking for her. He wiped his sweaty palms on his well-worn jeans.

"Unfortunately, Shiva has already left for the day," Andrea explained, picking up on his unsaid question. "She had to head home to take care of her father."

"Oh, Kareem. Of course." Sam mentally kicked himself, realizing his mistake. Naturally, Shiva would be at home to support her father—he was still in recovery from his surgery.

"You know him?" Andrea perked up, smiling with the interest of someone trained well in customer relations. "Well, I guess I'm not shocked. His art was pretty popular back in the eighties."

Sam scratched his head shyly. He had known Kareem was an artist before he retired, but he never realized that the man was *that* well known. It made him feel a little stupid for not realizing he was dealing with a small-time celebrity, but he quickly recognized that knowing wouldn't have deepened the respect he already had for the man. All he said was, "I'm his doctor, actually."

"Even better—so you're not a *lunatic* fan." Andrea gave a quick shiver of disgust at her own words.

Did that mean they often dealt with unpleasant people asking after Kareem? Sam couldn't help but frown at the thought. "No, no, I'm not. I was just here for Shiva," he confessed. There was no sense in crafting a lie, no matter how minor it is. He didn't want it to snowball later.

Shiva would certainly be hearing about him now. Preparing to excuse himself, he hunched his shoulders, his disappointment obvious.

"Wait," Andrea offered, "I can tell you where she is."

"Um... is that—I mean, is that allowed? Seems a bit dangerous if there are crazy fans looking for her and her dad..." Sam stammered.

"I'm not gonna tell you where she lives, but if you have something to say, you might be able to catch her at the grocery store down the block. I'd say she'll get there around, oh, seven o'clock." The young woman paused with a quick smile, pressing her hand against her chest. "I'm her personal assistant, too, sometimes," She happily clarified.

Trying his best not to feel like a full-blown stalker at this point, Sam thanked Andrea appreciatively before making his way to the grocery store.

Ch. 5

"Chasing Art"

Shiva was roaming the produce aisle, picking up fruit, feeling it, and dropping it back into the bins. He watched her cheeks curve to meet the reach of her smile as she brought an apple to her nose, inhaling the sweet fragrance; she put it in her basket.

As she paused in front of the avocados, Sam decided he had lingered long enough. Before her fingers could brush one of the purplish-green fruit, he grabbed it instead and held it up to his face.

She blinked, taken aback at first, but upon glancing at Sam's playful expression, she softened.

He demonstrated its ripeness, pressing down on the outer skin. "Not ready yet," he mused.

He grabbed another, this time jamming his thumb into the top of the avocado, and it caved. "Just right." He offered it to her so she could take it.

Still stunned, Shiva accepted the offering, a smirk creeping onto her lips. "Do you usually shop for your groceries here, Dr. Cooper?"

"Just thought I would stop by," Sam offered, shoving his hands into the pockets of his jeans with a shrug, but he knew it was a little too vague.

"Yeah? You live around here?"

His shoulders dropped. "No," he admitted, "I was at the gallery first. Looking for you, I might add. And a little birdie told me you'd be here."

"Ah, that must be Andrea," she said knowingly, with a hint of recognition in her voice.

"It's alright that she did that?" Sam asked as he followed her up the aisle.

Now she was headed for the dairy section, and her pursuit of a soft cheese overtook her shopping mission. She showed Sam a package of goat cheese with raspberry jam. "Thoughts?"

"Too mild," he replied after a brief inspection.

"Andrea's been trying to set me up for months," Shiva explained, good humor gleaming in her eyes. "But the last thing I expected was that she'd start sending you boys after me!"

"Oh, so I'm not the first?" They both looked away, blushing.

"You're the first to follow me to the grocery store, that's for sure." She eyed him up and down with a faint teasing judgment to her expression.

"I wouldn't say I *followed* you here," Sam corrected, embarrassed that he had ever agreed to the gallery attendant's plan. He should have just waited to meet Shiva at her workplace another day.

"It's alright," she said, filling her cart with a few items. "I don't mind. I'm glad it was you."

Sam's heart fluttered. "Do you always look this beautiful when you visit the grocery store?"

Shiva chuckled, waving off his compliment with a blush.

"What would you say to me walking you home?" Sam proposed.

"I'd love the company." She was dragging her cart over to a cash register, and Sam was close behind. "You just can't go inside."

"Are you afraid I'm not a gentleman?" He helped unload her groceries onto the conveyor belt.

"No, I'm sure you're the picture of a perfect gentleman." Her gaze traveled across his face again, then slipped down his tall form. A lot more appreciatively than before.

It made Sam's cheeks flare up.

She laughed at his surprised expression, gripping his forearm. "No, apart from wishing to remain the picture of a decent lady, myself, and not bring home the first man I pick up in the fruit and veggie aisle... I'm actually just worried about the conversation my father will trap you in. He's lovely, but my God, is he chatty."

She stacked her arms with bags as she thanked the cashier, who eyed the two of them smugly. Shiva didn't seem to notice, but Sam couldn't help but wonder if it was obvious to everyone around him that he was absolutely smitten with this woman.

Somehow, he hoped that it was.

Sam swiped all the leftovers with a grin. The plastic weighed down on his fingers, but he didn't mind the temporary discomfort.

He and Shiva exited the store. Before them, the sky was painted in breathtaking shades of purple and pink. Sam lingered for a moment, watching it, suddenly feeling as if he were back in the gallery, staring at the most stunning piece of art this city had to offer.

"Shall we?" Shiva asked with a smile softening at the corners of her eyes. Sam nodded and jogged to catch up with her. She turned down a tree-lined street, the yellow lamps starting to glimmer to life along the sidewalk.

It was a fragrant and gentle evening, and Sam was swept away by the romance of it all.

An ordinary task with a beautiful woman, the perfect weather, and a quiet, hopeful neighborhood to walk through.

Sam took a deep breath of the fresh air, picking up a hint of Shiva's perfume from how close she was to him. He looked down at her peaceful features and asked, "How's your father doing? After the surgery and all."

"He's good," Shiva replied. "Getting better every day, too. I can't thank you enough for sav—"

"Ah. Please, you really don't need to keep thanking me for doing my job," he interjected as carefully as possible.

Her eyes swam with emotion as he met her gaze. "Really, Sam, his condition has improved so much... I was scared I'd lose him too. I'm still not over losing my mom. You really saved him. You saved me."

"Oh, yes, I'm really sorry about your mom," he added gently after a brief pause. "Kareem mentioned it earlier. He held her in the highest regard."

He hesitated before continuing, "As I said, it's just my duty. And I would have worked just as hard to get the best possible outcome for *anyone*." While it was reassuring to hear that Kareem was recovering so well, Sam wished he could find a way to convince Shiva that he wasn't the hero she believed him to be.

"I know, I know..." Shiva sighed, resuming their walk toward her home. "Family means a lot to me, and knowing there's someone I can count on to protect them is a huge comfort. Job or not, you're making my life better."

She glanced at him, her expression softening. "And... yeah, it's been really hard for my dad—he was very attached to her."

Sam nodded, absorbing her words. After a moment, he asked, unable to keep the faint edge of emotion from creeping into his voice, "Are you and your father very close?"

As he waited for her reply, the emptiness of his own home crept into his mind. Though the halls were decorated with framed photos of summer vacations at the beach and cozy winters around the fireplace, his family was rarely there in person anymore. The memories only made the silence feel heavier.

"Of course." Shiva's mood instantly improved as she started talking about her family.

"My father was always a family man, and as we grew older, he worked hard to instill in me a sense of duty toward family. I think a lot of people grow up, move out, and feel resentment when their families ask for help. Part of me gets that—you want to be your own person, and you have your own problems. But I also believe it's rare to find people you truly love."

She continued, "I was lucky to be born into a family I actually like and respect, and I wouldn't ever want to toss that aside like it's nothing. When I have kids, I want them to value their relationships the same way—with each other and with their parents. People aren't disposable, you know?"

"That's an amazing sentiment. I think it is pretty rare to find that, so I definitely agree it's more than worth holding on to. I'm honestly a little jealous," Sam admitted with a slight chuckle. "I grew up around here, and yet I seem to be the last man standing. Everyone's spread out across the state, and it becomes hard to do more than send off a text every now and then. I miss how regularly we all used to come together when we were still kids."

"Do you get along with them, though?" Shiva asked sweetly, making it clear to Sam that she would be understanding if he said he didn't.

"Yeah, which makes it worse in a way. I'm not excommunicated or hiding from them; I'm just without them for no real reason other than distance and convenience and the fact that everyone has their own separate lives now. I think it'd be easier if we were fighting or hated each other."

"Well, we can't always get what we want," she said, teasingly bumping her shoulder against his arm.

Sam gasped in mock offense. "You think I *want* drama?"

"Doesn't everyone?" Shiva shrugged playfully. "Just enough to spice things up every now and then. Sometimes it helps to be mad at the world.

Makes you feel like you have a purpose—gives you something to fight for."

"Okay, so step number one to a life filled with drama—be mad at the world so you can fight for something," Sam nodded, his expression turning serious. "People say romance is worth fighting for... Does that count as an acceptable step two?"

"Depends," she said, trotting up the stairs to her house. Putting the grocery bags down, she unlocked the door but turned around before she opened it, a sly smile across her lips. "Do you plan on breaking my heart, Sam?"

The openness of her expression and the boldness of her question nearly sent him tumbling down the stairs. He met her gaze, studying the way the light of dusk illuminated the warm brown of her eyes.

"I wouldn't dream of it," he replied honestly. His heart pounded in his chest. It somehow felt both slower and faster than it should be beating. And he should know—he was a doctor.

She motioned for him to drop the groceries at her feet, and he followed her silent command. "Alright, then. No drama it is."

She was gathering as many bags as she could while she readied herself to go inside. Sensing their time together was running out, Sam knew he had to act quickly—and cleverly. "How about we start our undramatic first date tomorrow? Say, seven o'clock?"

She paused, narrowing her eyes thoughtfully, a small smile playing on her lips. "You don't waste any time, do you? Is that a doctor thing?" Her smile softened as she added, "But I think nine would be better. It's easier for me after my father has eaten and gone to bed. That way, I know he's taken care of, and we can have something a little more... relaxed."

"Of course. I'll be here—not a second after nine," he replied with a grin. "I wouldn't want to keep you waiting. And for the record, I don't usually waste time when it comes to what draws me in." He paused, his grin widening. "I'm looking forward to our... relaxed evening."

Shiva offered him an excited smile and a quiet goodbye as she entered the house, not shutting the door behind her until Sam had given her a quick wave and descended the stairs.

He strolled back to the grocery store, where his car was still parked in the lot, whistling as he gazed up at the populating stars, wondering how he had gotten so lucky.

***

A picnic blanket was spread out on the grass, displaying a delightful spread of food as Sam and Kate stretched out under the warm sun. Her backyard was massive, bordered by a towering hedge that offered the household the utmost privacy. Sara had a simple swing set toward the back wall, but the yard was notably free of toys, balls, and all the little odds and ends that Sam and his sister had once considered essential to the wild tales they would invent while playing outside.

Although the grass was tidy and the yard was well-kept, Sam could somehow tell that Sara and Kate didn't spend too much time out there.

The picnic was Kate's fulfillment of the promise to make things up to Sam, and he hated to admit that it was working, to some extent.

Chalk chased Sara around the grass, barking and jumping and wagging his tail furiously.

Sam was quieted by the scene, allowing the comforts of Sara's laugh and Chalk's playful barks to calm him as he settled in for a nap.

Kate rested a hand on his chest, gently stroking his muscles before she faded to sleep, too. Between the warmth from the sun and her affection, he was full. He would let himself imagine, just for a second, that this meant he and Kate were something real. He could pretend like he had finally found the woman whose hand he could put a ring on. A woman who wanted to build a family with him just as badly as he did.

As his mind drifted, anxiety ignited a flame within him, and his body twitched.

He had eased the guilt he felt over his endless dreams of Shiva by promising himself the fantasies were a search for attention that Kate wouldn't give him, and yet there they were, lying beside one another on a bed of grass, her daughter playing joyfully in the background.

This was a day spent as a family, the one he had tried to avoid cultivating because of his fear of becoming too involved, too fast. The last thing he wanted was for Kate to feel like he was pressuring his desires onto her, pushing her to enter into another serious relationship when she was still wrestling with the consequences of her failed marriage with James.

Shouldn't love, if it were real and meant to be, come with a certain fearless courage? The kind that urged people to risk it all, to take a chance, trusting that things would work out in the end?

Sam couldn't shake the feeling that such ideals only existed in the romance movies he'd been indulging in lately. Real life, he knew, came with baggage—complex, heavy, and far harder to set aside. All he wanted was for Kate to let him share some of that burden from time to time.

He had been telling Sara stories of his travels while they enjoyed their picnic treats of fresh fruit, heart bread, and decadent cheese.

He tried his best to answer her questions about math and science since her latest obsession was with space and astronauts. Sam drew on every bit of general knowledge he possessed. He had always been more of a debate team kid than a science buff.

Kate was observing their connection closely, staring at Sam as if she were meticulously evaluating every interaction he had with her daughter, and his willingness to participate in their lives.

Luckily, Sam had some experience with kids, thanks to his sister Judy's children. One was about Sara's age, and the other was younger. He didn't get to see them very often these days, but the playful tone of conversations with them was mostly the same.

Sam felt simultaneously disappointed and relieved when Sara eventually abandoned chatting with the boring American man and her mother, leaping up to play a game with Chalk that was a healthy mix of fetch and American football.

Kate winced every time Sara tried to tackle the sidestepping Swiss Shepherd in a vain attempt to win his blue ball back from him. At least, for moments, she had stopped staring so intensely at Sam.

Now, dozing peacefully in the sun, Sam tried to breathe deeply. He did his best to keep his mind from wandering from this scene. There was no need to think of Shiva when he had all this in front of him right now.

Kate's form pressing against his side was warm and comfortable. But, as he often found when they slept next to each other, she nudged him away or pressed her knees into his thigh painfully in an attempt to lay comfortably. Sam rarely said anything about it, despite the muscle aches he usually ended up with.

None of that mattered. He would fit with Kate even if it hurt if she was meant to be the one for him. He breathed in her scent of rose and shampoo.

He sneezed explosively, sending Kate scowling in annoyance at the unexpected break in their peaceful nap.

Sara laughed as she and Chalk raced back to the picnic blanket once again. The dog stood beside Sam, resting his full body against his owner for comfort, his tongue lolling out with each heavy pant. Sam realized he really ought to take him to the park more often, just like he used to.

"Mommy, Sam," Sara hummed.

"Yes?" Kate replied for them both, shielding her eyes from the sun to look up at her brown-haired daughter. Sara's braid was coming undone, and she tugged thoughtfully at its tips.

"I have a question."

"Another one?" Kate sounded mildly annoyed, so Sara trotted over to Sam and stood before him, a goofy grin on her face, which was sticky with juices of the watermelon they had enjoyed.

"Shoot," Sam said, pleased to have seemingly captivated Sara's trust.

He wondered what it would have been like to be a father from the start—passing his wisdom on to a curious, growing mind and seeing pieces of himself live on in this other person, this other world, as they grew up.

He didn't hate the idea of having children of his own one day, but... would Sara ever truly feel like his daughter if he and Kate got together?

With James constantly in the picture, how could he expect her to ever see him as a father?

Sara tilted her head a few degrees to the side, frowning seriously. "How come the world doesn't sink underwater?"

Kate snorted a laugh, laying back on the picnic blanket with a huff. She threw her arm over her eyes, using the opportunity of Sara's occupation with her interests to get another precious few minutes of napping in.

"The world is suspended in outer space by the gravity of the sun. There's no water out there for the world to sink into." Sam tried suppressing his amused smile. Sara deserved to feel like he took her questions seriously.

Fidgeting with a charm on the bracelet around her wrist, her frown deepened. "No, I mean, like, Japan and England. They're on the water."

"Yes, that's right, but—"

"She's just worried about her trip," Kate interrupted, seemingly not napping after all. She sat up again, rolling her eyes instinctively at the thought of James.

"It's a good question," Sam attempted, but Kate brushed him off.

"She hasn't spent this much time alone with her dad in... I don't even know how long."

Sara's small eyes filled with tears. The sight of it made Sam's gut twist. Maybe bringing up how cool satellites are would cheer her up, or telling her about the first dog in space, Laika... Remembering how that story ends made Sam clench his jaw shut.

"Why can't you and Sam come?" Sara muttered to her mother.

"Oh, honey, Sam's just a friend from work," Kate replied reflexively. She shot him a sideways glance, realizing the magnitude of her words too late. They stung Sam, despite him feeling the same way.

He wiped a hand across the edge of his chin to hide the way his mouth pulled to the side unhappily. He dimly realized he needed a shave.

Kate brushed past her stinging comment, over-correcting massively by telling Sara, "But maybe we can all go somewhere together, one day."

Sara's expression glowed once again. But somehow, seeing the hope flood to her face at Kate's words just made him feel more uneasy. He could tell it was an empty promise in the way Kate's eyes glimmered with guilt while she did her best to avoid Sam's eye contact.

How far could his understanding of her reluctance to remarry soon really go? How many more times could he push himself to squash any hopes before they even arose?

Could he really bring himself to say, "Just keep staying, stay a little longer," when he knew, deep inside, that Kate only wanted him for the luxury of a familiar, warm set of hands to hold?

He dutifully helped her as she started clearing up the snacks on the picnic blanket, complaining about the potential of bugs.

Any pretense of domestic bliss came undone within Sam. He hated to draw comparisons between a real woman and a figment of his imagination—no matter how vivid. But he couldn't help thinking about the romance, bliss, and tenderness that existed between him and Shiva while doing something as mundane as grocery shopping.

Wasn't that what he was supposed to be feeling for Kate?

He departed from Kate's home shortly afterward, his mind racing with questions and impossible solutions.

Every time he thought he had it all figured out, a new revelation—whether good or bad—would hit him, leaving his stomach tied in knots.

He longed for a change, to trade the familiar Singapore skyline for the golden hues of a California sunset outside his window. He imagined the feeling of his hands on the wheel of his SUV, driving toward Shiva's home. What he craved most was the simplicity of a connection unburdened by the pressures of a first date—no future to rush toward, no expectations to meet, just a bond free to exist in its own time.

His dream world—and the shining golden door in his mind that led to it—came swiftly that night. As sleep took him, the heavy ache in his heart dissolved into the grey mist of his dreams.

Perhaps there would be more answers waiting for him there.

***

Sam was singing along to the radio as he cruised down the highway to pick up Shiva that evening. The thrill of seeing her again made him feel as if all the habits he'd learned as an adult had flown out the window. For the first time in a while, he felt carefree—a welcome relief after another long day at the clinic.

When they arrived at an elegant seafood restaurant, a waiter led them to an intimate table on the terrace. They pored over the leather-bound menus in the soft glow of the candle between them, trading quiet giggles as they suggested dishes for each other.

"I don't know, you seem like a seafood soup kind of guy," Shiva teased, making Sam chuckle heartily.

"Hey! Don't knock it till you try it. Actually, it kinda does sound pretty good right now."

The sound of Shiva's clear laugh, the kind that came straight from the belly, made Sam's cheeks warm.

Running his gaze over her in a private moment while she contemplated the list of fruity cocktails, Sam was struck by her radiant face, awash in candlelight.

She had her hair pinned back behind her head, and she wore an elegant silk blouse with a high collar, in a shade of green that made Sam think of deep forest floors and vibrant, healthy leaves. The color seemed to bring an extra sparkle to her brown eyes as she raised them to meet his, catching him staring.

He expected her to shy away at the realization, but she matched his gaze, using the moment to admire his features openly as well.

"I don't know how the paintings in your gallery must feel when you stare at them during appraising," Sam half-joked, half-admitted, shaking his head gently.

Shiva smiled. Her tone was soft and private as she said, "Fine. I promise I won't stare at you like you are a piece of fine art if you promise to never stop looking at me like you want to take care of me."

Sam's heart raced in his chest. He wasn't entirely sure how to respond to that, so, after a brief hesitation, he simply reached over and slipped Shiva's hand gently into his fingers.

Thankfully, the waiter arrived to take their orders, and the conversation turned lighter in Sam's clumsy mouth once again.

He was deathly relieved when their drinks arrived.

Waves ebbed and flowed beneath the wooden boards at their feet, the gentle sound of the current drifting softly through the evening air. Sam watched in quiet tranquility as the moonlight danced and shimmered across the surface of the water.

"I never get sick of the ocean," Sam stated. "It's unpredictable, sure, and it makes our weather crazy, but I couldn't imagine looking out a window or across a parking lot and not seeing the water."

"So, you said you grew up here, right?" Shiva asked. It was such a typical question for a first date, but tonight, it felt like it was uncovering something deeper, as if it exposed an essential part of what shaped Sam into the person admired by Shiva, someone she was truly eager to know everything about.

"Never left," Sam replied. "Not much, anyway. The odd vacation here and there, but I mostly keep to the coast."

"I can't get enough, either. I get excited about having kids and how they'll wake up to this every morning." She paused and took a sip of her cocktail, her cheeks flushed. "Sorry, I probably shouldn't talk about kids on a first date."

"Why not?" Sam smiled at her playfully. "This isn't even the first time you've mentioned them to me."

She hid her face in her hands for a moment, then peered up again. "It scares men away. Works like a charm if you *want* them to run screaming, though."

"Personally, I think it's honest. Why get into a relationship with someone who wants different things? Everyone assumes they can adapt to wanting marriage or kids or learn to make compromises down the line for their partner, but I've never understood that. It seems like setting ourselves up for heartbreak by denying our true, significant desires."

"So, which is it? Kids or no kids?" Again, in that careful tone, as if she was ready to hear either answer without judging Sam's choice of response.

He leaned into the table, his eyes locked on her. "Kids."

A full grin broke out over her features as she took another sip of the fruity liquor. "Nice to clear the air about it right at the start of the night."

Later, they found themselves strolling barefoot along the beach, their pants rolled up past their ankles. The moon illuminated their faces as they spoke.

They walked side by side, their arms brushing against each other as they swayed. With each step they took, they drew nearer until their feet practically melded together and their hips were adjoined. Sam's limbs felt electric.

"What made you want to run a gallery?" Sam finally asked. Throughout the night, he found himself discovering more and more details he wanted to learn about Shiva—and to share about himself. The list was growing so quickly, it was getting hard to keep track.

"Oh, the usual. My father was a brilliant artist, and I wanted a place to showcase his work. I mean, he didn't need my help in that matter, but what's cool in New York doesn't always translate on the West Coast, so I had to craft a revamped gallery to get people to see his stuff. Along the way, I just really fell in love with art as a whole. I know it's so vague to say—*I love art, I love music, I love books*—but I truly mean it." The conviction in her body language confirmed it all the more. Sam listened with close interest.

"The history is endless, the rules are nonexistent, and how you showcase a piece is just as important as the piece itself. I create meaning by hanging something on a white wall in just the right way, and I think there's something so special about that."

They stood chest to chest now, Shiva buzzing with passion and Sam with pure admiration.

"I would love to see art through your eyes," Sam said, his chin down turned and angled toward her lips.

A moment passed between them, a silent exchange of choices. Finally, Shiva raised her gaze from his mouth, a playful spark in her eyes. "Not a fan?" she asked, her tone flirtatious.

"I feel like I just don't understand it as well as other people do. Unless it's a clear picture—humans and nature and scenes—it goes over my head. I'm a man of science, I guess."

"Maybe the problem is that you're thinking too hard." Shiva reached over and trailed her fingers over Sam's linen collar.

His throat felt thick with tension. "Yeah?"

"Yeah. Art is more of a feeling than a puzzle to crack."

Sam slowly ran his hands down Shiva's arms, their mouths inching closer.

A mischievous glint lit up her soft, delicate features, and she pulled away, the spell broken by her untouched lips.

"I should be getting home," she announced.

"I'll take you."

"You better," she grinned. "How else will I get there safely?"

The sky was dark as Sam pulled up to Shiva's little house—the light above the front door was on, illuminating the cracked concrete steps and the dusty curtains in the window.

Dropping her off was difficult. Sam didn't want the night to end, so he held onto the railing leading up the stairs like a life raft, silently hoping Shiva would change her mind.

Just five more minutes with you, he thought to himself. *That's all I need.*

Shiva stood with her back against the door, her flirtatious smile silently challenging him to resume what had been interrupted earlier.

"Goodnight, Sam," she whispered, her fingers tracing the curve of his cheeks.

Beneath her touch, he couldn't help but ask, "Can I see you again?"

"Of course."

"Tomorrow, my friends Mike and Julia are coming over for a barbecue. I'd love for you to join us."

"I'd love that, too."

She let herself inside. Decades of collected books were stacked on the floor in the hallway, and photos of kids of various ages hung on the walls. Some of them had to be of Shiva. Sam could smell the scent of freshly washed laundry, and something heartwarming, like the scent of sugar cookies, wafting from the house.

There was a full life waiting to be lived behind those windowpanes, and Sam felt a surge of joy at the thought of adding to their shared history.

After Shiva waved her final goodnight and shut the door, Sam stood on the front steps a while longer, his feet melted into the concrete.

He didn't want to go. He thought he had finally met the love of his life, and he couldn't spend another moment without her.

Life had already been long enough in solitude.

***

The next few days in Singapore passed in a blur for Sam.

Privately, Sam was floating on cloud nine from his date with Shiva in his dreams. Suddenly, it felt like he could see himself a little clearer—like he understood more about himself and what he was truly looking for in a relationship.

Maybe these dreams were less of a pathetic, lonely fantasy and more a glance into the life he wished he had...

The only way Sam could cope with the confusion about what these dreams meant for his future with Kate was to bury himself into work and long hours at the gym, as if staying busy would keep his thoughts at bay.

He mingled at functions and gave speeches that were heartily applauded; he took special envoys to the airport in ravishing cars and spoke about politics with an authority that denoted his many years of experience.

He used his refreshed spirit and sharpened sense of who he was to motivate him in his waking hours, trying his best to separate his brain functionality from the heavenly romance taking place behind the scenes in his dreamworld.

He shook hands firmly with political and public figures and kept a smile on his face that successfully hid all emotional confusion about his love life brewing behind his pale blue eyes.

He fought the persistent foggy sensation taking over his mind as he threatened to slip into daydreaming with each intense workout in the gym, laughing from his belly while playing fetch with Chalk in a local dog park, and found solace while jogging through the lush tropical nature reserve alongside his vigilant bodyguard.

At night, he finally surrendered all control, slipping into the tempting promise of a life that felt more and more tangible.

Ch. 6

"Lucid Dreaming"

"She fits into my life so easily," Sam mused. "It was like she had known my friends for years. She showed up with a bottle of wine and a bag full of snacks, arranging them with care on a platter she found in my pantry. I was amazed to see it—something I had long forgotten about was brought back to life by her. Mike and Julia just loved her, conversation was endless, and she stayed behind to help me clean. I can't remember the last time a woman helped me that way. It was like we were a part of a real team, you know? As a proper couple should be."

As Sam recounted the story to Tiffany in his office at the embassy, he vividly envisioned Shiva from his latest dreams. She was standing at the sink, scrubbing dishes, when he came up behind her. She turned to him with a devilish grin, bubbles of soap caught in her hair and on her forehead after she'd wiped her brow. Smiling, Sam brushed the soap away with his fingers as he leaned closer—a silent thank-you for how hospitable she'd been that afternoon.

Everything tasted sweeter when she was around, and he hadn't felt that intimate with his circle of friends in a while. He wanted more of it, for a life filled with Shiva.

She had mirrored his desires, and they leaned in for a kiss; but just as their lips were about to meet, the annoying beep of his alarm clock shattered the moment, pulling Sam abruptly from his dream.

As it continued to ring on his bedside table that morning, Sam stared at it hatefully, wishing he could return to his blissful dreamworld. His body felt like it weighed a ton, but he felt perfectly warm and comfortable. He did not want to move from his bed.

But he knew the day would reset in California by the time sleep took over again. He wouldn't be able to return to that exact moment anyway.

"What do you think it means?" Sam asked Tiffany, who sat across from him at his desk and munched on a bag of popcorn.

Tiffany shrugged. "I think you know."

He raised his eyebrows at her curiously.

"You've been saying it from the beginning—she's a family-oriented woman, perfectly designed by your imagination to be the ultimate adoring wife."

"Maybe, but I'm also not the kind of guy who just wants a wife to *serve* me."

"I'm not saying that, either, Sam." She swiveled in her chair to look out the window, her expression taking on an ironic look of meditation. "You just want to be loved in a completely normal way, where everybody has time to connect and your house feels like a home, not just a place to dump your dirty clothes."

"I guess..."

"Face it, Sam, Kate can't be *there* for you in a way that matters."

"That's not her fault, though. She's in a similar position with me." Sam rubbed at his heavy eyes, biting back a yawn.

"And maybe you don't like that, deep down. That doesn't make anyone the bad guy; it just means you want to settle down for once."

***

The hotel resort room was spotless when they arrived, and for hours, nothing disturbed its pristine condition.

Sam and Kate sat awkwardly on the bed, the covers still pulled tight against the corners of the mattress. They hadn't even ordered room service, unable to decide whether they were hungry. Their suitcases sat untouched, their belongings neatly packed inside.

They had spent the first few minutes quietly inspecting the luxuries awarded to them by the presidential suite, which included multiple televisions, a jetted bathtub, and an immaculate view of Singapore. But after deciding it was too extravagant for a single night, they ended up on the bed, struggling to make conversation, for their minds were both preoccupied with their troubles.

"Thanks again," Kate murmured, always the first to sacrifice herself to their awkward spells of silence.

"For coming, that is. I thought it would be nice to treat you—treat *us*—after such a hectic time."

"Especially after your fight with James," Sam added a little bitterly. This wasn't the way he imagined he would be wanted as a boyfriend. Then again, he wasn't even *really* her partner. He missed the simplicity of a barbecue lunch with his friends and Shiva.

The only reason he agreed to come see Kate tonight was because he knew she had been having a hard time. Did that make him supportive, or did it just mean that he was leading her on just as badly? His head and muscles hurt, and he squinted at the bright light in the hotel room.

"Yeah..." Kate admitted. It was a rough one. But you took my call and listened to me vent. You're always such a reliable shoulder to cry on." She patted him on the back like a friend.

He grimaced a little as he stared down at his hands.

"It's just so frustrating having to leave my daughter with him. I know he's filling her head up with fantasies about us getting back together. He can't take my no for an answer, so he's going to manipulate our daughter into wanting it so badly I have no choice but to agree."

"That's what the fight was about?" Sam asked. "Wanting you back?"

"In a way. He kept making comments about their trip to Japan—how he kept finding activities meant for a family: a husband, wife, and daughter. He always specified *daughter*, too, like I'm some idiot who thinks there are coupons targeted at couples with a girl. Sara is so upset to have to miss out on all this nonsense because I refuse to go. But I'm being blackmailed by the worst mistake I ever made, and I'm worried that one day I'll have to give in just to make it stop."

Sam opened his mouth to speak but hesitated. He wanted to ask if she was thinking of getting back together with him and if all her denial of him lately was just her way of laying the groundwork to make it easier for Sam to accept her eventual reunion with James.

That would have been a nasty thing to do, though. He was assuming the worst of her.

"I've said too much, haven't I?" Kate moaned as she brought her face to her open palms. She sighed deeply into her skin, the sound of her breath escaping through her fingers. Then she laughed. "I'm not helping us by constantly going on about that man. If anything, I'm adding to your list of reasons to leave me. Reason one: *can't be friends with an ex*; reason two: *always thinks my partners are the problem, not me."*

"I don't have some list of reasons to break up with you, Kate," Sam assured her flatly. "It's fine that you're venting. You're just having a day. I'm right there with you."

"Yeah? Things aren't going well at work?" She seemed to be making an effort to be soft for his sake, turning to give him her full attention for once.

"No, it's... I've been having these dreams," he began, his brain telling him to seize this opportunity to be vulnerable. A confession would put his mind at ease—Kate's reaction would affirm their connection and remind him of the illogical dreamworld he'd created.

Maybe she would recognize aspects of their relationship in his descriptions of Shiva, as he does, and they could promise to rekindle their spark based on a clear example of the relationship they both wanted. Well, Sam hoped they both wanted it, despite Kate's chilly attitude sometimes.

"Bad ones?"

"Maybe, depending on who you ask. They're just... very vivid," he said, gesturing to the length of his body. "I'm myself, exactly like this, from my head to my toes. Except I live in Los Angeles, and I'm a doctor in a clinic. I perform incredibly detailed surgeries, and I've started to date the daughter of one of my patients. Her name's Shiva, and I feel like

I know her. Not just in the dream, but when I'm awake, it's like I can still sense her around me. The days are playing out in real time, too—I go to bed here, and I wake up there to my morning alarm. I can spend a full day and night there, and then I'm back here in time for work. I don't miss anything in either dimension—except the only time I got interrupted was when... when we almost kissed."

Sam searched Kate's face for some sign of her inner world, but she wasn't facing him. Had she not been paying attention, or had he hurt her with his declaration?

Feeling himself panicking, he continued to explain Shiva. "Tiffany says this woman is just a solution to my loneliness. Not that I'm lonely with you, but we have to spend so much time apart because of our schedules and obligations..." The words were streaming out of his mouth now, anxiety and guilt making it hard to stop.

"She's not you; she doesn't even look like you. Well... that might be a lie. You're both very beautiful. My dates with her in my dreams have been mostly talking, so I guess I just need to hear myself. I want a sounding board—which... I know you would hate if I used you in that way. I'm not *using* Shiva either, though, I'm just—well, I don't know, really."

Kate laughed lightly. It was her laugh when she wasn't being genuine, when she was hiding her emotions. Sam chewed at his bottom lip. She shook her head at him. "You've got a wild imagination, Sam."

He braced himself; she looked to be composing herself, gearing up for something far worse than a forced laugh. "Is this your way of telling me you've met someone else?"

She didn't let him answer.

"I've been saying for a while now that you're bound to reach your breaking point with me. I just assumed you'd have the balls to leave me before you got yourself a new girlfriend. A bit classless, don't you think?"

Sam's jaw was slightly open, slowly absorbing her anger-filled reply while he considered her accusations. "That's not true," he argued, his own feelings on fire. "They're just *dreams*."

Kate's face was twisted with jealousy. Sam was taken aback by the expression. "Ah, so you're just a silly boy, then. Caught up in your sweet little fantasies of having a *regular* job and a *regular* woman. I thought you were supposed to want to be an astronaut or something? But you daydream about... this?"

"No, I'm asleep; it's just—you're not listening to me." He pressed his fingers against his temples, wishing his persistent headache would evaporate.

"Oh right, I'm sorry—I forgot to tell you how extraordinary your life is that you have to pretend to be someone lesser just to feel something new."

He winced, and Kate finally backed down. "That was meant to be a compliment, Sam."

"Yeah, sure..." Sam sighed. He didn't have the energy to argue with her over something so small. He just wanted to let her in on a part of his life, to maybe get her insights on the strangeness of his mind.

His life was being drained to fuel these fantasies, and he didn't know how to make them stop. He wasn't even sure he wanted them to stop, though. If anything, Kate's reaction only affirmed the sad truth—life was better with Shiva, even if she only existed in his head.

They went quietly to bed that night, each of them occupying their own side of the mattress. He listened to Kate's breathing, so out of sync with his own, and watched the world outside the window until it shifted into the Californian landscape of his dreams.

Sam was lying on the bed in his town house, and Shiva was wrapping her arms around him, inviting him to return his eyes to hers.

In his dreams, they made love for the first time that evening—it was tender and passionate, the kind of intimacy he didn't have with Kate.

Just when he thought he couldn't fall harder for the idea of Shiva, they solidified their connection.

Enveloped in the intoxication of their affair, Sam struggled to wake up in the morning.

He felt abandoned as his limbs fought against the tight covers to stretch and the scent of Kate's perfume invaded his nose.

She had been there beside him throughout the whole thing, an unwilling participant in his romantic evening with Shiva.

Even if he didn't let on to the events developing in his mind, he still ached for the touch of another woman while the one who actually existed, the one who was actually a fixture in his life, was probably waiting for him to come around.

When Kate began to wake, she seemed to be in better spirits, even kissing Sam delicately before getting up. Had he reached for her in the middle of the night, hoping she'd become Shiva so long as he kept his eyes closed? Was he acting out his love for another woman on Kate?

He couldn't ask her, and perhaps he didn't want to know the answer, anyway.

He didn't feel like the man he had claimed to be, and maybe Kate had every right to be angry with him.

Maybe he was a cheater.

Ch. 7

"Bonjour Paris"

Kate's expression was sour as she chewed her breakfast like it was a pile of something bitter. Apparently, the small shred of joy she'd experienced upon waking up next to Sam had been nothing more than a fleeting blip, a mere accident.

Sam, on the other hand, was feeling better after his intense, momentary regret when he woke up, and as soon as he and Kate were dressed and dining, with their bodies far apart, his mind inevitably drifted back to Los Angeles, where he knew he'd be waking up to a woman filled with love this evening.

He was seriously starting to consider if his life in Singapore was the true dream world—filled with confusion and misunderstanding.

Kate's aggression escalated as more time passed without Sam saying a word, lost in his own thoughts. Her knife scratched harshly against her plate and her teeth cut against the fork with each mouthful of speared pancakes.

Sam tried to ignore the hostility, not wanting it to push him back into the overwhelming sickness he had felt that morning.

"Are you okay?" He couldn't resist the question.

Kate shot him a stern look and pressed her lips tightly together before returning to her breakfast with renewed energy.

"The bed was a bit hard," he muttered, still trying to keep the conversation casual. He rolled his stiff neck. "I think I hurt my back a little."

"Next time, I'll spring for a nicer room," she replied bitterly.

For the rest of the day, Sam and Kate engaged in an odd battle. Neither of them left the room, which had been paid for through to the late afternoon, but Sam's attempts at a truce were useless.

Kate followed him around the suite, refusing to let him out of her sight—not only out of fear of his infidelity but also out of pride, too stubborn to admit her insecurity. She peppered him with questions about Shiva, pushing him away whenever he tried to touch her, and wondering loudly how Shiva might react if he approached her like that. She demanded to know whose skin was softer, whose hair was more beautiful, whose wardrobe he preferred.

Sam stopped answering after the questions became specific, feeling the urge to protect Shiva from Kate's vicious examination. Whatever he offered as an answer—whether true or as a white lie to spare Kate's feelings—was incorrect. She brushed off his sincere compliments towards her, insisting that he must be lying.

"We were never even really a couple, Kate," he finally snapped, frustrated by her accusations. "Even if I *was* actually seeing someone else... It's not like you ever wanted anything other than casual dates and a shoulder to cry on, which I don't mind! But would it have been so wrong for me to find someone who actually loves me?"

The hateful L-word did not improve her mood at all.

He had made a mistake by letting her in on his fantasy realm, and these were the consequences of his actions.

He had accidentally planted insecurity into a woman who claimed to be stubbornly independent, and now had to cope with the unfamiliar feelings that were arising within her.

He didn't mean to cause Kate any pain, but her bullying remarks left him feeling agitated. He had hoped that by sharing the vision of a relationship he really wanted, Kate would have agreed—that it would have brought them closer to the same page, somehow.

Would she be mad at him for having an imaginary girlfriend? Would she explain her feelings rationally and help him work through them?

Sam hoped he could control his dreamworld this way—he desperately needed someone to confirm he wasn't crazy and to dive into his mind to uncover the truth about his bizarre thoughts.

Eventually, Kate departed, notifying Sam of her leaving only when she had one foot out the door. She left him the access card so he could check out when he was ready, and finally, after too many hours tiptoeing around Kate, Sam was able to relax.

***

The world inside his mind was dark and shapeless that night. He experienced a single second of sleep, and then he was awake again.

It was his first dreamless night in a while, and Sam was unsettled by the disruption. It had to mean something, and he was afraid he wouldn't like the answer.

However, unlike the routine he had grown accustomed to, Sam was back in his residence in Singapore, surrounded by the emptiness of his pristine bedroom. It was his first night since the awful getaway to the hotel with Kate.

Perhaps he did deserve to be punished for his behavior toward Kate, but when he tried to call her, she didn't pick up. He wasn't all too surprised—she likely wanted all the space from him that she could get at that moment.

Still, he longed for a partner—without Shiva, he realized just how alone he was. It was a poor excuse to wish for Kate's company, but he didn't know what else to do. For all their imperfections, there was something between them—a history, a pattern, a bond. Despite his head-splitting bouts of confusion, Sam didn't want to sacrifice that for some dreams he had been having, no matter how real they felt. Given his position as an ambassador, he wasn't going to visit clubs and bars to meet potential women.

A couple of weeks passed, the silence between Sam and Kate stretching like an invisible barrier. He had given her space, unsure if his absence would heal the wounds he'd caused or simply deepen the distance between them. Yet, each passing day undermined his restraint and pushed him closer to reaching out.

Sam found himself rehearsing what he'd say, wondering if words could fix what actions had fractured. He knew it wouldn't be easy, but he had to try.

It wasn't just guilt that drove him; it was the unmistakable pull of their shared history, the connection they had forged in the short time they'd been together, however imperfect it might be.

He needed to hear her voice, to remind her—and himself—that there was something worth salvaging.

So, after wrestling with indecision, Sam picked up his phone and called her.

"Sam," she groaned after his third attempt that evening.

"Kate, I—"

"Listen, I don't want to talk."

"Can I see you? I know this is about the other night."

"*No*, no... I just want to be alone right now. It's nice with Sara away, and I never get the chance to be silent and motionless and do nothing."

Her voice echoed as the large, quiet room revealed her isolation. He knew she was lying; she often complained about her solitude, how she wished Sara was a bit older so they could talk about complicated things more and go on excursions that both of them would enjoy.

She needed company just as much as he did, but for whatever reason, they couldn't find solace in each other. Rather than running into each other's arms, they found reasons to push each other away. Sam had brought this upon them, but now Kate was hammering another nail in the coffin of their relationship.

"Enjoy your pathetic little dreams." And then she hung up. The blank dial tone made him feel worse than if he had never heard from her in the first place.

His thirst for affection only grew as his dreamlessness persisted.

Why couldn't he see Shiva anymore? Was Kareem doing alright? He was recovering very well, but Sam still felt the rush of responsibility to check in with the older man.

What about his other patients in Los Angeles? Were they being cared for?

Not doing double duty as a surgeon in his dreams meant he was less exhausted and more alert during his working hours as a diplomat, but his return to clarity didn't make him feel any better.

In fact, he was more aware of his emotional lows than ever, desperately trying to fill the void with nights out on the town, treating his staff to fun gatherings and fine dinners, and throwing all his effort and attention into his diplomatic responsibilities—or sometimes into workouts.

He ended each day exhausted, yet sleep felt cruel— an unwelcome thief robbing him of the oasis he so desperately longed for.

Finally, one night, after having a warm shower, Sam fell onto the couch in his baby blue T-shirt. He chuckled dimly as Chalk licked his cheek gently, as if he were concerned about how late his owner had returned home these past few nights.

The merciful wave of sleep rushed over Sam's mind within seconds.

***

The grey expanse felt familiar and welcoming to Sam. Mist curled around his ankles, and he breathed deeply in relief.

As he raised his eyes to the brown wood door that led to Shiva, he frowned.

The design of the door had changed completely. Now, it had a faded wood frame with stained glass panes down its length. The many colors of the glass lit up as light shone through from the other side without a source.

The sounds of chattering voices and the rush of traffic mingled with the distant clanging of church bells into a disjointed melody. Modern and ancient, all at once.

Excitement burst in Sam's chest. This was new. Grand and exciting. He reached out to the wrought iron door handle and stepped into the noise.

***

Sam jumped out of bed without missing a beat. His alarm went off at the same time—seven o'clock—and Sam strolled into the bathroom to take a quick, cold shower. Dressing in casual trousers, a neatly ironed long-sleeve polo shirt, and a blazer.

He took a breather before leaving the apartment, which retained the rich history Paris was known for. Between the original parquet floors, crown molding along the ceiling in each room, arched doorways that made him feel like royalty with each step as he walked through them, and the wire-fenced balcony he now stood upon, he felt like he was part of something bigger than himself.

For hundreds of years, occupants had been coming and going through these same doors, and now Sam was adding to it. Eventually, he shuffled down the steps of his vintage building, marveling at the polished black-and-white tiles he never grew tired of, and entered the bakery café just below his residence for a quick breakfast.

He sipped on coffee as he dipped croissants and fresh bread into a mug of hot chocolate, reading the newspaper alongside the elderly men who frequently stepped outside to smoke and the well-dressed women who fixed their lipstick in golden compact mirrors.

When he was finished, he generously tipped his waiter—an American sensibility he had yet to shake—and headed for the metro. The platform was as crowded as the train, and the trip to work was easily the worst part of his day. He couldn't complain, though—any big city had the same transit issues—too few options and too many people.

He arrived at the Haussmannian office building with the few firstcomers of the day. Sam, a top brand image consultant, had recently been transferred to the company's headquarters in Paris. The pristine building, with its gleaming façade, always looked freshly polished.

He nodded at the security guards as he walked across the glossy floors, his footsteps echoing softly in the grand lobby. Scanning his ID card, he passed through the gates with ease and stepped into the elevator. A few coworkers joined him, greeting him warmly as they ascended to their respective floors.

At the top floor of the brick building, Sam stepped out of the elevator with a cheerful *ding* and headed to his office where Tara, his assistant, immediately gave him a rundown of the day's tasks.

"David and Sary need you in the conference room to go over the redesign pitch; then, you have a lunch meeting with Gabriel to discuss their brand partnership. After that, the managing partner of Executive Media, Céline Kalotte, will be here to meet you and discuss the plans for the Fashion Week."

"And then?" Sam asked intentionally, knowing she had more to list off but was running out of breath.

"Well—" she sighed dramatically.

"I'm kidding, Tara. Take a break. We'll circle back once my meeting with Claudine?"

"Céline. Celine Kalotte," she corrected.

"Right, Céline—once my meeting with her is over."

***

The elevator doors were closing as Sam adjusted his outfit before re-entering the office. Despite spending his lunch hour in a meeting, Gabriel never criticized Sam or over-complicated their discussion, so Sam still felt refreshed after the excursion.

In the distance, a woman was rushing toward the elevator, waving urgently at Sam with clumsy gestures, pleading for him to hold the door. She had just crossed the security gate, juggling a handbag, a sleek laptop case, and her visitor badge from security.

Stunned by the loudness of her demand, shouted in French, Sam quickly held out his hand to stop the doors from closing. She slipped through just in time, breathless but grateful.

With her phone pressed to her ear, her bag falling off her shoulder, and her dark, windswept hair spilling out the ponytail she'd styled it in, she politely smiled at Sam as a gesture of thanks for holding the door open for her and continued her rapid conversation in French.

Despite her hurried arrival, Sam couldn't help but take note of her sublime beauty, even in her tousled state. Her pale, doll-like skin and curvy, tall frame were striking, while her youthful cheeks complemented the natural makeup accentuated by a classic French red lip. She wore a long, fashionable skirt paired with a collared shirt peeking out from beneath a tailored wool sweater. The faint scent of lilac and honey lingered around her as she remained oblivious to Sam's gaze, which he couldn't seem to resist.

"I'm on my way to a meeting," she said in her native tongue. "Ugh, some American I heard is a real challenge to work with."

Sam raised an intrigued eyebrow at the mention of himself.

"I'm not so looking forward to it," she continued as the elevator emerged at their floor and they both stepped off. Céline headed to the reception desk, and Sam coolly strode to his office.

He tried not to dwell on the comment, reminding himself that she came from an outside company that didn't have the same relationship with him. She could have gotten bad intel, or perhaps she lied for the sake of having a dramatic conversation with a friend. Regardless of the excuse he invented for her, he decided it was an honest mistake that wasn't worth spending energy on.

Later, when Céline knocked on his door, recognition crossed her marvelous face, and he watched her scramble to remain calm. She fixed her hair and adjusted her bag, extending a hand as she looked into his eyes, searching for evidence of his discontent.

"I'm Céline," she said, extending her hand. "We were—um, we were in the elevator together earlier. I'm sorry, but, do you understand French?" she asked with a slight wince. Her words tumbled out at light speed, and Sam found himself drawn to her energetic pace. He liked the way English rolled off her tongue, wrapped in her thick accent.

"I do," he replied honestly, and her forced smile dissolved.

"Look, I—I didn't mean it, I mean, I didn't know, and—"

Sam waved away her worries with an amused smirk. "Espresso?"

She raised her vibrant eyes to his, trying to read his intentions. "Um..."

"I brewed it just for the occasion—for you."

"Is it poisoned?" she asked with a small laugh.

"No, just a simple gift to show you I understand you meant no harm. Think of it as a gesture of peace."

"I think I'm supposed to be the one gifting things to you."

He sat in a stylish leather chair and motioned for Céline to join him. She dropped her bag on the ground and sat down enthusiastically, accepting the cup he offered and smiling at him pleasantly.

"Are you sure you're not mad?" she asked after a while. Sam had been preparing the documents and spreading them out on the coffee table between them. She drank quickly as she picked up the pages and scanned them with quick glances.

"I promise," he replied, laughing lightly. "I'll only be mad if our brand wouldn't shine at PFW."

"Right," she said, clapping her hands together as if to snap herself awake.

As they worked, they stole glances at each other, blushing over the rims of their coffee cups and trying to stay on task. Céline had a habit of cracking jokes, and Sam found it difficult to suppress his laughter. The sensation was unexpected but welcome, and when he escorted her out of his office, he made a mental note to ask Tara to schedule more of these meetings, even if they eventually became unnecessary.

Sam was collecting his things at the end of the day when there was a knock at his door.

Sary hovered by the entrance, a briefcase held in his broad hand.

"Are you coming to dinner?" he asked while chewing loudly on a piece of spearmint gum.

"Wouldn't miss it," Sam replied.

"Do you want to invite Céline, too?" he asked, a playful glint in his eyes. Their laughter during the meeting, it seemed, had echoed throughout the office. "You two seem to get along really well," he added with a teasing smile.

Sam shook his head, but a smile gave away his desires. "No need to mix business with pleasure."

Ch. 8

"A New Crush?"

"I met someone," Sam proclaimed.

Tiffany sat up in her chair, her shoulders rigid with her full attention on Sam. "Oh, yeah?"

"In my dreams," he added.

"Even better." She smirked, dramatically brushing her hair behind her ears as if to hear him more clearly.

"I could be wrong," he backtracked. "This new girl... she could just be a friend, or nothing, or gone by tomorrow morning entirely. I'm just thinking, based on my last experience, that this could become something." He paused. "I'm upset about it, though."

"What? Why?"

Nervously chewing on his bottom lip, Sam explained how he simply stopped dreaming of Shiva, spending entire nights without even the ghost of a dream in his sleep.

He deliberately left out the fact that he had stopped dreaming about Shiva after his argument with Kate. The memory of that night still made his stomach twist.

"But last night, I stepped through this mental door and ended up in Paris."

Tiffany melted into the cushions, pressing her hands to her chest. "The city of love! You're so lucky, Sam."

"I don't feel lucky; I think part of my brain is still in love with the idea of Shiva. I want to know how our story ends, if it even does. I could be with her right now and not even know it. I'm missing out on time with her, you know?"

"Lighten up." Tiffany sighed. "We agreed that Shiva is probably a stand-in for Kate, right?"

"In a way, but the more I got to know her—"

"Sam, this is your mind we're talking about. You're the one crafting these women and their stories. Shiva was a stand-in for what Kate lacked, and it's fair to assume this new woman is filling in for Shiva. What's her name again?"

"Céline. I mean, we haven't done more than look at each other a few times. She didn't like me at first, but after we had some coffee, I think she's, well... warming up to me."

"Haters to lovers in Paris! I wish *I* could dream about that. I've tried lucid dreaming, but I can't seem to get it right. I'm always very aware of being chased by robbers or killers or whatever, but never by charismatic gentlemen wanting to kiss me." Tiffany pressed the back of her hand against her forehead, sighing theatrically.

"She's gorgeous, too. I can't complain if she *is* a replacement or something." Sam chuckled awkwardly, running a hand through his hair. "I don't know, that sounds too harsh..."

"To whom?"

"To Kate... She deserves better than having me dream up how she could be a better partner for me. I should already see her as the perfect woman for me, not be dreaming up alternatives."

Tiffany reached across the desk, and Sam took her cold, clammy palms. It was always a shock to the system whenever she tapped on his shoulders or pulled his arm to lead him in the right direction.

"Sam," Tiffany began, "you have got to be open to this experience. You're having, like, a one-in-a-million-level elaborate fantasy. Just ride it out, see where it takes you." She let go of his hands and rose from her chair. "Speaking of going places, your flight leaves in a few hours—we should really get going."

"My suitcase?"

"Already in the car."

"You're the best, Tiffany," he said as she dismissed herself and started the remaining preparations for his trip to Washington, D.C. Sam attempted to clear his mind while packing his briefcase, double-checking the files he knew the President would want to see.

His duties to his country weren't over just because his life with Shiva had come to a halt. Rubbing his hands together, he could almost feel the familiar squeak of sterile rubber gloves. His purpose had felt so different in his life as a doctor. He screwed his eyes shut, huffing out a deep breath.

He had to keep living as himself.

Dreams were not going to get him anywhere in life.

***

Sam's knee was bouncing restlessly as he stared out the window at the Washington Monument.

It was a relief to be back on his home soil, but something was nagging at him, something telling him he couldn't relax. Perhaps it was his proximity to Los Angeles that was confusing him.

Though he was still on the opposite coast, it was much closer than being on the other side of the Pacific Ocean.

He thought about the house in California, how it felt cozy even when he was alone, without Shiva. The air there was warm and serene, and the winds carried with them histories and stories, as if they had secrets to share.

He had enjoyed the existence he developed in California, and now the bitter chill of the Potomac River made him uneasy. This wasn't the America he had dreamed about.

It didn't help that Kate had called, breaking their few days of silence. "Why didn't you tell me about your trip?" she asked.

Sam was irritated by the assumptions she was making—that he was keeping things from her when he had always tried to do the opposite, that she deserved to know where he was when she wouldn't talk to him for more than a few seconds.

"You said you needed time," he said finally. "I didn't want to bother you."

"Consider me bothered," she answered with quiet irritation.

Sam sighed into the receiver as his eyes adjusted to the skyline. Suddenly, the monument transformed into the Eiffel Tower, and the lights that dotted the city streets illuminated limestone façades, wrought-iron balconies, and the distinctive mansard roofs of Paris.

He wondered what kind of person Céline was. He hadn't really gotten to know her. Perhaps Tiffany was right—maybe Céline harbored complexities he hadn't yet uncovered. He shouldn't dismiss her so quickly. Maybe, just like with Shiva, there was something he needed to learn about Céline—something that would help him see himself more clearly, including his relationship with Kate.

Sam replied, defusing the tension, "I'm sorry, Kate. The trip came up suddenly. I'll fill you in on all the details when I'm back."

She sighed, and it was like Sam could hear her unspoken thoughts. She thought he hadn't informed her because he doesn't value her, that he doesn't see her as an important person in his life.

"Maybe... Maybe if we never agreed to try and keep things casual, we wouldn't be clashing heads about this kind of thing so much," Sam whispered into the receiver.

Kate gave a lifeless chuckle. "So, we need to label ourselves as an *official* couple for either of us to actually give a damn about the other? No, Sam. Don't pretend like that would somehow fix all our struggles."

Sam opened his mouth to protest but quickly realized from the sharp silence that Kate hung up.

***

The grey mists of Sam's dream world calmed his nerves, like the comforting embrace of a warm shower.

Sleep came easily after his long day of travel and preparations, letting the tension melt from his shoulders.

In front of him, the stained-glass paneled doorway to Paris shone brightly. He inhaled the sweet-smelling air deeply, feeling a rush of confidence surge through his limbs.

His dreams were his to explore, his to enjoy without reservations or guilt.

Stepping through the doorway, he vowed to do exactly that.

***

Céline's office was covered with file folders and papers. Empty coffee cups spilled out of the garbage, and now, her coworkers were attempting to stamp their takeout containers into the overflowing bin.

"Just leave it," Céline told them, her tone carefree as she and Sam opened the bottle of wine that had been sitting on the table, staring at them throughout their meeting.

They had spent the entire evening working on their collaborative project, and everyone was exhausted. Céline's team and Sam's assistant, Tara, had been trickling out over the past few hours. Finally, the last stragglers said their goodbyes, leaving Sam and Céline alone with a mess of food to organize and presentation slides to fine-tune.

"I'll get to that in the morning," Céline said, nodding to the remains of their work.

"How do you do it?" Sam asked, amused.

"What?" The wine had flooded her cheeks with a rosy glow.

"Go to sleep at night without having everything sorted and beyond organized."

"Ah, so you're a Type A, then?"

Sam swirled his glass, which had fingerprint stains along the stem. "Unfortunately," he admitted.

"It's alright. For every type A person, there's someone who's shamelessly messy who will drive them nuts at first, but then teach them to accept a little bit of chaos in their life, and vice versa." She refilled their glasses. "We definitely belong to opposite extremes."

"Do you think we'll even each other out?" The rhythm of his voice was flirtatious, the alcohol daring him to be more direct about his desires.

She looked into his eyes, biting her lip as she fought off a joyous smile. "Hopefully."

They locked eyes, staring intently at one another, for a beat too long. A small smile teases at Céline's full mouth as she looks out the window at the darkening city, breaking their eye contact. "My boyfriend has yet to get used to me and my messiness, unfortunately."

Sam coughed on a sip of his wine, smacking himself in the chest and waving off Céline's amused concern. "Ah… Sorry. Boyfriend, huh?" Sam hoped he sounded politely curious, like a colleague and friend *should* be.

The smile Céline aimed at him implied that, no, he hadn't hidden his frustration very well.

"You know, I do have a life outside of work," she said with a wink. "But don't worry, Sam—he's not the jealous type. I can have friends like you around." "She let her words hang in the air, testing his reaction."

Sam raised a humorous eyebrow at her, implying they were indeed friends. She looked relieved when he laughed along.

"Oh, I feel honored," he said, lifting his glass with a grin. "To go from someone who's apparently unpleasant to work with to a friend in record time—that's got to be some sort of achievement."

He chuckled again. "I'll try not to take up too much of your 'life outside of work' hours, then."

"Hey, I have high standards for friends," she replied with a wink. "Consider yourself lucky."

"Oh, indeed I will," he said, smiling. "And I promise I'll be the greatest friend you've ever known."

Céline raised an eyebrow, smirking. "I'll hold you to that."

"Okay, Annnd we're out," she announced, picking up the bottle of red wine and giving it a swirl. The silence that followed confirmed her assessment.

"Guess that means this evening's come to an end." Sam breathed out happily, satisfied that their workday had been a success.

She opened her mouth, frowning as if she was about to argue, but stopped herself. "Right," she replied, nodding awkwardly. Sam angled his head, watching her, curious about what was going through her mind. The way she carried herself always made it seem like her bright, excited thoughts were just one strong gust of wind away from lifting her off her feet.

They grabbed a large garbage bag from the supply closet and began clearing away the trash.

Sam helped Céline turn off all the lights on the floor, and he waited patiently with her outside while she fumbled with her keys to lock up the main gate. She had a water bottle, a purse, and a binder pressed against her chest, her chin holding them in place as she tried to free up both her hands to sort through her absurd amount of keys.

"Sorry," she murmured. "I know I have it." Her water bottle tumbled to the ground, and Sam picked it up for her. The embarrassment made her work faster, which didn't relieve her confusion, and he found himself chuckling at the unfolding disaster. "Sorry," she whispered again.

Sam gently took the keys from her trembling hands and held them up to the light. Céline leaned in, almost touching him as she tried to see what he was up to. The clean scent of her laundry detergent mingled with his own, creating a subtle blend in the small space between them.

The smell was intoxicating, but Sam kept a clear head. Although, his limbs locked when he heard the deep, intentional intake of Céline's breath.

"Did you just—" he grinned.

"Yes, sorry." Again, sorry," she replied, sheepishly. Her full cheeks were flushed.

Sam bumped his shoulder against hers teasingly, laughing deeply, as he jammed the right key into the gate. They both heard the glorious *click*.

Céline retrieved back her belongings from Sam with a grateful hum. "Well," she started, shifting between feet as she adjusted the objects in her hands to more comfortable positions, "I guess this is goodbye, then."

"For now." Sam nodded politely in farewell.

They broke off in separate directions, Céline hanging her head in shame and Sam occasionally turning back to steal a glance at her.

Even under the dim yellow glow of the street lamps, Céline looked as if she had stepped right out of the pages of a fashion magazine. Her appearance stood in stark contrast to her down-to-earth personality, Sam thought, and for some reason, it only made her seem more likable in his eyes.

He shook his head as he turned to take his short walk home, still smiling at the thought of her.

***

The next day, in the conference room adjoining his office, Sam closed his laptop with a sigh. The presentation had gone splendidly, but now it was time to dive headfirst into the final preparations for Paris Fashion Week.

Models, photographers, and designers had all begun to arrive, infiltrating the city and adding to the already dense crowds that filled the sidewalks and trains. This would be his first time handling the brand in the midst of the chaos, and he was nervous to even leave the office building, though his duties hadn't started just yet.

Céline rapped her knuckles on the door, and as Sam's attention was brought to her comforting smile, he felt himself melt a little.

"Congratulations," she purred. "All that hard work you did paid off."

"*We* did," Sam corrected. "You know I couldn't have done it without you."

She walked over to him slowly, her heels clicking each step along the way. "Still, you get most of the credit for it."

"Hmm... do I sense a bit of resentment?" Sam queried with a playful smile.

Céline rolled her eyes. "Yes, yes, I am beyond jealous of you, *Monsieur* Sam Cooper. I wish we could switch bodies like in *Freaky Friday*, and I could get all the glory for once."

"Just checking," he replied as he began shutting down the projector. "If I'm being honest, though, I wouldn't mind changing places for a day."

"Oh yeah?"

"Yeah, I mean..." He shook his head, and his eyes focused on the window. "I need help navigating that whole mess down there with Fashion Week coming up and all the VIPs and celebrities coming from all over the world. Wouldn't hurt to have the memories of someone who knows all the streets like the back of their hand for a few hours. Or maybe even the whole week."

Céline rested a hand on her hip. "I'll offer my services."

"Will you, now?"

"Listen, I remember what it was like when I first moved here—terrible. Even though I've lived in France my whole life, the city itself... it's impenetrable. Or at least, it feels that way until you understand its rhythm. Which I doubt you have, since you're still so bright-eyed and American. Europe hasn't crushed you yet."

"It hasn't," Sam concurred sincerely.

"I've got some tips, and I can show you around—landmarks, backstreets, good restaurants, and all that. It'll help you get acclimated."

"I'd like that."

"So, it's a date then?" She paled, realizing her mistake. "I mean, like, a playdate... Oh no, that's even worse. A normal date between two colleagues who are *professional friends*."

Sam's ears were burning as he tried not to seem too phased at her slip-up.

He grinned, gathering his belongings. "Like a classic get-together between school colleagues working on a science project."

She seemed to feel at ease at his joke, and they made tentative plans to meet up in a few days before the crowds of Fashion Week attendees became impassable.

Sam felt better about having to enter the world outside his office with a guide by his side.

***

The Oval Office was as intimidating as ever—the carpet was freshly cleaned, the walls were pristine, and the President stood behind his desk with the elegance of a man only the leader of the free world could possess.

Sam advanced to the desk confidently, shaking hands with both the President and the Secretary of State with the practiced calmness of a seasoned diplomat.

Moving over to the vintage couches, Sam pitched some ideas he'd been developing for months regarding the long-awaited trade between Singapore and the United States—an agreement that had proven extremely challenging to settle. He also reported on his time overseas as an ambassador and the details he'd already put in place for the President's upcoming visit to Singapore.

The speech he had prepared came so naturally he felt as if Céline was in his ear, whispering each line to him, just like she supported him during the presentation in his dream in Paris.

She was in the background, proofreading his work and offering suggestions that rounded out his ideas. He felt comforted by this thought and wished in that moment that he could tell her all about it. But the Sam in Paris wouldn't remember this meeting with the President, nor would Céline recognize the man sitting in the Oval Office.

No, he was a stranger to the people of his dreams. He did his best to remind himself of that fact—that they weren't real despite how vivid everything felt. The melancholy that accompanied that thought was silly.

He sighed in relief, grateful that he had managed to pull himself together at the last minute to accomplish this, despite how confused and hopelessly distracted he had been in the previous weeks.

But Kate's sentiment kept echoing in the back of his mind—maybe if they were truly meant to be, he wouldn't be able to steel himself after all this romantic turmoil. If she were his true soulmate, this conflict and the growing distance between them would have shattered him too completely to even think about focusing on his career.

"I knew promoting him was a good idea," the President applauded after Sam's business was settled.

"The finest ambassador in Singapore, sir," the Secretary of State agreed.

The noise barely reached Sam's ears, but he smiled appreciatively anyway, floating from reality back into his unusual fantasies.

Ch. 9

"A Tourist in Town"

"If you look to your left, you'll see the immaculate gardens," Céline said, gesturing toward the extravagant and impossibly large window. "I hear one man does all the maintenance—never sleeps, just works."

Sam was overwhelmed by the Palace of Versailles, his mouth hanging open and unable to combat Céline's jokes as she led him through the grand hallways and bedrooms. He gasped at the draped silk curtains, the canopy bed frames, and the gold that decorated every wall sconce, chandelier, and picture frame. They had been roaming the historic site for hours, with Sam completely entranced by the scenery Céline had grown accustomed to.

"This statue here"—she gestured toward an eight-foot masterpiece—"is of my ex-boyfriend. It's a bit of a shame things didn't work out between us, really. He's so rich... but very boring."

"Nobody's perfect," Sam joked, one of the only phrases he'd spoken so far that afternoon.

"Ah, another bedroom. I bet there's so much sweat just soaked into that mattress. You know, historically, they didn't bathe as much as we do now. Imagine a hot summer wearing a full-length nightgown and climbing in there..."

"Maybe whoever slept here had low iron."

"So, they were cold all the time... I see. Royals are anemic. That explains a lot."

"I'm glad we could make such an important discovery." Sam crossed his arms with a stern nod.

"Shall we alert the media?"

"Not before we have more breakthroughs to announce."

"You don't like to tease your audience?" She was staring at him now, her eyes magnetic as they seized ahold of his.

He gulped under her keen attention. "I don't like to be cruel."

Céline shrugged. "Sometimes a tease can be exciting."

She stalked into another room, where a series of regal chairs lined the length of a majestic walnut table. He followed closely behind, drawn to her vibrant presence with a force as strong as gravity—overpowering and impossible to ignore.

"I don't think this table is big enough," Sam announced.

"Someone's got their voice back," Céline remarked.

"I just needed a moment to warm up. A comedian never gets on stage without doing some vocal exercises."

"I respect your commitment to entertaining me."

They continued to make their way through the corridors and lavish rooms, their conversation flowing more naturally with each step as they settled into an effortless rhythm. It felt as if they'd bypassed all the typical awkwardness of early encounters and reached the comfortable ease of a well-established friendship.

The spark of newness was still there, but now they no longer stressed over each word or worried about appearances. Sam found this change refreshing—a comforting sense of ease that allowed them to simply enjoy each other's company.

"I've also got a surprise for you," Céline proclaimed. They were in the gardens, fanning themselves with their hands against the creeping afternoon heat. She led him to a gorgeous tree standing over a neatly trimmed patch of grass, where a picnic basket full of *gourmet* treats was already set up. "Ta-da! I had a friend come by and do this earlier."

"You weren't kidding about your ex having a statue here, huh?"

"Don't worry about my mysterious connections," she replied teasingly. She grabbed his hands and gently forced him to the ground. An assortment of cheeses, bread, butter, crackers, and deli meats were arranged on a glass platter, and a bottle of champagne was nestled into a bucket of ice. "Oh! And the grapes." Céline rummaged through the basket and brought out a host of fruits that were perfectly ripe and juicy.

"I have to say, I really do feel like a king."

"And we have an audience of peasants." Céline motioned to the tourists walking by in confusion.

"Who's better than us?" Sam grinned.

"Nobody."

After a lazy stretch of nibbling on snacks and engaging in random conversations, Sam finally summoned the courage to voice the question that had been lingering at the edge of his thoughts, waiting for the right moment to surface.

"So, how long have you and your boyfriend been together?"

Céline raised her eyes to the clear sky in thought. "Oh, I've been with Charles for about four or five months now. We met through a mutual friend of mine. He asked me out halfway through the night, and I had to admire that kind of forwardness."

As she spoke, she peeled the foil hood off the top of the champagne bottle and eagerly twisted at the wire cage over the cork.

"I met him when I was just out of a toxic relationship. It's interesting because he's not typically the type of person I'd usually go for, but I guess it was the way he climbed on the table to—"

Sam quietly held up his hands in defense as Céline secured her thumb against the cork, ready to let it pop. She was too busy wrestling with the bottle, chatting about the night she met Charles, to realize where she was pointing it.

"Céline, uh, just some basic gun safety—"

Before he could finish his joking warning, the cork burst from the bottle, catapulting with a foamy spray of champagne—right against his forehead. He fell back onto the grass from the impact, and a bellowing laugh ripped from his gut.

"*Sam*! Sam, I am so, so sorry! Are you okay? Shit, I almost killed my client—that has to be reason enough to fire me on the spot."

Céline rushed over, placing a hand on Sam's shoulder as he cracked with laughter. Her expression remained tight with worry.

"Don't *laugh*, Sam!" she said sharply. "Just tell me you're okay! Do you feel dizzy? Do you have a concussion or something?!"

Sam sucked in a breath between chuckles, wiping his eyes—watering from both pain and laughter.

"I'm okay. Damn—it hurts like hell, I won't lie, but I'm okay."

With her help, he sat up again. Céline carefully brushed the grass off his back, apologizing over and over again.

"You have a mark on your head now," she whispered anxiously, standing next to him on her knees as she brushed her finger over the red bruise. He fought the urge to wince.

"It's okay, it's okay," she muttered, "It's like my Mamie always said, there's no wound that can't be cured with a little spit from a kiss."

Without warning, Céline planted a quick kiss on his forehead, proceeding to smooth his tousled hair over the mark. "See, no one can even see it like that!"

With a shy laugh, Sam waved her off. Her proximity was making him feel warm—fascinating, given that he was soaked in icy champagne. "It's really okay, Céline. I played American football throughout my entire high school career; I'm sure I'll be fine."

Sighing, her guilt-ridden expression shifted into something bright and joyful. She laughed then, without restraint. Her hair fell back over her shoulders, exposing the strong column of her throat. She clapped a hand over his forearm, and he couldn't help but continue to laugh along.

With most of their champagne soaked into Sam's clothes, Céline gave a mock frown at their lack of drinks.

"Okay, I have an idea of where to go," Sam offered. "On me, to prove there is no harm done, despite almost taking my head off just so you can steal all my brilliant ideas."

Céline shot him a look glittering with good humor. "Fine. You Americans love spending money, from what I know, so I'm not saying no to a free drink."

Gathering the few things that were left over from their lunch and shaking the grass off the blanket before folding it up together. Sam couldn't help smiling.

"Don't tell me you're still bullying me mentally," Céline griped.

"Nah... I was just thinking about how we could make friends so quickly when we were kids. Like you know each other for a few days over a family trip, then all of a sudden you're best friends..." Céline shook her head dramatically. "Oh, that doesn't happen with us French."

Sam rolled his eyes playfully and gathered up the picnic blanket, leading Céline off to one of the few spots he knew with a grin.

***

Sitting on the concrete terrace of a local brasserie, Sam and Céline sipped their drinks beneath the soft glow of twinkle lights draped along the perimeter. The place overlooked a quiet street lined with low-rise buildings and winding alleyways. Céline seemed to have shaken off her earlier embarrassment, and the two were now immersed in a heartfelt conversation.

"It's hard dating as a successful woman," she announced, sweeping her hair back with a casual shrug.

Sam laughed. "Are you trying to brag?"

"Of *course* I am. Why are people so shocked when someone brags? There's nothing wrong with being vocal about how great you are," Céline insisted, huffing lightly through her nose.

"Cheers to that," Sam nodded, raising his glass towards her.

"But on a serious note, what I mean to say is that it's harder to trust people. I think Charles is different because he earns a lot more than I do, but some of the others have been wild."

She let out a short laugh. "I once went on a date where the other person insisted I pick up the bill—in a way that wasn't even subtle. He didn't want to pay a cent because, apparently, I earn twice his salary."

She shook her head tightly. "Not that I mind paying, but I feel like it's just the principle of the matter. If you ask someone out, you can't expect them to pay for everything. Right?"

Sam scratched the back of his head. "Well, damn, seems like you ruined my plans for these drinks then."

Céline glared at him sharply but couldn't help laughing, nonetheless.

"But in all seriousness, I do get what you mean. I feel like dating just gets more and more complicated the older you get. Especially if you aren't able to get out much with work," Sam murmured into the last sip of his beer.

"Oh, I do like to get out and be social, *specifically because* I'm stuck in an office all day. I need some excitement in my life, and I live in Paris, for Christ's sake—I can't be a shut-in. Does that mean I want to date around forever? No. But finding someone who treats me well and appreciates what I do without trying to take advantage of it feels almost impossible."

"Charles isn't good to you?" he asked, tilting his head to the side. "How has he made it to almost four months then?"

She scoffed lightly. "I think, with him, it's more of that only-child syndrome—where they don't really want anyone getting too close? Like, the dates are luxurious, the passion is exciting, and there's a thrill when we actually spend time together, but there's none of the softer moments. None of that dancing in the kitchen while cooking breakfast together kind of stuff."

A gentle pulse echoed through Sam's heart like he understood the feeling in a deep, personal sense that he couldn't put his finger on.

"We'll see where things go with Charles, though. He's pretty easy-going and he knows how to spoil a woman, so maybe if he asked me to marry him at some point, I might just say yes for the hell of it. He seems like the type of husband who'd still just let you do whatever you want without any issue." She shrugged unconcernedly like it was the last thing she could care about.

"Doing what you want, of course, but shouldn't there still be some sense of sharing your time together when you're married?" Sam asked genuinely. He remembered vividly how his parents always enjoyed their hobbies alongside each other. His father would build his model war airplanes or go fishing, and his mom had a little sketchbook or travel painting kit that she used to set up near Jeffrey. They were engrossed in their own worlds but still together.

"I mean, sure, that sounds nice in theory. Sharing little moments, having hobbies together... But to have my partner make demands because of my lifestyle?"

She refilled their glasses, though her pour was far from perfect—the drinks were mostly foam. Céline shook her head with a faint smile as they tapped their glasses together, each choking back the bubbly layer. "I don't know... I guess I'm still a bit hardened from my last relationship before Charles."

"How long ago was that?"

"Two years," she admitted. "He just wanted my connections, contact lists, party invitations. He cared more about my social circle than his, not because he wanted to make a good impression on my friends but because he saw them all as opportunities. He talked down at me for working and claimed I wasn't enough for him—my job wasn't good enough—and yet he wanted to reap all the benefits of it. God, even now the idea of him makes my skin crawl."

Sam frowned deeply. "I didn't realize people like that actually existed—who make romantic connections purely out of greed. I can imagine it makes it hard to trust someone again."

She looked cheerlessly at the scratched table. "I'm trying to work my way out of that, I really am. I don't like how bitter he made me. I don't like treating other people like they're my enemy before I even get to know them. It doesn't help that I'm still such a workaholic that I don't always have time to emotionally connect with people. My mind is just elsewhere..."

"I get that," Sam confessed. "I'm trying to get through that myself. I don't realize how sheltered and unemotional I make myself sometimes, because I *am* talking to people and all that as a part of the job, but sometimes it still feels like there's nobody in your life who you can call when you're stressed or feeling down. Like you could have a host of acquaintances and people you can date for a night or two, but nobody to genuinely *be* with. It's hard. But I know I want someone who I can live my life with. My apartment is too perfectly Parisian and romantic to roam around in alone…"

"A hopeless romantic and a bitter pessimist in Paris. We are doomed, Sam," Céline moaned as she ran her fingers through her elegant hair.

He looked at her for a moment, a smile forming on his lips. "We're total lost causes."

"Maybe I should break things off with poor Charles and join a nunnery," she mused, and Sam laughed.

"As long as I can still come sneak you out for drinks," he grinned.

She cheered loudly and called for another round.

Maybe it was the alcohol, but Céline seemed to shimmer, her smile so vibrant and pure it felt almost unreal.

Sam closed his eyes to savor the feeling, and his mind seemed to drift away into space.

***

Unsure of where he was, Sam swayed in his seat, wrestling his anxious thoughts under control as he reacclimated to his surroundings.

He was on a plane, the wind beneath his feet rushing against the thick layers of metal that contained him. The window beside him was small and showcased only blue skies and puffy white clouds they tore through as turbulence shook the aircraft. He looked to his right, where a cabin crew member still had a hand on Sam's shoulder.

"Sorry to wake you, sir," he said. "But we've begun our descent. We'll be in Singapore shortly."

"Right... Sure... Thanks," Sam replied breathlessly. He attempted to mask the shock on his face as he grinned at the employee.

Once off the plane, Tiffany ushered him into a black sedan. The car had been packed already, one of Tiffany's many great conceptions as his assistant, and she was going over his schedule as he buckled in. Sam, however, didn't hear a single word, for his phone was buzzing in his pocket, and his heart was still in France.

He checked his messages while Tiffany continued to chatter—Kate wanted Sam to join her for dinner.

He also had a text from his sister, Judy, that he had received and read while in D.C., but hadn't found the heart to respond to it yet. He could practically hear her comforting voice—back then, it had been as familiar to him as his own.

Her message read:

Hey, Sammy! I hear you're on home turf again for a bit. How long are you staying? Hopefullyyy long enough for you to come visit home soon. Zack and the boys send their love. Bob and Eddy have been saying that Uncle Sam should come back because they need your help running their lemonade stand again... Please, for the sake of preserving my sons' entrepreneurial spirit, try to come home soon, okay? Mom's doing okay, though. I know you worry about her, but I promise I'm doing my best to check in with her as much as I can during the week, as promised. Maybe if my brother wasn't half a world away, I'd have more time to myself.

Kidding! ... Or not. We miss you a lot, Sammy. Lots of love from your big sis.

Sam had read and reread the message a few times but opted to wait before replying until he was back on Singaporean soil. Somehow, making the admission that he wouldn't have the time to visit while he was already back here seemed easier.

He felt sick with how much he had lost his bearings. Since when did he run away or ignore his problems until they had to be faced? He did not like this change in himself. He could attribute it to feeling burnt out lately, but he knew it was no excuse to treat the people who loved him so coldly.

"What time is it, Tiff?" Sam asked, interrupting before she could finish her rundown.

"Uh, your phone doesn't say?"

His confused frown, paired with the way he awkwardly looked down at his phone, made Tiffany giggle.

"It's, uh, still on U.S. time..."

She had mercy on his confused mind and answered him patiently, "It's about four in the afternoon."

"Alright, could you schedule a dinner with Kate for later this evening, please?"

"No problem, sir." Her eyebrows lifted high, and a question seemed to hang from her lips.

"You can ask, Tiff," Sam said, smiling at her dryly.

His assistant looked relieved at the permission. "Are you two going to try making it work again?"

He sighed, his posture deflating. "I'm not entirely sure what lies ahead, but lately, I've been wondering if maybe we should focus on building a good friendship first instead. It feels like we rushed into trying to create a stable connection built on trust—without truly getting to know each other, and now, because it's been going on for such a long time, it feels like we've started expecting our romance to be further developed than it truly is."

Tiffany smiled. "Let's hope Kate shares that sentiment with you tonight, then."

"As long as I don't mention any women from my dreams again," Sam muttered somberly.

"You dream about that French chick again?" Tiffany asked with a fascinated gleam in her eyes.

"Yeah, but she has a boyfriend, so we're really just more..."

"Friends," Tiffany completed the thought for him, nodding knowingly. "Well, just remember, Sam, they're just dreams. You're not cheating on Kate by dreaming about other women. You guys are just going through a rough patch, and so you're escaping in your head every night. That's fine and totally normal."

"It's not," Sam disagreed. "Céline took me to discover the streets of Paris and the Palace of Versailles, and being there with her... it took my breath away. I had never connected with somebody like that before, and the conversations we had weren't from some romcom movie, or anything close to what Kate and I talk about. They were original. They were unique to us. That's not normal."

"Well, it is when you've found your soulmate," Tiffany shrugged. "You said similar things about Shiva, remember."

Sam rubbed at his forehead. "I don't know anymore."

Exhaustion was overpowering him once again, and he couldn't bring himself to discuss his feelings any longer. It felt like torture to be so indecisive and confused—two traits he barely recognized in himself. He felt as if he were slipping away. What had happened to the man who never hesitated or doubted his choices? What had truly changed in him since that night at Istana Palace?

As the car pulled away from the airport, Sam felt an unexpected sense of relief wash over him. It was good to be on his way back to his home in Singapore.

Ch. 10

"Mixing Business with Pleasure"

Their food was hardly visible in the dim light of the supposedly chic restaurant. Kate had picked it out, claiming it had outstanding reviews and would certainly add some excitement to their otherwise regular date night with its chic interior and experimental dishes.

However, Sam found the place to be remarkably dull and generic—just another restaurant trying to present itself as something intimate and special. The food, overall, was tasteless and, if he were honest, ridiculously overpriced.

Not that he voiced this opinion, though.

Their evenings had been carrying on like this for a while since he returned from his trip to Washington, D.C., and he was growing tired of the trendy entrées and recurrent conversations.

Perhaps it was a good thing that he couldn't see his flavorless noodle soup or the woman sitting across from him, because he wasn't in the mood to confront what was bothering him. But then—"We need to talk," Kate declared.

Sam stopped scraping his spoon against the rim of his soup bowl. "Oh?"

"Yeah."

"About what?"

"About us."

"That's never good." Sam gulped.

"No, well, I mean, yes, maybe, I don't know." She sighed, dropping her utensils and bringing her hands to her chin. "Sam, you and I both know we haven't been *right* lately. Admit it."

Yes, he wanted to admit. In the beginning, he and Kate could go on pleasant dates, make some lighthearted jokes, and then go to Sam's apartment to spend a few hours together before Kate left again—and that was just their way. Practiced and simple. Sort of like eating a familiar bowl of cereal.

Sam sighed. Even his analogy of Kate and his relationship seemed lifeless...

Was he really someone who needed constant change and new experiences to keep his interest alive? He didn't think so, since he found comfort in a steady routine. But maybe that was exactly the point— maybe he needed someone who wasn't bound by a strict schedule to pull him out of his comfort zone.

His thoughts drifted to his most recent dream about Céline.

She had taken him to a seafood house overlooking a bustling harbor, where catamarans and fishing boats swayed gently in the water. He watched as fishermen counted their day's catch, sorting through massive nets filled with wriggling fish. He couldn't help but enjoy the sight of them, dressed in their oversized overalls and sporting thick mustaches—features he had once assumed were simply stereotypes created by animators. Yet here they were, in the flesh—the real thing.

He and Céline had taken a train out to a small, charming town to get away from all the noise. Sam was hesitant at first—he was a city boy at heart; he wasn't sure that he'd like the quiet of the countryside.

But Céline had proven him wrong. He was captivated by the rolling hills and stone cottages blowing smoke into the atmosphere. He liked the coolness of the breeze as it whipped through the empty fields and brought with it the scent of flowers.

He picked her a makeshift bouquet of wild grasses and unusual weeds he found along their path to dinner, and Céline smiled, opting to tuck a few of his gathered finds into her hair.

Their conversation flowed effortlessly, and she seemed to radiate laughter and genuine warmth. Sam couldn't help but be amazed at how she looked even more beautiful every time she cracked another silly joke.

With Kate, it was the opposite. Her lips were veiled in shadows, but he could still see their sour frown. She was obviously gearing up for something unpleasant; otherwise, she wouldn't have been so determined to hide her face.

It made Sam even more frustrated about her choice of location. Céline was taking him on journeys to broaden his horizons, while Kate wanted dark corners so they wouldn't have to look each other directly in the eye.

"It's my fault," Kate went on, her hair pulled back into a tight, precise bun. Everything about her tonight seemed rigid, from her posture to the turtleneck tightly wrapped around her neck. "I think the real problem is that I introduced you to Sara way too early—and if I remember correctly, I did it without even telling you beforehand."

"I wouldn't say that," Sam replied, shaking his head at Kate. Her words stung more than any of her previous assumptions.

"It's true," Kate continued somberly, "and even if it weren't, Sara likes you an alarming amount. I'm scared I'm going to end up hurting both of you by holding back."

"Holding out on what?"

"This. Us. Progressing further. Let's face it, Sam. It's been a year. Things were great between us, and then I brought Sara into the mix after only a few months, and we haven't recovered. You're great with her, don't get me wrong, but she does add pressure to our relationship that I don't think we need, or can handle, for that matter."

Sam's hands were in tight fists under the table, fighting to hold back the hurt. "Kate, meeting Sara was one of the greatest things to me. I... I felt so honored when you introduced her to me. I thought it meant that you wanted things to be serious between us—for us to actually work *towards* something."

Kate dropped her perfect posture, shaking her head in annoyance. "Sam, for the love of God, will you ever give up on this idea of some perfect wife and child? Sara and I are not that, alright? You're never going to get that with us, so either we both agree that things are simply casual pleasure between us, or we break this off now." She hissed a sigh through her perfectly white teeth. "Because I don't think we want the same things anymore."

"I've known that since the start, Kate. I still wanted to try with you—"

"*Why?*" Kate spat with all the venom of a cornered cobra. "Because you thought you could *convince* me into being your perfect little American dream of a wife? When will you stop living in that annoying dream world of yours? Stop pretending like you don't know what's going on."

Sam's stomach twisted.

The rest of the memories of that dream with Céline in the countryside overtook his mind, despite Kate's insistence to abandon his fantasies.

But Céline had said nearly the same thing to him.

"Don't pretend like you don't know what's going on, Sam."

She had leaned back in her seat, her cheeks bright with playfulness. The way she stared at Sam, with adoration and affection filling her eyes, made Sam's chest glow with shyness. "Face it, Sam—we're falling for each other."

He had pressed his knuckles against his lips, letting his gaze settle on his bowl of mussels swimming in a rich, buttery sauce, just to keep himself from smiling back at her. The confession emerged low in his throat. "I think I have been, ever since that day when I held the elevator door open for you."

"Precisely. But we've got a bit of a problem."

"I would never overstep with what you have with Charles," Sam said firmly. "Besides. We're supposed to keep things—"

"Professional. Right."

"So, then working together will be... a pleasant challenge, but that's nothing I didn't know from the first time meeting you either."

Céline laughed in mock offense before throwing her hair over her shoulders. "Think of it this way. So long as we're aware of how we feel but don't act on it or let it affect our work together, then we're being mature adults about it. We don't need to worry about things getting too messy or complicated as long as we stay honest about how we feel."

"And when you eventually *do* marry Charles?" Sam asked jokingly.

Céline had reached over, her eyes warm and bright as she took Sam's hand and squeezed it. "I am sure you and I can keep being friends. We ride it out, see where it goes."

Sam had felt strangely confident in agreeing with her. He loved Céline's company, and his attraction to her was completely undeniable, but if he could only have her as a friend, he would still be content.

So, in the dark restaurant in Singapore, when Kate said, "I think we should scale it back," Sam's ears were burning as his worlds were crashing into each other.

How could he feel so relaxed and at ease with the idea of just being friends with Céline, yet struggle with the mere thought of that with Kate? Did it mean he was truly, deeply in love with Kate, just unable to express it? Or was it that Kate simply wasn't the kind of friend he would naturally choose for himself?

"Bring it back to just us," Kate clarified when Sam failed to respond for a few long seconds. "Let's just focus on what we *used* to focus on before."

"Let us focus on just entertaining each other so neither of us feels too lonely?" Sam snapped. He couldn't hide the frustration on his tongue.

"Well, why not?" Kate seemed completely pragmatic. "We refocus on each other and what we *actually* want out of this agreement, not what anyone else does. I meant we should take Sara and... all of the family drama out of the equation again."

Sam's jaw clenched tightly. He knew there was nothing inherently wrong with what Kate was suggesting. He'd had relationships before that were based mostly on physical attraction, with simple make-out sessions and little else tying them together. But that was back when he was younger—before this looming ache for something deeper had settled in him. Now, he longed to belong to someone, to build a family, to be bound to a woman he loved more than anything else in the world.

Was he stupid for pushing away a woman as attractive and willing to simply fulfill their basic desires for each other with no strings attached by being an overly sentimental and emotional idiot?

"You're mad," she said worriedly as she watched his face twinge.

"No," he responded, "I'm just shocked, is all."

"I'm doing this *for* us," she insisted. "I'm doing it because I like you, Sam, and I feel like we're spinning in circles rather than moving forward. You can understand that, right?"

"You just want it to be the two of us. No fairytale romance, just friends with benefits," he stated.

"Yes, exactly," Kate frowned. "Not that the fairytale part won't help with the benefits part, but that's the general idea. Yes."

Doubt curled in Sam's chest like a worm in the crispy flesh of an apple. "Are you sure that we'll be able to do that, though?"

"Yes, I promise." Kate reached over, her fingertips tracing the faintly raised muscles and veins on his hands. Her eyes gleamed with a dark fire—the very same look Sam had seen on each of their first dates.

It sent a familiar rush of pleasure through him, settling deep in his core.

For some reason, he didn't believe Kate's promise.

***

Sam previously thought it would be an escape from his emotional decay to be immersed in work, but he found his realities shifting around him.

His wants, his desires, his loves, all merging into one shapeless form.

He was busy preparing for the President of the United States to meet with both the Singaporean President and the Prime Minister, meticulously coordinating every detail. Yet, in the back of his mind, he was also juggling the speeches he needed to draft for the exclusive parties that Céline's company, Executive Media, was hosting at Fashion Week. The dual responsibilities pulled him in opposite directions, each demanding his focus and creativity.

Tiffany gave him the rundown of his duties in his life in Singapore, which sounded coincidentally like the ones fed to him by his Parisian assistant, Tara.

He stayed in his office at the embassy all night, worrying over the exact wording of his address to a group of influential politicians, hoping to finally secure the trade deal in the President's presence. When he reread it the next morning, he noticed it was laced with a mix of French and British accents, along with cultural references from both. He found himself torn, wishing he could have *Kate*—no, *Céline*—no, *Kate*—to go over it with him. She always knew what to say. *Both* of them did. In the end, he had to scrap the entire draft and brainstorm something fresh with Tiffany.

He wished he could meld them together, creating one perfect woman he wouldn't have to give up or sacrifice anything for. The thought sounded awful, and he knew it. He was beginning to hate himself for even thinking that way.

A wave of illness swept over him as he hurried into the long-awaited conference to deliver the speech he'd worked so hard on—only to spot Kate sitting among the attendees. He'd been distant with her ever since she suggested they scale their relationship back to something purely casual, something simple. Now, seeing her there, he couldn't shake the creeping guilt, the sense that he was punishing her for simply doing what she thought was right.

Just before he stepped onto the stage, Kate reached out and took his hand, giving it a reassuring squeeze. "You'll do great," she murmured softly, her voice steadying him more than he'd expected.

He smiled at her warmly, he wondered if they might somehow see this through after all.

Still, he could practically feel and smell Céline close to him, remembering how she dusted off his blazer in his dreams before she took the podium, hedging the judgmental crowd for Sam. She knew they wouldn't appreciate being lectured by an American, even though Fashion Week was an international event. But the crowd eased mercifully with her magnetic charm.

His speech was a resounding success, drawing enthusiastic applause from the attendees, including both presidents and a distinguished crowd of politicians, diplomats, and public figures. Each point he made seemed to resonate, his words capturing their attention and reinforcing the importance of their shared goals. As he concluded, he noticed nods of approval and even a few smiles among the high-ranking officials—a clear sign that his message had hit its mark.

Kate was watching him from the sidelines, her expression one of genuine pride and admiration. As the applause died down, she met his line of sight, giving him a small, approving nod that filled him with a sense of accomplishment he hadn't anticipated.

It was more than just a successful speech; he felt, for a moment, that he'd regained her respect.

That night, Kate was stuck to Sam, her hand possessively resting on his chest as they walked up to his home. She pressed his tall frame up against the door, grabbed his tie, and kissed him with a fresh surge of passion. He pulled her close, allowing himself to give in to her desires as he eagerly guided her inside. Later, Sam lifted her onto the kitchen counter, savoring their closeness before they moved to bed to continue what they'd started. Wrapped in the comfort of each other's presence, Kate eventually rolled away. He knew she was bound to wake up and leave soon.

He sighed, a quiet, heavy sound as he wrestled with the unfamiliar weight in his chest. This was what he'd agreed to—casual, uncomplicated, no expectations. But in the dim light of his empty kitchen, the reality felt sharper. He gulped down a huge glass of water, hoping the cold clarity might wash away the ache settling inside him.

He set the empty glass on the counter and braced himself with both hands, staring down at the gleaming surface as if it held the answers he sought. The silence of the house pressed in around him, heavy with unspoken thoughts, while the faint trace of her perfume lingered—a bittersweet reminder of everything he couldn't quite hold onto.

Without realizing it, he wandered into the living room and sank onto the couch. His mind raced with half-formed questions and quiet wishes he hadn't admitted even to himself. Before he knew it, exhaustion won out, and he drifted off right there, the soft haze of city lights outside his window was the only witness to his restless sleep.

***

The colorful glass on the door's windowpane flashed with multi-colored lights. Sam could hear the faint echo of trendy house music pulse through the wood. He felt his spirits lifting.

On the other side of this door was an adventure. Excitement and heart-stopping opportunity. And he knew, between it all, like the eye of a glittering storm, was Céline.

A grin spread slowly across his lips as his hand lingered on the door, pushing it open to step into the warm, intoxicating press of attractive bodies awaiting him.

***

At the after-party of their main brand event, Sam glued to the wall, drink in hand, quietly observing as models mingled with journalists and photographers. The room pulsed with flashes of light and the sparkle of disco balls. Despite Céline's best efforts to draw him out of his shell, he still felt oddly out of place in the crowded room. Back home, he was never like this—he frequented clubs and regularly hosted gatherings. Usually, he could flirt and mingle with society like this with no issues. In fact, a part of him had to admit he sometimes liked the engagement; he enjoyed dancing and connecting with people, even if it was just for a night.

Maybe he was simply nervous about making a mistake in front of Céline. Now that it was out in the open that he was harboring a crush on her, he didn't want her to catch him dancing with someone else and assume he'd lost interest. Even if they were technically just friends, and she was already taken, he couldn't shake the desire to keep her focus on him.

He groaned inwardly. He felt like he was back in high school.

Like a sunflower turning toward the sunrise, he looked toward the other end of the room. Céline held a microphone and stared out into the audience before motioning for the DJ to pause the music for a moment.

As the crowd settled and turned their attention to Céline, a model strode over to Sam, leaning against the wall with a sigh before casually clinking her glass against his.

"Cheers to the wallflowers," she declared in a thick British accent, raising her glass with a playful smirk. Her golden hair was swept back into a sleek, stylish bun, and the roaming spotlights occasionally caught her angular features, highlighting the hollows of her cheeks.

Sam squinted, a flicker of recognition sparking in his mind. She looked familiar—perhaps he'd seen her face on a magazine cover or towering over a city street on a billboard. Her beauty was both striking and elusive.

"And here's to your keen eye" he replied, lifting his glass in sync with hers before taking a swallow. The drink burned just enough to remind him he was still rooted here, surrounded by flashing lights and glossy strangers. The model's smirk widened as she matched his pace, her eyes glinting with a mix of interest and curiosity.

She raised a thin eyebrow, a teasing glint in her eyes. "Oh, an American. Forgive me for using you as an oasis in the midst of a European desert, darling."

He let out a surprised gasp, then chuckled. "That's okay. Thankfully, you don't seem to hold a grudge over that little *Boston Tea Party* incident." Sam said, referring to the *1773 protest where American colonists dumped British tea into Boston Harbor in defiance of British taxation.*

The model looked at him quizzically, then laughed as she deciphered his joke, hanging onto his shoulder.

Sam politely smiled at the model, "I'm quite new to this scene, but at least the French champagne is good enough to see you through it, right?"

She frowned slightly, a flash of pity mixed with irritation crossing her face at his lack of flirtation. Sam sensed the subtle shift in the atmosphere, his awareness sharpening as the charged silence thrumming through Céline's microphone cut through the background noise like a warning.

She had faltered over a key part of her speech. Her eyes were locked on Sam. Meanwhile, the model clinging to his arm leaned in, whispering something about Paris's free-spirited nature—words Sam barely registered.

His eyes met Céline's—steady and reassuring—and in that silent exchange, she seemed to regain her composure. A slow breath escaped her, and relief softened her expression. Her posture relaxed as she continued with newfound confidence.

"Um... Apologies! As I was saying, the spirit of Fashion Week is truly in the art that we all get to create together," Céline continued, her voice strengthening as she delivered the familiar lines Sam had helped her rehearse just hours earlier.

He followed her every word, heart pounding, feeling a rush of nerves tightened inside him. Had she really been jealous? It didn't make sense—not with her having a boyfriend. Yet the possibility persisted, unsettling and oddly thrilling.

Sam swallowed the last of his drink, feeling the warmth spread through him as the British model scoffed softly and slipped back into the crowd, her figure vanishing under the glimmering lights.

***

He could feel himself beginning to fade away, his senses completely overwhelmed as his body overheated under the bright lights of the Parisian party. His limbs were heavy and tired, like he hadn't slept in years.

Suddenly, Céline's hand gripped his arm, anchoring him back. Her eyes were wide with worry. "Sam. Let's go outside."

He felt the steadiness of her touch and instinctively drew closer to it, allowing her warmth and reliability to penetrate the fog. Without resistance, he let her guide him through the crowd, trusting her to lead him to the fresh air he so desperately needed.

After a few minutes, they found themselves walking along the Seine, the refreshing air drifting from the water, cooling Sam's flushed face as they strolled down the quiet pathway. He inhaled deeply, each breath settling as he gripped Céline's hand, her touch anchoring him.

"You shouldn't be doing this, Céline," he murmured, managing a weak smile as he gestured to their interlaced fingers.

"I'll stop holding you when you stop breathing like a bull," she teased, a playful glint in her eye. "Are you sick or something? Or did that cork to your head cause more damage than we thought?"

Sam's laugh was weak, but he felt his spirits lifting high above the city, soaring over the glittering Eiffel Tower.

Peace spread through him as they turned and looked out over the water, his skin vibrating with heat each second they drew closer together.

"I just want to be with you like this," Sam whispered, "Out in the open. Somewhere we can just breathe."

She stared at him with an expression he found hard to read, but he felt himself melt in the care of it. She was so close, her entire essence enveloping him. Her eyes kept shifting from his curious eyes to his lips.

They were standing on the edge of something.

But the world began to dissolve around him, grey mist spilling into the corners of his vision.

All he could hear was Céline's final words.

"Sam, I'm thinking that maybe we could be..."

Ch. 11

"Conflicting Emotions"

The scent of cologne filled the luxurious car as Sam sat across from the President of the United States. The tinted bulletproof windows prevented him from looking outside, while he avoided fixing his gaze on the regal man before him. Just because they were on good terms didn't mean he could become overfamiliar.

"This has been a wonderful visit," stated the President.

Sam looked up from his tightly clasped hands. "I'm glad to hear that, sir."

"You've been reliably professional—handling the reception, coordination, management... and finally, and most importantly, concluding the trade agreement. Everything Sam Cooper touches turns to gold."

"I appreciate your kind words, Mr. President. I just performed my duties."

The last two days had been a high-speed excursion between his worlds. He thought he had been slipping, losing track of his tasks as one event bled into another.

He wouldn't have been able to keep his head on his shoulders if it hadn't been for the people supporting him.

Pictures captured him shaking hands with the President of the United States and the President of Singapore, both leaders beaming at the camera, though he could barely remember the interaction at all.

He had only caught glimpses of Kate in crowded halls and missed her phone calls at night, returning them with apologies about being overworked and exhausted as he prepared to announce the success of the trade deal to the public—only to fall asleep on the couch again.

Kate had offered to help him relieve some stress with the promise of emotional support and a welcome distraction. In the end, he gave in and allowed her to come over. Fortunately, it seemed to work—at least enough to give him something else to hyperfocus on for a few precious hours.

He stood outside the car, watching as the President boarded Air Force One. Sam gave a steady wave from the ground. Once the door was sealed and he was certain the President was safely inside, he instructed the driver to take him back to his residence.

The chaos was over—for now.

He found himself daydreaming about the charm of the French countryside—wandering through its scenic landscapes, savoring every corner of its renowned cuisine, and indulging in the region's finest vintages. In his mind, Céline was always there, her laughter mingling with the gentle breeze, their days flowing into a serene rhythm of *simple pleasures* and tranquil solitude.

***

Kate appeared in the doorway with a slight sway, her eyes gleaming with tipsy delight as she smirked at Sam, a bottle of wine swinging from her hand. Her hair was spread in loose waves across her chest, the hemline of her dress short, her shoes already stripped from her feet, the straps hanging from her free hand.

She didn't greet him as she strolled inside. Instead, she handed him the bottle without a word and headed straight to his bedroom, settling onto his bed as if she had always lived there.

He followed her lead, silently pouring them both a glass, though he gave her a smaller pour than usual. Glasses in hand, he joined her on the mattress, settling beside her as she stretched out deliberately. She tossed her hair back as she accepted the wine, her fingers brushing his as she breathed his name, then reached to run her fingers slowly through the hair at the back of his neck.

A slight, awkward shiver passed through him, and he found himself staring into the deep, scarlet pool of wine in his glass. He couldn't explain why, but something about her recent, heightened desire unsettled him. She seemed almost ravenous for his attention, a desperation he didn't remember even in the first moments of their relationship. It was as if her need for him had intensified, becoming something somehow unfamiliar.

"Look at me, please, Sam," she begged with a low, desperate voice, a hint of urgency underlying her words.

He obliged, turning to meet her gaze, his cheeks more flushed than he would have liked to admit.

"Come on, Sam, what's wrong?" she pressed, her hand sliding down his spine in a slow, intentional motion. Goosebumps prickled across his skin, and her lips curved into a devious smirk as she noticed his reaction.

He opened his mouth but hesitated, unable to tell her that this was starting to feel wrong. It was becoming clearer to him that they were just *using* each other, and he knew that was, in part, the point. But somehow, he couldn't bring himself to see Kate in that detached, casual sense.

"Are your dream girls doing it better, Sam?" she muttered, leaning in closer and gripping his jaw in her hand. "Do you want me to try to be more like them?"

He winced, instinctively trying to pull away from her grasp, but she held him there, her fingers firm and unrelenting, as if determined to force him to pay attention, to make him truly see her.

"What would they do to make you feel good, Sam?" Kate asked in a dangerous tone. She stretched her bare legs across his lap as she grabbed his glass of wine and finished it off for him in a few eager mouthfuls that left her breathless. "Tell me."

"I don't like this game, Kate," he replied, gently trying to push her off.

"It's not a *game*, Sam. I'm trying to figure out what you want because it certainly doesn't seem to be me."

"They're just dreams," he told her. But how many times would he find himself tossing and turning over this exact phrase?

He was living his dreams. He was breathing it.

They were something more than just pictures in his mind, and yet nobody could comprehend why he tried to make them materialize in the real world.

"But they mean something to you, right?" she continued.

"No." *Yes*. That sickening feeling of betrayal sat on his tongue like acid.

"There's someone else, isn't there?"

Sam looked at her in confusion.

"There's someone else?" Kate repeated, her words slow and drawn out this time. "Some new dream woman you're obsessed with."

He thought of Céline, of Shiva—of everything that they made him feel. The love and admiration that he received from these women were real, in some way, even if they were made up.

His mother had always told him that real love is something that changes you forever yet allows you to be exactly who you have always been.

That has never been him and Kate; he knew that. No matter how much pleasure they could give each other, they could never make something real and pure magically appear between them.

So, against all logic and reason—knowing full well how their last discussion about this had ended—he looked her in the eye and said, "Yes."

She climbed off his lap and sat beside him on the mattress, her shoulders dropped and the straps of her dress falling down her arms. She looked almost like a heartbroken teenager, rejected on prom night.

It was a cruel reflection of the conversation they shared on that night of Singapore's National Day celebration.

When Kate didn't speak or move, Sam took a measured breath and continued, "I think I already told you about her. Her name is Céline. I just… I really enjoy getting to know her. It's been nice, working with someone I feel so strongly about."

"Someone you feel strongly about?" Kate asked with a sigh. But her sadness dissolved as soon as it surfaced, replaced by the cold fury he'd grown used to. "That's *silly*, Sam."

"I know nothing I can say will ever convince you of how *real* it feels for me—"

"It's a figment of your imagination. I mean, why can't you dream of a better life with me, for heaven's sake? You control all of it. Why don't you make things easier for us in that goddamn head of yours?"

"But I don't have control."

"Bullshit. This is so typical of you, Sam. You never wanna take responsibility for anything. Have you ever heard of meditation or lucid dreaming? This whole helpless-victim-of-female-sexuality act is absurd for a man your age. And she's French?"

"Yes—she's French."

"Good luck with that. Real or not real, this woman is going to break your heart. They're a lot less rigid about monogamy and commitment, the French."

"Céline's not—"

"*Not like the other girls*, oh, I'm sure. You've created this perfect fantasy where you're not a complete fool and only idealized women want you. You think you've got it so bad with me because, *what?* I actually expect things from you? This isn't even the second-class treatment you would've gotten from those women if they were alive and sitting here on your bed instead of me. And that reality would've caved your little head in. So don't think I'm going to indulge you the way your dream women do. You have no grounds for complaint and no reason to be acting like this."

"Maybe I'm sick of always doing things *your* way, Kate."

"How?" She folded her arms across her chest. She was standing in front of him now, glaring at him.

"How?" Sam repeated, irritated at her petulant demands.

"Yeah! How have I silenced you, Sam?"

"We never really collaborate, Kate. We never actually try to figure things out together—it always has to be your way. I'm sorry we have problems, Kate, but they're not gonna disappear just because you demand that they do."

"Tell me, what have you done for our relationship, other than look down on me for wanting something more? Something better than a casual girlfriend who can barely stand me?"

The words rushed out of him with the relief of a frozen river finally thawing. He placed a hand over his chest, trying to ignore the rapid pounding of his heart.

"Is it so crazy that I feel like the only place I'm wanted is in my own dreams?"

Kate made a sound of disgust in the back of her throat. "Always with the victimhood. *You're* the one who can never make any decisions!"

"Listen, I know I've been stagnant. I've tried to go with the flow because I thought that's what you wanted, Kate. I knew how hard things were with James, how he rarely gave you the space to do things the way you wanted, to make choices on your own terms. So, I tried to be different. I thought if I stepped back, gave you that freedom, you'd feel safe with me—like you finally had the room to be yourself. I thought that's what would make this work."

"I never wanted you to be the antithesis to James," Kate murmured. "I just wanted to have fun with you, Sam. Something carefree for once in my miserable life!"

Tears welled up in her eyes. This was anything but carefree.

Reaching his limit, Sam stood up and wrapped his arms around Kate's tense form. He aligned his mouth with hers, pressing into a deep kiss as his fingers sank into her hair, trying to convey all the words he couldn't say.

She let out a soft sound of relief and pulled him closer, her fingers tightening in the front of his shirt.

This was what Kate wanted, right? To be overtaken by lust, to let it gloss over their problems and reset everything between them. He gripped her hip and kissed her deeply.

Sam couldn't shake the feeling that Kate was provoking him, pushing him until he proved his commitment to her. And while he didn't appreciate the bait, he took it anyway. Maybe, in some unspoken way, he needed to prove something to himself, too.

As they fell onto the bed once again, he couldn't help but think about what he'd felt for Céline in their last scene by the Seine in the Paris of his dreams—even though nothing physical had happened between them, nor did he know if it ever would. The feeling had been just as intense and wild as whatever was brewing between him and Kate right now, and maybe it was his subconscious reaching back into memories of his past with Kate, before they'd lost that spark.

But he didn't want to muddy his perception of Céline by dragging her into the confusing, fragmented, and often discontented world of modern romance. He wanted to preserve her in his dreams—yes, she existed in an idealized state, but wasn't all love, at its core, an attempt to convince each lover of their partner's perfection?

And yet, he wondered, wasn't that very quality that made Céline feel so divine, in some way, an essential part of Kate as well?

Maybe they were woven from the same fabric, similar in their design. So, Sam pulled at every thread of Kate, searching for the pieces he needed—the bright essence of connection, of friendship. Something clear and tangible, something that made him believe she was meant to be his after all.

Yet, every thread he pulled seemed to slip from his fingers, leaving him uncertain.

When Kate finally collapsed, exhausted, onto his chest, all he could think about was returning to Céline. He needed to reaffirm that what he saw in Céline, that pure essence, still existed somewhere within Kate.

But Céline would not come. There was nothing—no ancient, beautiful streets, no office building, no coworkers. Paris, as he knew it, had become a black void where all his thoughts and hopes vanished.

It went on for a couple of days, maybe even longer. Sam had stopped counting after he reached three, recognizing that what had happened to Shiva had now happened to Céline.

His bed felt empty once Kate had taken her fill of him, his mind was a blank, drifting stream, and he returned to his regular duties with a dull, mechanical repetition that exhausted him. Reality had descended upon him, a dream he could neither escape nor wake up from.

**

Fog surrounded him utterly. Above, below, filling his vision with endless grey. His chest felt tight.

The cool sensation against his back made him realize that he was lying down. He stretched his hands out, making sure there was enough space around him before he stood.

He was back in that misty space between his worlds.

Mist swirled around him as he turned, desperate to find a door glowing with potential.

His heart sank when, once again, a new door stood in front of him.

A new place. A new connection?

He didn't know if he could do this again. He had already lost two women before—their names already starting to fade from his knowledge in his disconnected dream state.

The door was heavy and made of oak. Its gilded gold designs were intricate and ancient.

A relentless itch to see what lay beyond it started to scratch at Sam's consciousness.

He walked toward the door and pressed his ear against the wood. It was faint, just a whisper in the background, but Sam could swear he heard the distant sound of car horns. The thrum of music pulsing through streets. A city.

He tightened his grip on the handle. Where would he be this time? Would he be going back to Céline? To Shiva? Or stepping into a totally new adventure?

With a deep breath, Sam stepped through the door into the shining light, desperate to find out where—and to whom—it would take him.

Ch. 12

"Not Again!"

Sam was sitting in bed, a steaming mug of cardamom tea pressed to his lips, his gaze lingering over the cityscape beyond the window. An assortment of pillows was carefully arranged behind him, cocooning him in comfort. The curtains were already drawn back, allowing the early morning sunlight to spill into the room, casting a warm glow over everything. He sipped slowly, savoring the quiet, watching as the first rays illuminated the skyscrapers in soft shades of gold and orange. It was a small ritual, but one he'd come to cherish.

He had grown accustomed to waking before his seven o'clock alarm, slipping quietly out of bed to make tea, and then returning to his king-sized sanctuary. Here, in the stillness of dawn, he could settle back into the pillows, take slow, unhurried sips, and let his mind drift before the demands of the day closed in. This was his time, a buffer against the world outside, a rare pause in an otherwise demanding schedule.

Even after a late night, he felt more rested by taking this time for himself. Without consciously setting aside this ritual each morning, he knew he'd be swallowed by the endless demands of work, lost in the constant bombardment of emails, meetings, and decisions. This simple act—just him, his bed, and his tea—grounded him, offering a moment of calm in a life filled with chaos.

The Dubai escarpment was remarkable, unlike anything he had seen in the United States. Normally, he wouldn't find an expanse of towering buildings and revving cars to be a marvel, but the wavelike shapes of the architecture were something to behold.

He could get lost in its sights for hours, watching as the lights in buildings came on and people started moving about. His floor-to-ceiling windows amplified the view, making him feel as though he were floating in the air, suspended over the city. It was electric; his whole body buzzed as if it were real.

With a sigh, Sam pulled back the sheets, made his bed with crisp corners, and showered in his en suite. He dressed in an immaculate suit, tailored to perfection and dry cleaned regularly, as well as a glossy pair of loafers.

He made an espresso shot in his shiny café-grade machine and downed it before he headed off for work. He couldn't survive on just one form of caffeine alone.

Locking the door behind himself, Sam entered a hallway stepping on a marvelous, marbled floor—

which was always shining and free of stains—and walls dressed with satin wallpaper. He waited at the assortment of six elevators positioned on both sides of the hall.

He certainly wasn't a lonely neighbor and often thought of his apartment building as a town of its own. When he first moved in two years ago, he doubted if he would ever meet everyone he lived with—not even the ones on the same floor—but he slowly acclimated to the environment and was able to at least recognize everyone's faces. Something about the densely packed tower made sense. It brought comfort to him, and he didn't mind all the traffic.

He heard the sound of doors sliding open, and he strolled over to the sole elevator waiting for him. As he stepped inside, his heart skipped a beat. There, at the back of the cab, leaning against a golden railing with her hair reflected in the mirror behind her head, was the most gorgeous woman he had ever seen. She had almond eyes that peered up at him through a mass of thick black eyelashes. Her long brown hair fell in soft waves, with bangs sweeping elegantly across her forehead. He had never encountered her before and was certain she had to be new to the building.

She blushed under his focused attention as he continued to take her in, debating whether to strike up a conversation or let her continue her morning in peace. But the soft pink glow on her angular cheeks made his decision for him.

"Morning," he said, his voice warm and casual.

"Good morning," she replied, her tone polite yet guarded.

He tilted his head slightly, his curiosity evident. "You're... new here?" he asked, drawing out the word with teasing emphasis.

She squinted at him for a moment, her compelling eyes narrowing as though weighing his intentions. "I recently moved in," she replied at last, her tone softening as if she had decided he wasn't a threat.

"Don't worry, I live here too," Sam said in an attempt at a joke. When she didn't react, he continued, "So, you haven't given your address to a total stranger. Only a partial stranger—one with excellent manners, I promise."

She seemed to turn inward, nodding at Sam's words but struggling to add any of her own. Her shyness endeared him.

"I'm Sam Cooper." He held out his hand for her to shake, and she quietly laughed at the formality of the gesture but took his hand in hers anyway.

"I'm Lara," she replied timidly.

"No last name?" Sam teased.

"Maybe you'll find out later." She smiled enough to let him know she was being playful.

"That's a bit bold," he said with a smirk, leaning against the elevator wall. "Most people try to win their neighbors over with cookies or a casserole, not a mystery. But hey, maybe it'll work. People usually love a good enigma."

"Ah." She nodded.

She was tough to crack, and Sam found himself talking just to fill the silence, grasping for anything that might retrieve more words from her. There was something captivating about her slowly melodic voice, and he wanted to hear more of it. Perhaps he needed a simpler approach. "What do you do for work?"

"I'm a financial consultant."

"Wow, that's high stakes."

"Yeah," she concurred with a light, breezy chuckle. "It's definitely not easy with all the long working hours."

"Well, I'm an investment banker."

"Also not easy."

"No, but it is fun, depending on the client."

"Hm, that's the first I've heard that."

"I'll just have to take you on one of my business trips to show you what I mean."

"Networking this early, Sam?"

He shrugged, his eyes bright at her joke. "Finance never sleeps."

The elevator came to a halt on the ground floor, and the doors rolled open with a *gentle tone*. Lara stepped out first, slightly blocking Sam's path as she turned to face him. She gave him a half-smile he couldn't read.

"It was nice meeting you," she said with a sort of practiced formality.

"You too," he replied.

Sam lingered for a moment, as she faded into the crowded lobby.

He watched her, hoping their interaction had meant something more than just a chance encounter.

***

Sam sat in his car, letting the final notes of the song he was blasting wash over him. This morning, he felt unusually cheerful as he navigated the familiar traffic, his windows rolled down and the radio cranked all the way up. Yet, despite the upbeat tune, his thoughts kept circling back to his brief interaction with Lara. Unanswered questions about her swam in his mind, infiltrating every note of music, making her presence feel as vivid as the melody itself.

He wasn't one to believe in true love, love at first sight, or any of those overused clichés, really—but he couldn't shake the unbearable urge to talk to her again. Curiosity tugged at him, persistent and insistent, fueling his need to uncover more about the woman who had captivated his thoughts.

He was refreshed as he skipped out of his vehicle and locked the doors with a click of his keys, all while humming the melody of whichever pop tune was racing around in his head.

Entering his office building, Sam was greeted by every doorman, secretary, and colleague with a courteous nod.

Some of the women stole glances at him, which he sometimes responded to with a wink or a thankful smile. Hushed whispers, telling of crushes and butterflies, followed in his wake.

He barely noticed it at all today.

Waiting for him at his desk was his new assistant, Raya.

She carefully put a takeaway coffee cup on a coaster for him and spread across the tabletop his client folders that she had meticulously arranged in order of his appointments for the day.

She pulled his chair out, which was a gesture he'd normally wave away, but today, he accepted her overly generous offering.

"Raya." He sighed with an earnest smile. "You're the best."

"Thank you, sir," she said with a polite nod. "Your day is fully booked," she continued. "You've got five meetings with potential investors, none of which are in the office."

"Your first stop is at Mr. Mohamad Bin Farhat's home. After that, you'll head to Dubai Hills Golf Club, followed by lunch at Em Sherif Café. In the afternoon, you'll visit La Casa Cigar Lounge, and to finish the evening, you'll have dinner at Roberto's."

"Another endless day ahead, then," Sam murmured sarcastically. He opened the first folder before him and studied its contents, his eyes scanning the pages with practiced intent.

All of this was in pursuit of a private island resort, a haven promising solitude, security, and unparalleled serenity for its exclusive guests. Sam envisioned this getaway project as the perfect retreat to suit his own needs, but indulging in a vacation there wasn't an option—not until he secured the commitment of all the financiers to back the investment.

As much as he delighted in his ability to party while still handling his business responsibilities, the last few months of his life had been nothing but that—drinking, smoking, and even traveling when the moment called for it.

His clients needed reassurance that he was one of them, that he belonged in their exclusive circle, and only then would they entrust him with their millions. Sam never doubted his capabilities or his value as an asset, but the numbers certainly worked in his favor—especially with projections showing that the resort would steadily appreciate in value, virtually guaranteeing no losses.

It seemed like a mathematical impossibility, but Sam and his team had gone over it time and time again—the numbers always checked out.

"Well," he concluded, "we'd better be off to Palm Jumeirah."

***

As their car pulled into the expansive front yard of Mohamad Bin Farhat's residence, a well-known pearl trader in the Gulf region, another vehicle arrived almost simultaneously—a sleek, convertible Mercedes. The unmistakable strains of an old Arabic song wafted from its open top, adding a nostalgic undertone to the crisp morning air. Mohamad stepped out gracefully, dressed in an immaculate Emirati kandura, his confident stride perfectly complementing the timeless elegance of his car.

Sam couldn't help but notice the deliberate care Mohamad put into every aspect of his appearance and surroundings, a man who clearly appreciated the finer things. Mohamad wasn't merely a car enthusiast but a true collector of classic beauty. His collection included vintage Porsches, Jaguars, Bentleys, and a handful of rare Mercedes models—each one a tribute to a golden era of craftsmanship and sophistication.

He greeted Sam with a warm handshake, his expression brightening when his gaze landed on Raya, standing composed at Sam's side.

"Mohamad, let me introduce you to my new assistant, Raya," Sam announced, gesturing toward her. "She's the one who will keep everything running smoothly from now onwards."

Raya extended her hand with a polite smile. "It's a pleasure to meet you, Mr. Bin Farhat."

"Please, call me Mohamad," he said, shaking her hand warmly. "The pleasure is mine. Sam's lucky to have someone as sharp as you on his team."

Raya inclined her head appreciatively. "Thank you, sir. I look forward to assisting with today's discussions."

Mohamad turned back to Sam, his smile widening with familiarity. "The last time you visited, I mentioned my car collection. Today seems like the perfect opportunity to show it to you."

Sam's eyebrows lifted with interest. "I've been waiting to see it. You're not going to make me plead for access, are you?"

Mohamad laughed, his voice rich and easy. "Not at all. I've just been waiting for the right moment. After our meeting, you'll finally get the tour."

The trio walked toward the grand entrance, the Arabic melody fading as the heavy doors swung open to reveal the opulent interior. Sam's thoughts wandered briefly, picturing the dazzling collection that awaited him after their business discussions were concluded.

His seaside mansion was marvelous. It looked like a Grecian sculpture, with marble columns that held up the immaculately sized structure and statues that adorned the walkway. Each stone in the path was carved with a pattern or picture, and the beach that expanded beyond the residence was perfectly landscaped, as if someone had run a vacuum over the sand and left it in neat rows of varying shades of brown.

Raya stood quietly at the edges of the room, observing as Sam moved confidently through the space, engaging animatedly with Mohamad over a lavish brunch of scones, croissants, and an array of flaky pastries. The client clearly had a sweet tooth that seemed impossible to satisfy.

To keep herself occupied, Raya alternated between scrolling through her phone and reviewing Sam's agenda, pausing every now and then to take notes. Both she and Sam maintained an air of understanding, though it was clear they were struggling to keep up with Mohamad's unpredictable and eccentric behavior.

Sam did his best to match the gentleman's energy, but eventually, he had to admit defeat. It seemed he was off his game today, despite his otherwise cheerful disposition. This marked the second instance where he just couldn't manage to connect with someone as effortlessly as he usually did.

Once they had finally finished, Mohamad escorted Sam and Raya out of the elegant meeting room, his energy as bright as ever.

True to his word, Mohamad led them toward a different section of his grand estate to showcase his renowned car collection. As they stepped into the vast garage, Sam found himself momentarily speechless.

The room resembled an art gallery rather than a typical storage space—each vehicle was displayed under carefully placed lighting that accentuated its polished curves and flawless finish. The walls were adorned with vintage automotive posters, plaques from exclusive car shows, and even a few signed photographs of iconic racers.

Mohamad gestured with pride toward the lineup. "And here we are. Please allow me to present my dearest treasures."

Sam's eyes roamed over a stunning display of classic automobiles—a pristine Porsche 356 in a soft silver shade, a sleek Jaguar E-Type with its unmistakable silhouette, a stately Bentley S1 adorned with its original fittings, and an iconic Mercedes 300SL Gullwing that seemed to radiate timeless elegance. The vehicles weren't just maintained—they were celebrated, their details restored to perfection.

"These aren't just cars," Sam remarked, his admiration evident. "They're masterpieces."

Mohamad chuckled, his laughter warm and infectious. "Indeed. Each one has its own story, its own character. I've spent years tracking some of them down, ensuring they're properly preserved." He walked over to a Bentley, running his hand lovingly along its fender. "This one was my father's favorite. He used to bring me along for long drives in it when I was a boy. It's what first made me fall in love with the artistry of these classics."

Raya snapped a quick photo on her phone, unable to hide her own enthusiasm. "They're incredible," she said, her tone respectful. "I can see why you're so passionate about them."

After an hour of exploring the collection, peppered with Mohamad's memories and stories, Sam felt a renewed sense of appreciation for the skill involved in crafting these vehicles.

As they prepared to leave, they exchanged firm handshakes and polite farewells, reinforcing the sense of progress and mutual respect. Mohamad clapped Sam on the shoulder. "I'll see you both again soon, I'm sure."

"Absolutely," Sam replied, already deciding that the collaboration was a certainty in his mind. He turned to Raya as they approached their car, his tone resolute. "List him as an official financier. At this point, we're not accepting no for an answer."

Raya nodded with a small smile. "Consider it done, Sam."

Silently, he vowed to himself to do a better job of getting through to Lara if their paths crossed again. This constant preoccupation with her, like some lovesick daydreamer, was a distraction he couldn't afford. The stakes were too high, and billions were on the line.

Ch. 13

"A New Adventure"

"Oh, God," Tiffany groaned, "another one?"

Normally, Sam might have tried to combat her irritation, but the growing fatigue in his own mind left him with little energy to do so.

With Shiva and Céline, he experienced emotions he thought had evaporated from his body, and he got to visit new corners of the world. That was enough for him.

But Lara had come along when he least wanted it.

The Sam Cooper of his dreams was thrilled by the idea of falling in love with some beautiful stranger, while Sam of the present was struggling to keep up.

He was confused by her revelation—why had Céline been taken away from him?

Was he destined to endlessly mourn the women he lost, even as he rushed toward another in his dreams?

He knew none of them were real, yet the tangled complexity of his emotions was becoming harder to navigate. He felt perpetually hollow, haunted by visions of memories both tender and painful, all while wishing desperately for a sense of control over *something*.

Just one small part of it.

"I'm not happy about it, either," Sam protested. "I adored Shiva, and I liked Céline... I mean, Céline really checked all my boxes—except for the fact that, unfortunately, she was in a relationship with another man. And don't get me wrong, Lara seems great—"

"Lara is nothing more than the boogeyman of your REM cycle."

Sam winced, feeling an insane urge to defend a woman his brain had completely made up. "That's a bit much."

"It's like she's Freddy Krueger sucking the life out of you when you're most vulnerable. You can't escape her until you wake up. You can't escape any of them until they decide *they're* done with *you*."

"It's not that serious."

"Okay, do you feel good, Sam? Because you look awful."

Sam sighed. His entire body tingled with oversensitivity. He squinted at the fluorescent lights in his office, and even the familiar tightness of the tie around his neck seemed to choke him. He felt like every nerve in his skin stood at pinpoints, ready to take offense to even the smallest bit of sensation.

He rubbed at his gummy eyes. "I feel like I haven't actually been relaxed in my sleep for years."

"Exactly, so these women are great in theory but are literally ruining your life. Total sleep paralysis demons."

"I thought you were into this?" Sam couldn't help but ask with a humorous twitch to his lip.

"Into what?"

"My dreams, Tiff?"

"Well, I was—until you started self-destructing your relationship with Kate and spending all your free time thinking about these hallucinations!" She paused, took a deep breath, and gathered herself. "I've just noticed a change in you, that's all. You don't seem happy anymore. And I've been doing a lot of research on sleep to see what's been going on with you."

"You have?"

"Yeah, you're my boss, and when you're in the pits, we're all in the pits, okay?" Tiffany tried playing off her interest as pure business, but Sam still felt an ache of appreciation in his chest. She was the closest thing to family he had here.

She straightened her spine and clapped her hands together. Sam tried not to recoil at the sound. "So, the only thing I can determine is that you're hitting your REM cycle each night, which means all of your senses are fully engaged while you sleep. We all need it, we all go through it, but your cycles are probably too long, so you're not feeling rested."

"That's a very... clinical answer."

"Yeah, yeah, yeah, it's no magical fairytale fantasy, but it's the truth." Her eyes were tense and uncompromising.

Sam was disappointed by such a short response. It couldn't have been something as simple as an overactive imagination and a problem he needed to go to a sleep clinic to solve.

What if the women were real and this was his brain's way of urging him to go after them? Maybe he was suffering from an odd case of amnesia, and the memories of his romances were coming back to him in elaborate montages he couldn't break free from until he addressed the reality of his lovers.

What he thought were dreams were actually scenes from his life. Maybe, though, the women were just lessons—experiences meant to guide him toward choosing the right partner in the real world.

He groaned, dropping his head in his hands. He couldn't even think of a logical reason for his dreams. Maybe he did need medical help; even Tiffany was tired of it all.

His dreams likely held power over him because he allowed them to. Because he spent his waking hours thinking about them and analyzing the details.

The more he gave energy to the women, the more clearly they could appear in his sleep.

He was creating these illusions; he just didn't want to admit it. Just like how Kate had accused him of avoiding responsibility, he felt himself doing it now. He resolved to put an end to his dream girls by stopping his thoughts about them once and for all.

The day dragged on, but with a hearty meal and some caffeine in his system, he was running a little better.

When he returned home for the day, he shot off a message to his mother in the States, telling her how much he missed her.

The message read:

I'm planning on taking a vacation or something soon, so hopefully, I get to come home for a little while. If you visit Dad's grave again this week, would you put some flowers out for me again, please? I love you, Mom.

No response came yet, which Sam was used to, given the time difference between Singapore and the U.S. He fell asleep remembering how the sunrise slipped into his childhood bedroom when he was growing up, recalling the peace of knowing that it was summer and a few more hours of blissful sleep were promised to him.

***

Sam felt his shoulders droop as he woke up before a grand door, its surface engraved with intricate gold designs.

Here he was again. Beyond the shimmering light of the doorframe lay the promise of a new adventure. Should he give it up now? Should he choose not to step through the door, staying in his grey void until he eventually woke up in Singapore? Perhaps it was better to stop before anything more could develop between him and the woman with the alluring almond eyes.

He clenched his fists. He would resist it. He turned in the opposite direction of the door and started to walk.

His movements were sure, determined, fueled by his insistence to stay grounded in the real world.

But the further he walked into the curling, misty expanse, the more his footsteps slowed.

There had to be a reason why he dreamed about this woman. That brief interaction couldn't be all there was. He had to understand more—maybe then he would see why he was dreaming in the first place.

When he raised his eyes from the featureless ground, the door was in front of him once again.

Fine, *he concluded.* Just one more time.

***

Sam woke up at his usual time, following his typical detailed morning routine, though there was a quiet anticipation hanging in the back of his mind. As he stepped into the hallway and waited by the elevator, he found himself hoping to bump into Lara. She'd been occupying his thoughts since their last brief interaction, and he couldn't help but imagine running into her again. But as the elevator doors opened and he was greeted with only an empty cab, his hopes deflated.

He was sure of it—he was the kind of guy who liked to believe in serendipitous events brought to him by fate. But something about Lara compelled him to take matters into his own hands, orchestrating his own version of divine intervention.

He went to work as usual, but he made sure to finish his tasks quickly and postponed a few afternoon meetings to free up his schedule.

As soon as he arrived at the tower, he began his light stalking mission, starting in the lobby where the café was located. He scanned the room, hoping to catch sight of her sipping a latte or chatting with someone. The barista greeted him warmly, but there was no trace of Lara.

Not ready to give up, Sam stopped by his apartment to quickly swap his business attire for something more casual and sporty before heading to the top floor of the towering building, where the rooftop terrace and pool were located. There, the water glimmered under the golden hues of the setting sun, casting a warm glow over the peaceful scene. Children played near the water's edge, scattered towels lay forgotten on lounge chairs, and other tenants reclined, soaking in the sunset. But still, there was no sign of her.

Eventually, he decided it was best to head to the gym after checking all the lounges and recreation areas within the tower. He figured he would stay there as long as necessary to accidentally-on-purpose bump into her. His body could use the exercise, anyway—it was a good opportunity to make up for all the missed workouts.

As soon as he walked into the gym and scanned beyond the array of machines and grunting weightlifters, he spotted Lara trotting on a treadmill. Her hair bounced with each step, tied into a high ponytail, while a few stray strands clung to her forehead.

She didn't notice him at first—not until he stepped onto the treadmill beside hers and casually tapped the buttons to start. He tried to appear nonchalant, as if his choice to be near her was pure coincidence, but the moment his machine whirred to life, she did a double take. He met her gaze with an easy smile and gave a small wave.

She took an AirPod out of her ear.

"You found the gym," Sam remarked with an impressed smile.

"I didn't really need to," she replied. "Wandering around this place is a workout on its own."

"In a few weeks, you'll be able to find the spa and finally get to unwind after all this exercise," he said with a hint of humor, reluctantly starting to jog. He couldn't help but feel overly conscious of his own stride compared to Lara's smooth and effortless rhythm.

The tiniest of frowns appeared between her dark eyebrows. "A spa?"

"Of course, a spa."

"God, this place is intimidating."

"It takes a while to acclimate, but after a few months of getting familiar with it, it's really not too bad."

"I'm doing the best I can." Her tone was flat and emotionless. Sam chewed his lip, wondering if he had somehow offended her.

He took a breather before the speed of his treadmill increased. He didn't want to appear out of shape in front of Lara, for she had barely uttered a word despite the rapid motion of her feet. He was still so disoriented when it came to her.

He could feel the conclusion to their conversation approaching—without ever getting to anything more than neighborly small talk, Sam asked, "Are you new to Dubai?"

"Yeah," she said, confirming his suspicions, "I'm from Lebanon, which doesn't seem worlds apart, but it really is. It's how I imagine Canadians visiting

America must feel. Same continent but entirely different lifestyles and people."

"That's always the worst kind of culture shock—the one you don't expect." Sam clicked on his timer and started to jog once again.

She gave him a brief smile before turning her attention back to the television mounted on her treadmill.

Maybe he was chasing someone who simply wasn't interested in him. What was he basing all of this on, anyway? A few fleeting glances in an elevator and polite answers to his questions?

Sam realized he had no choice but to rip off the Band-Aid and find out if all this yearning to connect with her had been worth it.

"You know, I could always show you around Dubai," he suggested, his tone light but sincere. "You can easily consider me a pro—I've played tour guide to every investor visiting here for the first time, not to mention the occasional family or friends who've come by."

He gave her a grin. "So, I promise you, no fancy landmarks or tourist traps, just the real magical side of the city. I'm confident you'll have a great experience." He paused with a playful expression. "And as an added bonus, I'll make sure you don't get lost in this building. Think of it as a full-service tour."

"Really?" She raised an eyebrow, a mix of skepticism and curiosity glimmering in her eyes.

"You bet."

She glanced at him sideways for a moment, as if carefully weighing her options. "That's a kind offer... but I'm not sure how far I can trust a stranger with my tour plans. And how do I know you're not just trying to get me lost in this building on purpose?"

Sam's heart tightened, a knot forming in his throat—and not because of the jogging. He steadied himself before replying, his voice firm despite the nerves bubbling beneath the surface. "Well, you'll have the chance to get to know me better during our outing. To be honest, I'm just hoping it'll be a good start to showing you I'm worth trusting."

Lara let out a quiet sigh. "I don't know, Sam. I'm not certain if that's a good idea. I mean, we just met..."

Sam's expression fell slightly, the disappointment was clear in his eyes, but he nodded nonetheless, "I understand. No pressure at all."

"Please don't get me wrong," Lara explained gently, her tone careful. "It's not that I don't appreciate the offer. I just... I'm not sure if it's the right move. We've only just met, and I don't want to give you the wrong impression."

"No, no worries at all—I get it," Sam replied, his tone calm and genuine. "And no wrong impressions, I promise."

Lara wrapped up her workout session, slowing the machine to a stop before reaching for the towel draped over its handle. With a soft but genuine smile, she turned to Sam. "I've got to head back," she admitted, dabbing her forehead. "There's a project I need to finish—it won't work on itself, unfortunately." Her tone was light, but a trace of regret was evident as she slipped her gym bag onto her shoulder and prepared to leave.

"Well, good luck with the project. I'm sure you'll nail it," Sam mentioned with an encouraging tone. He hesitated for a moment before adding, "Maybe next time we'll actually get to have a proper conversation—when you're not rushing off to save the day."

"Sure," she called casually. "See you around, Sam."

As she walked away, Sam couldn't help but feel a mix of anticipation and uncertainty. At least she hadn't shut the door completely. He made a mental note to figure out how to make *next time* happen sooner rather than later.

***

For the next several days, Sam's nights were filled with vivid dreams of his routine life in Dubai—poring over documents in his sleek office, negotiating with high-profile investors at their luxurious mansions, and socializing over gourmet meals in upscale venues. These scenes unfolded in a swirl of polished settings, from elegant dining rooms to dimly lit lounges steeped in the scent of premium cigars.

But no matter how busy his day seemed, his evenings always found him drawn to the gym at the same hour, hoping to cross paths with her again. Each time, he scanned the treadmills and weight stations, a flicker of hope in his chest. But every effort ended the same—she wasn't there. A quiet disappointment settled over him as he left each night, wondering if she had vanished from his world entirely.

In the real world, Sam found himself questioning her absence. Where was Lara? Why wasn't she appearing in his dreams anymore? Had she never truly been the one he was meant to meet in Dubai? The thought unsettled him, pressing at the back of his mind no matter how much he tried to shake it. Maybe everything had simply shifted course, or maybe she had never been meant to stay. Perhaps someone else was waiting for him, another presence woven into this experience, yet to reveal herself.

Until one day, as his dream began, he found himself at the gym as usual, the clang of dumbbells and the hum of cardio machines filling the space. This time, however, he finally spotted her just as she was heading for the exit, her gym bag resting casually against her side.

"Hello there, it's been a while..."

"Hey, Sam, it's been a while indeed!" She greeted him with a cheerful smile that brightened her face.

"Workout already done?" Sam asked, his voice light but carried with surprise.

"Unfortunately, I just got interrupted by a phone call about a last-minute meeting—ruined my workout plans again."

As she tossed her bag over her shoulder, Sam extended a handwritten invitation card—one he had apparently been carrying around, waiting for the chance to bump into her. His gesture was lighthearted. "Look, I know you turned down an informal invitation the last time I saw you, but I thought I'd try again with something a bit more formal this time," he remarked, grinning as Lara took the card, her hesitation giving way to curiosity.

The card read: *First, let me officially welcome you to our special community! As a token of this welcome, I'd love to invite you to explore some of Dubai's most magical places with me as your private tour guide. Afterward, we can enjoy a cozy, casual dinner—no expectations, just good company and interesting sights. Signed, Sam.*

Lara glanced up at him, her lips curving slightly. "You really don't give up, do you?"

Her eyes lit up, and before he could answer, she let out a soft laugh, holding the card delicately between her fingers. "But you're not bad, I have to say. You really surprised me with this—plus, there's a dinner included. That's very optimistic of you."

Then, she added playfully with a wink, "Can I ask you, Sam—how many ladies have you already impressed with those letters of yours?"

Sam smirked, leaning in slightly. "Well, actually," he said, his tone teasing, "I'd love to say you're the first, but the truth is... I've been saving the best for now."

She finally smiled. "You're persistent, I'll give you that. And since I'm in a hurry right now, I'll make a quick decision and say yes. Let's do it. But just as neighbors, okay?"

"Of course," Sam replied with an understanding nod. "How about we set it for Friday at six PM?"

"Friday's going to be tough, especially at that time," Lara pointed out, glancing at the card briefly. "Do you mind moving it to Saturday instead?"

"Saturday it is," Sam agreed happily.

"I'll meet you in the main lobby," Lara said with a quick wave before hurrying off.

"Awesome. See you then," Sam called after her, a spark of excitement glowing in his eyes as he turned away.

***

Kate had reached out again, and just like before, Sam melted at her touch.

They sat in bed when he felt the energy in the room take that turn again, now that the heat and rush and blissful freedom of thought had evaporated.

"So," she inquired in a quiet, even tone, pulling the sheets up to under her pearly shoulders, "who've I lost you to this evening?"

Sam sighed, his shoulders heaving as he braced himself for another miserable argument. He and Kate were going around in the same circles he was suffering through in his sleep. There was no relief from the unrest—only regret and confusion, chaining him to the ride he couldn't escape. Maybe it would have a happy ending. He knew he had to be honest for that to have any chance of happening.

He felt Kate's insistent eyes on his, so he admitted, "Lara."

"So, Céline ran out on you?" The question was salted with arrogance, but she said it in a way that gave her room for denial.

"No," he breathed, "she just... disappeared."

"That sounds like she left you." Her eyes sparkled with barely contained amusement, as if she were on the verge of laughing. He realized, with a sinking feeling, how pathetic all of this must seem to her. And honestly, he couldn't blame her.

"No, Kate," he repeated with more firmness this time. "My brain just stopped putting her in my dreams. There's nothing else to it. Plus, Céline was just a friend and a professional business partner."

"Oh, sorry," she replied softly. "Guess you're still not over it." She waited until he laid back into the pillows again. "Where's this new girl from? Lara?"

"We're in Dubai."

"Oh... that's nice." A strange look crossed her face. She was staring out into the darkening expanse of skyscrapers and threads of traffic, her eyes and voice unfocused on him. "Have you ever been there before?"

Sam shook his head. "It seems like a lovely place."

"Yeah, I've heard great things about it."

An awkward silence fell between them.

"So, this Lara... Are you with her, like, currently?"

"I'm not with anyone, Kate," he assured her as he began to unwind again. "Except for this, between us, right now."

The city lights from his window illuminated the glaze over her eyes, and Sam wondered if she was about to cry. He reached out to her, but she didn't sink her cheek into his palm the way he wished she would.

"Oh, that's a shame."

Sam's voice was unsteady and unsure as he asked, "What's going on, Kate?"

Kate looked down at her lap. "I don't know... I guess I'm just waiting for you in your dreams, too. Do you... do you ever see me? Or is it always them?"

He bowed his head, a quiet heaviness settling over him. "Maybe one day you'll show up, Kate. Dreams are weird like that. I can't—I don't control them."

"Hmm..." She regarded him thoughtfully. "I think I might try to go to Dubai tonight. Promise to meet me there?"

Sam leaned in, guilt and desire wrestling in the pit of his stomach. He kissed Kate slowly and willed himself to remember to try.

Ch. 14

"Sleepwalking"

Shifting into his dream world, Sam smiled as the captain anchored them in the middle of the Persian Gulf, offering an astonishing view. The waves gently kissed the bottom of the boat, where he sat with Yanis Kolomontanos, a Greek millionaire and potential investor.

Yanis had taken a particular interest in stringing Sam along, inviting him on extravagant adventures, only to dismantle the topic of business with long-winded tales about his life.

Sam didn't mind the charade, as it was part of his strategy to conclude deals, to build a personal relationship with his clients, and establish mutual trust.

He saw something in Yanis that reminded him of himself, and he couldn't decide whether he was pleased or horrified.

The yacht, M/V Saya, named after Yanis's beloved and only daughter, was an experience in itself. The sun bathed them in warmth, while chilled beers were served regularly by attentive staff. Both of them leaned back, savoring the rich, smooth flavors of hand-rolled Opus X by Fuente cigars, a perfect accompaniment to the serene atmosphere.

Sam didn't even have to flag down the staff before another bottle was smoothly placed in his hand. The seats beneath their tired legs were upholstered in pristine white leather, cool and luxurious to the touch, adding to the yacht's understated sophistication.

"What are your goals, brother?" Yanis asked in a dense accent. His shades glinted as they caught the sun's rays and reflected them back at Sam. "For me," he went on without waiting for Sam to answer, "I want to be a billionaire."

"This isn't enough for you?" Sam queried in jest, motioning at the sea.

"Nothing is ever enough for Yanis," he said, his tone carrying a mix of pride and determination. "I can always strive to be better, to have better things—and so should you. Honestly, I think I'll die chasing money."

The statement sounded like a burden, not something to brag about. Would there really never be any rest? The whole point of acquiring luxuries was to one day enjoy them, and even though Sam was taken to exclusive clubs and natural wonders and fed the finest foods, he still wanted it to amount to something.

It couldn't be just a stepping-stone to bigger things. That wasn't the kind of life he wanted to live; he was already exhausted as is.

Yanis was typically a solitary figure, having been divorced long ago. His daughter, the namesake of the yacht, ran a high-end restaurant in Mykonos during the summer and managed a boutique hotel in Athens the rest of the year, along with her husband.

Yanis spent most of his time reveling in his achievements through extravagant trips he took alone or purchasing properties that remained uninhabited. He collected wealth and possessions purely to brag about them, rarely indulging others in the luxuries he surrounded himself with. He was greedy with what he had, and Sam was beginning to feel that way about himself, too.

He had the largest bed he could buy, just to sleep on one quarter of it. His apartment could house six people—he had two extra rooms and many closets he simply could not fill—and yet he resided in it alone.

He had more space than he needed, more money than he could spend. He wondered what it would be like to have someone like Lara, practical and self-efficient, out on the water with him, providing some solace to his vacant decisions.

Yanis was right—this lifestyle would never be enough.

Sam needed much more than this. None of the luxuries mattered if you never had anyone you loved to share it with.

"I cannot invest in your property if you do not have this mindset," Yanis continued. "How can I trust that you and your people will keep improving the project? That you will bring in guests with more and more attractions? That you will continue developing when change is demanded? This is also something you must do."

"Don't worry," Sam assured him, "that's all in the plan. We'll be assigning the management of the resort to one of the most renowned hospitality brands. We never intend to stop reaching for greater heights—giving people what they both want and need. As society progresses, so will we. That's the only way to keep up."

"Great, man, now we're talking." Yanis waved down his staff for a plate of oysters and a bottle of champagne.

***

At night in the lobby, Sam watched curious-looking fish swim around the neon aquarium, running his fingers through his hair mindlessly while he waited for Lara. Sam made sure to arrive earlier than the agreed time—he didn't want to risk having her wait even a second for him.

Following his excursion on the sea that same day, a wave of gloominess settled over him, heavy and unshakable. It wasn't just a passing feeling—it clung to him like an unwelcome shadow.

For the first time in a long while, he found himself questioning everything—the choices he'd made, the paths he'd taken, and the people he'd allowed into his life—all tangled with the pieces of advice he'd absorbed from Yanis.

It was as if the clarity of the open water had magnified his uncertainties, each ripple in the ocean reflecting a decision he feared had been the wrong one. The excitement he felt over Lara was fading, turning into ash as he went over the possibilities of their relationship in his mind.

He began to recall their conversations, noting how he bulldozed his way into a date, and now, he had little to hope for. This was going to be another routine dinner, wherein they shared basic information about themselves and wound up feeling lonelier than when they had arrived.

How many more times could Sam share the highlights of his life story before the novelty wore off? Even though he had been sure of Lara when he saw her, how could he guarantee his brain would keep feeling that way?

He had a tendency to expect too much in a relationship, deducting points from women as if they were players in a game, always trying to measure them up to fluctuating standards. He told himself he was being deservedly picky—you *should* be strict about the kind of people you introduce into your love life.

But now he was aware of his own resistance to change—he was simply scared to settle down despite all his moaning and groaning about his isolation. He blamed his hectic work schedule for his coldness when rejecting women and his inability to forge a deep connection, but he continued to put himself out there, hoping for a different result.

He had problems he refused to confront, yet he kept trying to move forward regardless. In doing so, he was dragging innocent women into his chaos, only for it all to lead nowhere. An unsettling sensation surfaced as these thoughts began to align in his mind, taking shape and creating voids within his chest he didn't know how to locate and patch.

Any doubt he had quickly vanished when she swept out of the elevator. Sam marveled at the effortless elegance in the way she carried herself, as if every move was deliberately measured and refined to perfection.

Lara smiled at him, for the first time, with an openness he hadn't seen from her before. She looked comforted by the sight of him, waltzing over as if on air. Her beautiful hair was loosely curled and fell in waves across her shoulders. Her pointed chin highlighted her heart-shaped face. She looked like an angel, wearing a wine-red dress that elegantly hugged her waist and thighs. He stood up to greet her, his hands automatically adjusting the lapels of his jacket as he prepared for their joining in the center of the carpeted lobby.

"You look wonderful," he said earnestly as she stepped into earshot, his eyes lighting up at the sight of her.

"Oh, thanks. You're not so bad yourself," she responded with a warm smile, handing him her jacket to hold so she could slip it on with ease.

"Shall we?" he asked, gesturing toward the door with a slight tilt of his head.

"You lead, Mr. Guide," she said with a playful inflection, nodding toward the parking lot.

***

They began their *Dubai by Night* experience with a visit to the enchanting old town by the port. The narrow streets, lined with traditional markets and the faint scent of spices wafting through the air, seemed to come alive under the soft glow of lanterns.

The rhythmic lapping of the water against the docks added a soothing backdrop to the animated chatter of locals and tourists alike. Sam seemed particularly at ease here, his gaze lingering on the old stone walls and the shimmering water.

It became clear that he had a fondness for old towns and the sea—they always seemed to play a part in his dream getaways, places that offered a blend of history and serenity.

From there, they drove along Sheikh Zayed Road until Dubai Marina, where the modern side of the city unveiled itself in all its glittering glory. The streets buzzed with activity, the weekend energy filling the air. Shops, hotels, and restaurants shone brightly, their signs and facades sparkling like jewels against the night sky. Crowds of people milled around, some leisurely strolling, others dining outdoors or heading to the latest hotspots.

Lara couldn't hide her amazement. "So, this is JBR? I've heard about it, but seeing it is something else," she murmured, her gaze gliding from one dazzling storefront to the next. "It's so alive... so electric."

Sam chuckled, clearly enjoying her awe. "This is just the beginning. Dubai doesn't slow down, especially on weekends. Wait until we hit the famous Madinat Jumeirah."

She admitted sheepishly that this was her first real chance to explore the city, especially at night. "I've been so caught up trying to find a place to live," she explained, glancing out at the striking coastline. "Between work and moving out of the hotel, my free time has been... limited."

"Well, I'd say it was worth the wait," Sam replied with a warm tone. "Tonight's all about catching up on what you've missed."

The smile on her face grew, the city's lights reflecting in her eyes as if they were her own. Her delight was unmistakable as they continued their vibrant and exciting journey.

Dinner at a dynamic Latin American restaurant nestled within Madinat Jumeirah, an Arabian-inspired touristic village, offered a unique charm, though it was far more understated than the opulence Sam typically chose for a first date. The warm glow of hanging lanterns mixed with the rhythmic beats of salsa music in the background, creating an atmosphere that felt intimate yet lively. The aromas of grilled herbs and freshly made tortillas wafted through the air, inviting them to relax and enjoy the ambiance.

He couldn't help but notice how the simplicity of the evening brought out something different in him—an ease he hadn't felt in a long time. It was a departure from the usual extravagance he relied on to impress, but perhaps that was the point. With Lara, it didn't feel like he needed the grandeur. Instead, he preferred to give her the space to breathe, to truly come into herself around him, before he introduced more elaborate elements to their future outings or dates, if the chemistry developed.

The setting was cozy, with rustic wooden tables and colorful mosaics lining the walls, adding to the charm. Their waiter was quick but didn't linger, and Lara ordered a cocktail with a silly name, which she blushed about but Sam found adorable.

"I'm not much of a drinker," she said, "so when I go out, I like to order something I can't fix for myself. It makes everything more fun, don't you think?"

Sam had joined her, and in front of him was a blue cocktail drink of rum and syrups, adorned with an umbrella and a gummy shark. He was embarrassed to admit it was delicious. "Only for you," he replied as he held up his glass to toast her.

"Still going for the machismo thing, huh?" she asked teasingly.

"Whoa, where did that come from?" He scoffed out a surprised laugh.

"This is why I don't drink, Sam; I let go of all my self-control."

"Well, you must have liked the *machismo thing* if you agreed to go out with me."

"Mmm..." She shrugged her athletic shoulders. "I could tell there was more going on under the surface."

He felt like every single aspect of him, every inch of skin and beat of his heart, was visible to her in the way she was watching him. He swallowed his sudden shyness with a gulp of sweet cocktail. "Really?"

"Yep." She seemed more cheerful, knowing she was getting under Sam's skin. "I have very good instincts about people. Despite the self-control issue."

"I don't know, you seem pretty reserved to me."

"That's just my facade. I've been trying to step away from that level of shyness..." Lara brushed a few loose strands away from her forehead self-consciously, her voice tense as she asked, "Am I doing well?"

A grin spread across Sam's face. "So far so good."

"Glad to hear you're slightly entertained," she replied dryly, her expression falling into a mask of pure frustration. She clearly needed more convincing affirmation than his teasing.

"That's all you can really hope for in life—just mild satisfaction." Sam gestured playfully toward her with his gummy shark before biting into its head. He enjoyed testing Lara's boundaries—they seemed to shift with every passing moment. She was like an ever-changing maze, and he was eager to find its center.

"Sounds like my last relationship." Lara's eyes darkened, the playfulness from her tone evaporating as she seemed to be pulled into some grim memory.

Sam sensed the need to tread lightly. He didn't want to risk accidentally hurting Lara if this was a sensitive topic. He watched her carefully, choosing to ask a tentative, "Did you—would you wanna talk about it?"

"No... no..." She put down her drink and clasped her hands on the table, her body shutting down. "I'm pretty sure it's rule number one to not talk about exes on first dates."

Sam's heart skipped at her choice of words. *A date.* She'd called it *a date*. The flutter of excitement stirred within him, but he quickly masked it. "We can be unconventional." A rush of unexpected protectiveness filled him. "Besides, playing by the rules is usually very boring."

She giggled slightly, gazing at him, almost as if she were scolding him for wanting to be a rule-breaker. Then she said, "Well, it certainly didn't help me with my previous boyfriend."

Sam met her gaze and nodded, encouraging her to share if she felt up to it—or to simply wave away his interest.

She settled for the prior option. "We got as far as engagement, but I really didn't want him to waste his time forever on me. It wasn't like he was a bad guy or mistreated me in any way... I just never felt that spark with him. Maybe I did on the first date or two, but by the time he became my boyfriend, all of that had faded. I don't even know why I said yes to him either time. Maybe I was just afraid of being alone."

Sam felt a dull ache of understanding, but he let her speak. He wasn't going to interrupt her now.

"It's our nature to couple up," she said, meekly unfolding and refolding her napkin, "to find that *someone* who will be by our side no matter what, and after so many years of dating and being let down, I was just tired. And there he was—perfectly nice, waiting for me with open arms. Sometimes, I wish I could have made it work for his sake, but you can't live for other people like that. I would have made him miserable with my misery, and that wouldn't be fair."

"How long were you together?"

"Just over two years."

Sam leaned back in his woven bamboo chair. "I know it may seem strange to say, but I'm proud of you for walking. Once you're comfortable with someone or somewhere, it becomes terrifying to break away from that. Like you're tossing your whole life away."

"You've been through the same thing?"

"Yeah. Maybe not with love or relationships, but I know the feeling."

The tension seemed to thaw from Lara's muscles, and she offered Sam a small, grateful smile, "Well, I'm glad I'm no longer alone, then."

***

"And somehow, you look worse," Tiffany noted as Sam shuffled into his office on Monday morning.

"Unfortunately, I agree," Sam replied, rubbing his hands across his forehead. He felt as if he were in the grips of a migraine only a strong, black American coffee could cure—the kind he used to endure in his early twenties, back when he thought himself invincible, surviving on just a few hours of sleep while intensely poring over his textbooks.

Age had moderated his lack of self-care, but apparently, that familiar sickness of an overworked body found new ways to infiltrate his system.

"Are you trying to stay awake so you don't think about the girls?" Tiffany asked in a concerned tone, ever the Mother Hen.

"No, quite the opposite, actually. I slept for twelve hours last night. *Twelve*. I can't seem to get enough sleep, but I'm pretty sure I'm having more than enough for the entire world. It's like I developed narcolepsy."

"Maybe you're a vampire or something. You been to a club recently?" Tiffany leaned in and wiggled her clawed fingers at him with wide eyes. "Did a stranger bite you on the neck, and now you're thirsty for blood?"

"Come on, Tiff," Sam managed to huff out a laugh, shaking his heavy head at her with a smile. "This is really messing with my head... I need... *someone*, alright? I need a partner. In the real world. I need what my dreams are showing me, and the fact that I can't is—is driving me nuts."

Admitting it all made Sam's empty stomach clench with displeasure. He'd forgotten to have breakfast again.

He sighed as he settled into his comfortable office chair, Tiffany following with a now-serious expression. "You know, I go home, and I can tell nobody lives there, including myself. I can't get comfortable because none of my furniture was picked out by someone who wants it to be *ours*. I don't cook because it's pointless to do all that work for one person. I don't talk to anyone before bed. I just sit there with my eyes open, waiting for something to happen, or for Kate to maybe come over for a few hours every week."

"Damn," Tiffany sighed. "I don't think that's something I can fix. Sorry..."

Sam laughed softly again. "Thank you, Tiff. For caring about me as much as you do. But I promise, I don't need you to fix this for me... Maybe once I've found her, I'll have the peace I need to get a good night's sleep."

She frowned slightly, "Find who?"

The simple question felt so much heavier than Tiffany ever intended. Sam's migraine pounded at his temples with a renewed fury.

"I don't know anymore."

***

Kate was stepping out of the Minister of Foreign Affairs' office just as Sam was heading in. They crossed paths in the hallway, and she quickly averted her gaze, avoiding eye contact. Almost immediately, her expression shifted to one of regret, an unspoken apology shining in her eyes as she slowed down to greet him.

He wasn't in the mood for another emotional conversation, but not communicating with Kate never got them anywhere. He stopped to meet her reaching arm.

"I've just..." She looked over his shoulder. "I've got to tell you something really quick."

He waited for her to continue. She took in a sharp breath, her collarbones tensing as she braced herself for the announcement—"I'm being relocated to the United Arab Emirates."

Sam was stunned. The information ripped through him like a shock wave. "Oh?" was all he could utter.

"In a few weeks. Sara still has to finish up school, and I need to get all my paperwork sorted, but it's happening," she mentioned with a note of regretful excitement. "I was just officially informing Minister Lim."

"Oh, wow, um... That's great, Kate. You've done an amazing job around here. I'm happy for you." The words kicked around hollowly in his chest. He meant it, of course, but he didn't want to be saying it.

"Thanks, Sam. And, well, as you know, James tried to reconnect, but I finally gathered the courage to reject him. Again," she added quietly. "I'd rather be unmarried than with someone who doesn't even really like me."

Sam was struggling to catch up. The advice he gave to Lara somehow transpired in Kate. Was it a coincidence, or did it mean something?

He cleared his throat, trying to ignore how achingly numb he felt. "I know things have been tense between us, but I'd really like to have you and Sara over one day. I'd like the chance to say a proper goodbye."

"I'd appreciate that," she replied then squeezed his arm lovingly. "See you soon, then?"

"See you soon."

As he watched her fade into the crowd of busybodies and suits, he felt a weight lift off his chest. The feeling caught him by surprise, but somehow he couldn't help but realize that this might actually be a good thing.

They could finally stop entangling their lives with conflicting desires and unmet expectations. And maybe, just maybe, Sam could meet someone who truly shared his feelings, someone who wanted more than just the physical side of a relationship. Perhaps, too, this experience would give Kate the clarity to decide what she really wanted in a partnership, rather than both of them blindly diving into the unknown.

With the distance between them, Sam and Kate's romance would surely diminish on its own, dying with the time and space that would continue expanding and never cease. They could both start new lives and be free of some of the guilt of actually breaking things off in a messy fight.

Maybe it was another version of the easy way out, but at least it was happening. This was a step in the right direction for both of them.

Ch. 15

"A Sandy Day"

He had gone days without seeing Lara, and the hope of finding her was starting to fade. They had agreed to meet again, but she hadn't shared her phone number or unit details. He strained his mind, trying to recall the floor she had gotten off on, but even if he remembered, knocking on random doors and pleading for her to appear wasn't exactly an option.

She was nowhere to be found at her usual time at the gym, so he resorted to his familiar routine of touring the building, hoping it might lead to another encounter. But lightning never struck twice, and his search felt increasingly futile.

Once again, a nagging thought crept in—maybe she hadn't enjoyed their outing. Maybe she was deliberately avoiding him so he wouldn't get the chance to ask her out a second time. Perhaps she hadn't shared her contact details on purpose that night. The possibility stung more than he cared to admit, making him feel even more foolish for continuing to chase after her.

Having run out of coffee beans at home, Sam headed down to the coffee shop in the lobby of their building for his morning fix.

He had left the apartment a bit earlier than usual and settled at a table with his double shot espresso, savoring a rare moment of quiet before venturing out into the world.

As he creased the magazine left behind by a previous customer, he happened to look up just as Lara stepped through the door and approached the counter.

If he only had one coffee yesterday rather than two, he never would have found himself here, waiting in the perfect place to bump into her.

He smiled to himself as the usually shy woman placed her order, speaking to the cashier with a self-confidence she had recently admitted to lacking. He let her collect her café latte before he bounded into the picture, his own drink in hand.

"I was hoping to run into you again," he said cheerfully.

After her initial surprise at being approached, she seemed to be relieved to run into him.

"Sam..." she murmured, her voice light and airy. "I'm glad to see you. I meant to—to find you. I wanted to text you and thank you for the other night, but I realized we never exchanged numbers. And I've been drowning in work the past few days, so I haven't been going to the gym. I hope I didn't sound bad—like I was avoiding you or being careless. I promise, that wasn't my intention."

"I guess that's on me—I should have asked for your number," he said with a patient smile, taking a slow sip of his drink. "But I suppose I was a little overwhelmed by your presence."

Her eyes flicked to the ground, and she bit her lip. "I really enjoyed our time together—I mean, our *outing*."

Sam reached out and gently squeezed her elbow. "Same here, and most of all, I really enjoyed our conversation."

"Oh, well, honestly, I wasn't sure about your thoughts, but I personally enjoyed it too."

"Okay then, since we both agree we enjoyed it, how about we plan another one soon? Maybe something a little more adventurous than just dinner?"

"Hmm, sounds tempting... and a little scary," Lara laughed hollowly.

A grin lit up Sam's entire face.

"Oh, no, nothing scary, I promise. Let's just say it's a little victory lap celebration for my work achievements. I'll fill you in about it during our excursion," Sam said, proud to have successfully secured his investors for the resort project. "Shall we meet here in the lobby at eleven on Saturday?"

Lara giggled at his sudden business-like attitude. "How formal of you."

"Well, I've learned from my last invitation to you—the more structured our plans are, the more likely we are to follow through."

She reached into the practical handbag hanging from her elbow and pulled out a sleek card that read *Lara Khalil—Financial Consultant,* with her workplace address and contact details typed in a neat font. "And here's my business card, just to continue with the formalities—in case you need to call or text me if there are any changes."

Sam laughed. It wasn't how he was used to getting a woman's number, but it would do the job. "I'll be sure to call, even if the plans don't change, Miss Khalil."

Lara carefully brushed her hair from her face. "Again, I'm really sorry—"

"Hey, it's seriously fine, Lara. I'm just happy we bumped into each other."

She nodded, though her apologetic expression remained. "But I also can't on Saturday. Go out, I mean. I've got so much work to do. But I'm free on Sunday if you are."

"That works perfectly for me. Shall we say Sunday at eleven?"

"Sure, but what do you have in mind? Anything specific?"

"Let it be a surprise," he announced with a wink.

"I do like surprises, though I'm not an adventurous person, so you'd better make it worth my while."

"Great, then make sure to wear something casual."

"Okay, sure."

The way her mouth parted in an intrigued gape made Sam wish he could fast forward straight to Sunday.

***

Sam opened the door to the SUV for Lara, holding her hand as she took a big step to climb inside.

The air conditioner was on full blast, and she settled into the cool environment, sighing in relief. Sam instructed the driver to be on his way, and soon the Dubai cityscape disintegrated into dust, and they were surrounded by oceans of sand.

The dunes rolled like waves across the terrain, the wind gently picking up crystals and threading them through the blue sky.

Lara was quiet on the ride over, giving only brief responses to Sam's questions about her week. Despite her impressive job, she never seemed to want to talk about it much.

Perhaps she was exhausted by numbers and clients and would have rather contained those notions to her paid working hours.

Though, she was just as vague about her diet, her plans, her friends, and Sam was having a difficult time trying to make conversation.

He wanted to believe that this was just her shy outward manner, that she was naturally reserved, but he was starting to wonder if he was just out of practice at making conversation with a woman he was this interested in.

"My week was insane, but that's pretty typical for me these days," Sam answered her returning question while she watched him with quiet attention. It made him feel pleasantly shy, and he ended up chattering a little more than he expected to.

"I had some back-to-back meetings with investors to secure funding for the project I told you about—the one I invited you on this trip to celebrate. I got to traverse the islands around Dubai and spent a few days on the golf course. Schmoozing, convincing, and closing deals, of course—I'm always schmoozing. But you know? I get to do it in these stunning mansions. I thought our apartments were fancy, with everyone having a Jacuzzi on their balcony, but these houses? They blow that right out of the water."

"Do you always do business around Dubai?" Lara asked, her tone light but curious. Shifting the focus away from herself seemed to come more naturally. "Or have your ventures taken you to other parts of the world?"

"For this particular venture, I've stayed in Dubai—my company's been working on it for a while. But I've traveled all over Europe, especially the Mediterranean, for other projects earlier. Once, I was even flown to Antarctica by an incredibly eccentric client, a Swedish businessman named Eric Puntintin, who had fallen in love with researching penguins there. It was bizarre, to say the least."

"You've really lived," Lara commented appreciatively, her eyebrows drawn together a little. Her olive skin looked velvety, and Sam wished he could lean in and kiss that cute frown away from her forehead.

She seemed to be holding back frustration, her hands clasped tightly in her lap, "And here I was, thinking I was all adventurous for finally leaving Lebanon. And then people like you come along, with all your fascinating and rich stories... Makes me think about all the things I might be missing out on."

Suddenly, Sam shared her frown. He felt terrible for making her look at her life compared to his and think it was any less wonderful. "I thought you studied abroad?"

"Yes, in London and Philadelphia. But I don't know—I stayed in cities primarily, which meant going to restaurants and shopping. I guess all the places just felt the same after a while."

"You must have done a great American road trip or something. Gotten out into the mountains, camping in a state park." That was something Sam missed deeply about the States—camping with his family or friends during the long summer months.

"I regret to inform you that no, I did not. As I told you earlier, I'm not an adventurous person," Lara remarked, tilting her head in reluctant confirmation.

"I'm sorry. I'm not trying to make you feel bad—"

"Oh, goodness, don't be silly. My insecurities are my own. I'm glad you tell me everything. I like hearing it."

"If it's any reassurance"—Sam hoped his voice would be enough of a distraction to hide his reddening cheeks; Lara's sentiment had touched him—"going out to the dunes with a man you hardly know is pretty adventurous."

She shifted in her seat, facing her legs to his. "It is, isn't it?" She thought for a moment. "Well, I can't pat myself on the back too hard. I only agreed to this because I know where you live—and so do all my family and friends. Haha."

He chuckled warmly. "Touché, Lara."

They returned to silence, but this time, it was comfortable.

***

Dune buggies and built-out cars were racing across the sand, driving at full speed over mounds and ripping through obstacles. Sam and Lara watched as they stood among a crowd of tourists, whooping and shouting along with them.

Tents lined the perimeter of the attraction, and Lara asked if they could explore the activities awaiting them inside. Men looking after camels offered them a ride, and Lara jumped at the opportunity. Her pledge to spontaneity began today, it seemed.

Lara was no natural, and though she tried to mask her screams with hearty laughter, her awkward struggle was unmistakable.

Sam was equally terrible at the exercise, unable to maintain his balance as the animal trotted unevenly through the soft sand. His legs faltered with each step, and his arms jerked wildly in a futile attempt to steady himself, eliciting amused chuckles from the group. Lara didn't hesitate to poke fun at his struggles, but their shared talentlessness sparked a lighthearted connection that eased any tension. In their mutual clumsiness, they discovered a shared humor, laughing at their bumpy progress as they bounced along the trail.

The tension had broken, and Lara was more animated and engaging than Sam had anticipated.

A buffet was being served for lunch, and the couple joined the rest of the tourists for a meal. Sitting cross-legged in the sand, they dined on local dishes with their fingers, sharing food from each other's plates in the traditional Gulf way.

Lara didn't look away in embarrassment every time she chewed, like she had at their previous dinner, and Sam felt more confident about their connection.

She did want to be here, he reminded himself. *She just has a less expressive way of showing it.*

After a long day, Sam called for their car to return and take them back home.

"This was great," Lara said serenely. "Thank you for including me in one of your adventures. Now, I finally have a story of my own to tell."

"There'll be more to come," he replied happily.

She took his hand, intertwining her elegant fingers with his—a silent gesture of admiration for the way he treated her—and a swarm of butterflies stirred in his stomach.

***

In the evening, Sam stood outside Lara's door, his hair almost dry and his excitement barely contained as he waited for her to answer. In one hand, he carried a small box of pastries—something he had ordered online earlier, figuring she might enjoy a treat. She had invited him back to her place but insisted it was a casual affair—she would be in her lounge clothes, glasses on, with a mug of tea in her hands.

He accepted her request, and after taking a quick shower, he changed into sweatpants and a funky T-shirt. He was ready to join her.

As the decorated oak door of her apartment croaked on its hinges, Lara revealed her little world to Sam. Small embellishments had already made their way onto every surface, with massive and exquisitely designed rugs lining the original floors and mismatched decorative plates hanging on the walls.

However, the extent of her personality stopped there, for everything else was still stored in boxes, which were dispersed throughout the kitchen, dining, and living room. The vast space felt small, crowded in cardboard and packing tape.

"Welcome," she said, stepping out of his way. She shut the door and led him to the middle of the living room, where she offered him a sole cushion to sit on.

"Oh, and thank you for this," she added, gesturing to the box of pastries. "You really didn't have to."

Only then did she glance around the space, her expression turning a little sheepish. "I don't have much furniture yet," she remarked before letting out a small laugh. "I guess we should have gone to your place," she added meekly, realizing her mistake only after the words had already left her mouth. She let out another laugh and waved a dismissive hand. "Or not."

"Mine isn't much better," he admitted. "You at least have the excuse of recently moving. Me? I don't even know what mine would be." He landed on the cushion as Lara strolled back to the kitchen, her long hair woven into a loose braid that somehow still looked refined.

"I've been too busy to really settle," Lara continued, "and I can be very picky about my things. It all needs to be a perfect reflection of me, and that takes time. Though, my own process is weighing on me right now. It sucks walking into a place that's meant to be my home but doesn't feel like it at all."

"I get what you mean. I love it here, but it's definitely a struggle not to feel stuck in place. My apartment looks like I'm expected to leave at a moment's notice."

She shuffled around the counters, adding water to a kettle and turning it on. She pulled an assortment of cups from an open box and rinsed them in the sink, drying them off as she went and neatly placing a few in her cupboards.

"I can always help you shop for home goods," Sam proposed.

"I really appreciate that, but I usually prefer to do things on my own. I promise—you'd hate the experience." She paused. "Tea?" she asked, holding up two boxes as he turned to look at her.

"Please," he confirmed.

It was comforting to listen to her move around in the kitchen. The hum of the boiling water, the gentle ringing of the ceramic mugs, and the preparation of his drink felt familiar.

Maybe it was just that she reminded him of himself—they both wanted their apartments to be filled with items that brought them joy, and yet they fumbled when trying to bring that to life.

But there was more to it, an undercurrent of emotion he couldn't make sense of, though it rang through his body like the regularly scheduled buzz of a morning alarm.

Reliable, knowable, and always on time. He felt himself grow dizzy as he tried to put the puzzle pieces together.

But soon, Lara joined him on the floor, passing him his tea and whispering for him to be careful. "It's hot," she softly warned.

"This is nice," Sam said as he sipped his drink. "Thank you for forcing me to calm down."

"What do you mean?" she asked.

"I'm so used to rushing everywhere... trying to be flashy with dates or constantly traveling from one place to the next. Sometimes, I forget to just settle into my space—except for my morning coffee, you know? I actually take the time to assess my surroundings. I like meeting you at your level."

"Is that really a good thing?"

"Yeah..." He thought about it more. "Yeah, it really is. We balance each other out."

The déjà vu struck him again, but he suppressed it the only way he knew how—by letting himself get lost in Lara's eyes.

She smelled of soap and shampoo, and the steam from the tea curled around her face as she took an absentminded sip, staring right back at Sam.

Lara winced, covering her mouth. She had scalded her tongue, forgetting her own considerate warning to Sam.

He reached out, his fingers pressing along her jaw delicately to get a good look at her. "You okay?"

"Yeah, I'm..." The words died on her tongue as she realized how closely he was staring at her lips.

Thick tension twisted between them. Sam wanted to comfort her. Hold her and keep her safe. But he also wanted to take her on more adventures, to make her laugh as fully as she did on the day's *experience*. He wished to plan getaways to stunning destinations where they could both unwind and disconnect from work.

He wanted more of her—more *with* her.

Lara's breath brushed against Sam's lips. He couldn't recall how they'd gotten so close, but he slipped the finger cupping her jaw to the nape of her neck.

Lara slowly closed her eyes and tilted her lips to meet his.

He inhaled the sweetness of her breath, the lotion still soaking into her skin, and the delicate aroma of her tea—then, in an instant, it was all gone. He snapped awake in Singapore, the cool air pressing against him, the silence swallowing the last traces of his dream.

Ch. 16

"What Would I Do Without You?"

Sam and Kate watched Sara play with Chalk in the yard. They could hear the pure delight in her voice through the glass windowpanes when she giggled, the dog barking at her as it chased her around in their favorite game, fighting for ownership of Chalk's bouncy ball.

Kate picked at a bag of chips that sat between her and Sam. They had decided on a casual venture, opting to only purchase prepackaged foods and to make a meal out of scraps.

Nobody wanted to cook or clean, just nibble on an assortment of treats Kate would no longer be able to purchase in the U.A.E. It was just the three of them, too—no bodyguards, assistants, or friends. They were free to talk to each other without reservation, and yet they spoke only as old friends, not lovers.

"I wonder how different the TV channels will be," Kate said with a sigh. "I've really gotten into some local dramas over here."

"You can stream anything you want from anywhere you are, Kate," Sam teased with a smirk. "What year are you living in?"

She rolled her eyes. "You know I can't figure out all those doodahs and cables."

"They're just apps you download—"

"You've lost me already. I'm intelligent in every part of my life except for figuring out the TV. In that respect, I am a total granny." Kate held up her hand, completely dismissing the very idea, as she delicately popped a kimchi-flavored chip into her mouth.

"Sara is doomed, then, isn't she?"

"It's not *doomed* to only be able to watch cable and DVDs. Maybe she'll have a deep appreciation for history. I'm setting her up for success if you think about it."

"You are, Kate." The sincerity in his tone made his voice thicker, gravelly. "She's gonna be great as long as she has you as her mom."

They paused and locked eyes the way they only really did between kisses.

It would have been the perfect moment to say something about their relationship, to put their emotions out in the open and finally receive the closure they were both lacking. They never discussed what they would do going forward; the definitive amount of Kate's remaining time in Singapore was a marker for what they couldn't say out loud.

It was too hard; despite their problems, genuinely letting go of each other was a challenge they weren't ready for.

Sam ran through all of the dialogue of the romantic comedies and dramas he had watched so much of. What did the characters always say when someone had to move away or leave for some unavoidable obligation in London or something?

None of it seemed appropriate. None of it could put into context exactly the bond he and Kate had. He threaded his fingers through his hair.

Once again, reality was much harder to deal with than fiction.

Sara bounded into the room, breaking the still air suspended between the pair. They both uncomfortably cleared their throats as they turned their full attention to the little girl.

"Sam, I'm gonna miss Chalk *so much*," Sara announced with short, quick breaths. Chalk was waiting for her by the door, wagging his furry tail and hardly containing his energy.

"What about Sam?" Kate asked her daughter with a faint smile. "Are you gonna miss him?"

"Always," Sara replied.

"Yeah." Kate reclined into the couch and whispered, "I'm gonna miss him, too. Always." Her eyes moved to Sam and slowly trailed down his form like she was trying to commit everything about him to memory.

Sam's chest ached. He wished things could have been different. Or at least, he wished he could have been more decisive about what he wanted from his relationship with Kate from the very beginning. He wished that they could have met at some different time in their lives.

But his head swiveled back to Sara, and he changed his mind. He felt deeply appreciative that he got to meet this sweet, endlessly curious, and energetic little girl. He wished he could express how much hope he had for her, growing up and making the world her own.

While it was the better decision for both of them to part ways cleanly and not look back, it didn't feel so good anymore. Sam still found Kate to be a wonderful friend. She was the type of person who would have your back and fight for you relentlessly if she cared about you, and that was something that Sam admired so deeply about her.

He knew he could use a little bit of that determination within himself.

"I'll visit you guys," Sam proclaimed, "in Abu Dhabi, when you're all settled."

"We'd really appreciate that," Kate said. She looked at him meaningfully, her eyes swimming with all the things she couldn't say.

He understood.

***

An airplane roared overhead, the powerful hum of its jet engines dripping down to the world below. Sam and Tiffany were in a courtyard, sitting down to lunch, and the noise from above reminded Sam of Kate. She had gone sometime in the past few days, but he didn't know exactly when.

She never really said, and he never really asked. They promised to stay in touch, but all he received was her new address and a new mobile number to reach her at. He figured he'd give it a few more days and then text her in order to plan a trip to see her.

"What am I gonna do, Tiff?" Sam asked as he unwrapped his sandwich.

"Still no dreams?" she inquired before noisily shaking her salad.

"Nope. And now no Kate."

The last week had been nothing but emptiness and long stretches of time without talking. The embassy was quieter than usual and now, so was his mind.

He should have seen it coming—the dream women were always snatched from his unconscious mind so abruptly, but with Lara, their development had been more brief than he was used to.

While he wasn't exactly over the moon to be thrown into love again, he was beginning to appreciate Lara. She felt safe and secure—someone he could truly unwind with after a long day.

The absence of all the women he'd cared for felt like a punishment—it came at once, ripping them out of his life without remorse. He wasn't blameless in his current isolation, but getting out of it was distressing.

But at the same time, his body hadn't felt this good in months. He had gotten back into a more regular exercise routine under the guidance of Jack, his bodyguard and private trainer, and had been much stricter about sleeping a more reasonable amount. He'd even turned it into a game—staying awake just long enough to catch his early-rising mom in her cozy apartment on the outskirts of New York. When the time was right, he'd phone her to catch up on their days.

The little bit of normalcy in hearing his mom's voice more regularly both calmed and pained him. He didn't know how much longer he'd been able to live in an entirely different country from his family.

"You should put yourself out there," Tiffany suggested. "I mean, the dating scene... It's not great. But when has it ever been great? Besides, you obviously want a girlfriend, and with Kate being gone, this is the push you need to finally put that into action."

"I'm not interested in meeting new women. Even dream Sam Cooper was tired of the back-and-forth, exchanging the same old information over and over again, expecting different results. I think that's why I held on to Kate for so long—we already knew and liked each other in the ways that mattered the most to us."

There was no need to impress her, no pressure to recount our entire life stories over dinner dates. She could simply walk into my house, and we'd pick up right where we left off. If I could find that kind of effortless familiarity with someone who truly loved me and whom I loved in return... I'd be the happiest man alive.

"You guys really didn't love each other?" A look of profound sadness softened the corners of Tiffany's mouth. "I mean, I knew that you and Kate had a fluctuating relationship, but I always assumed you stayed together because you loved each other despite the arguments."

Sam shook his head. It felt simultaneously awful and relieving to admit this to someone. "No. It sounds cruel, but she never tried to say it, and neither did I. It was just a shared sentiment between us. I personally tried to give our relationship a try, but she insisted on keeping it strictly casual."

Tiffany crunched on a piece of watery lettuce as she stared blankly into the distance. "By the way, have you tried looking for the dream girls?"

He narrowed his eyes, asking, "Like, assuming they're real?" before taking a huge bite of his sandwich.

"Yeah! Crazier things have happened, right?"

A muted unease settled over him. He was just beginning to accept that the women of his imagined world and Kate were no longer part of his life. Was he really about to plunge himself back into the same obsession?

"I don't know... I've spent so much time convincing myself they don't exist that I almost believe it now. Maybe I should *believe it*. I can't keep wasting time chasing something intangible." He sank back into his chair, running a hand through his hair. "Then again, I've already lost four women, so clearly, my current approach isn't working."

"I hate to be blunt, but no, it's not," Tiffany said, emphasizing her point by wagging a tiny chunk of carrot on her fork.

"And," Sam continued, the ideas he'd been suppressing were rising to the surface, "there's no harm in trying, right? Like I said, I've already lost them technically, so all I'd be doing is trying to rekindle a few romances. That's only if they're real, of course. If I search their names and find nothing, then fine—that's my answer."

Tiffany nodded her head with the steadiness of a wise sage. "You can't go through life not knowing what could have been. Especially when you're just a few clicks away from the truth. Frankly, I'm surprised you haven't tried weeks ago."

"It just seemed—well, *still* seems impossible. It's not like I *really* could have been in two different places at once. Right?"

Shrugging, Tiffany motioned to his tablet, resting on the small table between them.

He sighed, relenting as he reached for it and opened Google, then took a deep breath as he began with his first dream crush: Shiva.

Just as she had appeared in his mind, she now emerged in his search.

She was still in the same place she'd always been—Los Angeles—and now she was running an art gallery near the downtown core. His mouth went dry as he scrolled through her pictures on her public account of the social media platform. The paintings in the photos stopped him cold; he had been there before, seen these works with his own eyes.

There, the painting of that thoughtful and melancholic face staring into the distance, crafted from thick brushstrokes and pure artistic talent. Sam's heart thudded in his chest.

He had seen all of this before. The more he scrolled through the posts, the more his memories surged to the forefront, vivid and undeniable, as if it had all happened yesterday. The sights, the smells, the sensations—they all came rushing back, so tangible they felt etched into his mind.

The only bond he and Shiva shared existed in that surreal realm, though, as there was no indication he had ever encountered her in his *real* daily life.

There were no webpages that had already been visited nor a follow associated with her Instagram account. But it was her.

He showed Tiffany his screen, needing her to confirm what his eyes were seeing—after all, they could easily be tricking him, projecting illusions to satisfy his desires.

"Her name is Shiva, alright," Tiffany confirmed. "Oh my God, Sam, she looks exactly like you always described her."

"I really can't believe my eyes... it's surreal. Like seeing a piece of my imagination come to life?"

His hands trembled as he typed Céline's name into the search bar. The result was immediate—just like before, she was among the first suggestions to appear. Her profile was accompanied by familiar images, and Sam felt his head swim as he scrolled through her Instagram account. There she was—immaculately dressed, flashing that slightly goofy grin he remembered so well.

A few clicks later, he landed on her professional LinkedIn profile. And there it was, plain as day—credentials that perfectly aligned with what he had dreamed. Managing Partner of Executive Media agency. She had even been involved in Paris Fashion Week, exactly as he had envisioned.

Lara, too, was a Lebanese woman, and her profile picture was exactly as he remembered her. However, her social media accounts were private, leaving him unable to view her posts. The only exception was her LinkedIn page, which listed her position as a financial consultant in Dubai—exactly as it had been on the *business card* she handed to him in his dream.

As for Shiva's and Céline's pages, they were filled with photos of their travels, and some of them featured the same locales they had explored with Sam. Yet, curiously, none of the images revealed partners or the unmistakable shine of a wedding ring.

Shiva's profile was harder to judge—she primarily shared posts showcasing her artwork and advertisements for her most recently acquired collections.

With every new link he clicked and photo he swiped through, Sam turned the screen toward Tiffany, as if he wanted the essence of these women and their lives to be ingrained permanently in her memory.

"I can arrange your trips for you, Sam," Tiffany offered, her tone calm and confident as Sam sat back, his mind spinning.

"Seriously, Tiff?" he asked, staring at her in disbelief.

"Why not? You owe yourself a vacation," she replied with a small shrug, as if it were the most obvious solution in the world.

"And then what? I just show up to these women and say, *You're the woman I met in my dreams! Are you single and open to a relationship with me?* like some cliché romantic lead in a cheesy novel? Yeah, that's a surefire way to land myself three tidy restraining orders."

Tiffany burst into a loud laugh, clearly amused by the thought, but she gave his hand a reassuring pat. "Just don't make it weird. People meet each other all the time through dating apps and social media. Why not through a dream?"

"Hmm... how sentimental of you," Sam muttered, his tone laced with skepticism.

"Come on, Sam! Besides, you promised Kate you would visit her in Abu Dhabi, so you can start from there, and your mother is expecting you in the states, so you will be going back there anyway."

"That... I mean it couldn't hurt to try and find Lara while I happen to be in the same country?" He chewed on his bottom lip while Tiffany nodded knowingly. "Just to get some closure. Or even just to see them and know that I'm not an absolute nutcase."

"And from Dubai, I'll send you to LA, then from LA to New York. After that, Paris, on your way back here. I'll make the layovers short and book your seats in business class."

"Tiffany!" Sam burst out laughing. "What would I do without you?"

He looked down at his screen, and his heart raced.

There, still imprinted on his tablet, were his dream women staring back at him.

***

Arriving in Abu Dhabi, Sam stepped out of the airport spotting Kate's driver, who held up a sign with his name written neatly in bold letters.

Earlier, as soon as he'd discovered his dream women, he messaged Kate for the details of her daily life and fed the intel to Tiffany, who was bartering with airlines, trying to get Sam's trips booked with perfect precision.

She'd arranged for everything prior to his visits—hotels, chauffeurs—and even investigated restaurants for Sam to take his partners to, should they accept his invitation. His assistant was either just as crazy as he was, or she was desperate to get him a wife so he could stop complaining.

He made sure to tell her just how much he appreciated her care, regardless of the reason, as she waved him off at Singapore Changi Airport.

Sam requested a stop along the way once he was in Kate's driver's car—a pet store, where he'd already orchestrated a puppy, outfitted with a bow on its collar, to be retrieved.

She was the same breed as Chalk, and Sam was certain Sara would be overjoyed to receive her. He had run his plan by Kate, and she was reluctant but willing to give it a shot.

Anything to make her daughter's transition less overwhelming and lonely.

When he arrived at her residence, gift in hand, Sara sped out of the front door at the sight of the little dog. She barely acknowledged Sam, lifting the crate from his fingers and rushing it indoors to set the puppy free. She was relentlessly *ooh*-ing and *aah*-ing over the fluffy little thing, squealing happily as she licked and nibbled on Sara's fingers, Sara decisively announced from where she sat, "I will name her Lilly."

"Well, that seems to have been a winning decision," Sam smiled at Kate as he continued up the walkway. She stood in the doorway with her arms folded across her chest. "Did you tell her I was bringing her a dog?"

"No," she answered. "But I guess she just loves animals more than people."

Sam shrugged while whispering sarcastically, "Maybe that isn't such a bad thing."

They awkwardly hugged once he got closer, a tension between them that neither had anticipated. It felt like an embrace shared between two high school friends who had always gone to homecomings and prom nights together out of convenience. However, their dates had been to glamorous political receptions and celebrations in national palaces, where they had to sneak around just to be with each other—just like on Singapore National Day.

He thought back to how they'd sat on the carpet in his living room. Life had seemed different back then, before the dreams began—simpler, but much duller.

His mind was also overwhelmed with excitement at the thought of chasing the dreamworld ladies.

The usual lust that Sam felt stir within him when he and Kate touched had faded almost completely. He couldn't decide if it was like someone had extinguished a fire or simply switched off a light bulb. So much of her had always left him confused about himself, even if he did appreciate her familiar presence in his life.

Perhaps it was a mistake coming here and they should have let sleeping dogs lie, but he couldn't backtrack now.

She led him into the house and gave him a brief, stiff tour, mumbling as she introduced him to empty rooms she didn't know what to do with, making remarks about the mess that was around the place.

She hid her face under her fingers whenever they passed by a box or a pile of clothes, but Sam was too busy marveling at the place to notice or care. It was massive, with high ceilings and multiple sunrooms. He could see the little patch of nature that surrounded them from all four corners, and the floors were made of precious stones that added to the exotic ambiance.

He found himself feeling a hint of jealousy over her new home, wishing his embassy residence in Singapore City had even a fraction of its charm. He could easily imagine himself living in a place like this, surrounded by warmth and soul.

"It's truly exceptional, Kate," he murmured, his neck craned to look at the skylights. "Does it ever get hot with all that sunshine?"

"No, we have a lot of shady trees around here, and I keep the air conditioner cranked all day long. I'm afraid they're gonna kick me out for practically killing the environment."

Kate concluded the tour of her new place for Sam before they settled into the dining room for a seafood lunch prepared in the traditional local style.

Sara joined them, alternating between taking bites of her food and slipping pieces of shrimp under the table for Lilly to nibble on.

The playful energy of the little puppy and the sound of silverware against plates filled the room with a quiet warmth—a stark contrast to the unspoken weight between Sam and Kate that hovered like an unwelcome guest.

On their way out, Sam reassured her, "This has been a needed change for you. One you deserve, too."

She softened and joined him in his wonder at the world above them. "You think so?"

"Absolutely."

They locked eyes, and he could see the hesitation etched across her face as she parted her lips to speak. But the words wouldn't come—that maybe the last few months had been a mistake. Despite their flaws, they *had* been something, something real, even if imperfect.

They didn't have to give it all up. She didn't have to leave him behind.

But he knew there would be no response that could satisfy them both. The remnants of their relationship were beyond repair. For as much as they fought for their connection, it wasn't built to last, and it was time they accepted it in order to move on.

He leaned down and kissed her—a short, simple peck on the lips. It wasn't passionate or melancholic; it simply was, perfectly encapsulating their history. When it was over, they exchanged sweet smiles in a quiet moment of understanding, knowing it would be their last kiss.

"I will always be there for you whenever you need me, Kate," Sam declared, before he set out on his mission.

"I know, Sam. Likewise," she replied, trying to hide her emotions. Those were the final words she spoke, closing for good a bittersweet chapter of her life.

It had been good with Kate, but it never would have been good enough for either of them.

Ch. 17

"Reality Kicks In"

The Dubai streets were all too familiar as Sam proceeded from the taxi drop-off to the tower that he'd envisioned in his dreams. It was surprising how accurate his subconscious had been in crafting such a world, for the cityscape was exactly how he'd imagined it—the buildings crisscrossed above him, friendly people roamed around on the hot concrete sidewalks, and the scent of the sea not too far away drifted through the air.

He knew exactly how to navigate traffic in order to get to his former apartment, and once he arrived, settling into rhythm was easier than he expected. He kept wondering if he was truly awake or if the Sam Cooper of his nightly dreams had finally acquired his conscience.

Maybe his sleep had taken on a new layer of depth, and now he couldn't distinguish reality at any level of wakefulness.

He checked his pockets for any identifiers of his dream world. There were no mysterious keys to the building, and his wallet was lined with identification for the real Sam.

He was still an American diplomat simply traversing the United Arab Emirates to meet up with people who mattered to him. He sighed in relief; he wasn't losing his mind.

Sam decided to start at the coffee shop, drawn by the familiar hum of espresso machines and the rich aroma of freshly brewed coffee—a perfect replica of the place he had envisioned. He ordered a decaf latte and found a seat at a corner table, strategically positioned far from the entrance. From there, he could discreetly watch the street and anyone passing by, all while sipping his drink and pretending to scroll through his phone.

He was going back and forth with his thoughts—had he given in to his worst impulses? Was he only trying to ease his troubled brain, or was this truly a grand romantic gesture?

It was hard to comfort himself when he felt as if all eyes were on him, watching like a predator waiting for Lara to arrive—only to snatch her away before she even realized it.

He tried putting himself in her shoes, contemplating what her reaction would be. The women of his dreams were outright beautiful, and their personalities were nothing more than constructs of his imagination.

Unless he had somehow managed to perceive their personalities as well, it only added to the bizarre strangeness of how vividly their lives existed inside his mind.

Would Lara be receptive to his determination? Who else could say that a man flew all the way to another country just to catch a glimpse of the woman he'd been musing about?

After an hour, though, his patience began to fade, and so did his spirits. The crowds thinned out, and the sun sank lower on the horizon. People were beginning to prepare for dinner, which meant Sam couldn't justify sitting around aimlessly any longer.

He sighed, tossing out his garbage and heading to the lobby of the apartment building.

Without thinking, he trailed behind a couple entering the main access hall to the residences and slipped through the door, the suddenness of the act going unnoticed by everyone, including himself. As he stepped inside, a strange déjà vu gripped him.

The tenants he came across in the lobby felt oddly familiar—faces he had seen during his dream adventures. Even the concierge at the front desk and the security guards stationed around the building seemed no different.

None of them seemed to recognize him, though. Perhaps, since he was already inside, they simply assumed he was a guest visiting. He allowed his body to take him where it wanted, and that meant hopping into an elevator and searching the building from top to bottom, just as he had done on those fateful nights in his sleep. Every detail seemed to align with what he had seen before, amplifying the surreal nature of his search.

He stormed through the corridors with confidence, fueling his air of mania—how could it be that he genuinely knew what each floor harbored, where every door led, and what tenants lived where? Was he misinterpreting his own judgments, willing them to be real just to validate his desires? Was he hallucinating every unlocked door and social interaction?

He moved from level to level, making sure to get on a different elevator every few floors, roaming through the places where he had run into Lara before. But the gym had emptied out, much like the rest of the common spaces, and eventually, Sam had to pack it in for the evening. Despite his seemingly all-knowing senses, he was certain he couldn't sneak his way into his dream apartment and rest his head for the night.

As he crossed the lobby, however, he caught the eyes of a gorgeous woman. He almost didn't halt, simply acknowledging her beauty and continuing toward the glass front doors, when every muscle in his body compelled him to stop dead in his tracks.

Her sight remained fixed on him, those almond-shaped eyes narrowing as she studied his expression, searching for answers. Her slim fingers gripped the arm of a man he didn't recognize, pressing into the soft cotton of his loose-fitting shirt.

Sam and Lara smiled in unison, her lips curling softly and a look of recognition crossing her face. Sam's hand twitched in his pocket, dying to gesture to her.

But he knew he couldn't, especially as she glanced up at the man beside her, smiling as their conversation continued. They walked further into the building, stopping only when they reached the elevators.

Lara seems to be taken, and there was nothing he could do to change that. This was the real world.

Then again, he couldn't assume their relationship was perfect or even intimate. The man in her company could have been anybody—did he really come all this way just to bow out without trying?

However, when he decided to at least march over to her and confirm that it was Lara and that she had known him in some capacity, she was gone. She had disappeared behind a set of elevator doors and was launched into space, to an apartment—a life, a love—that he didn't know about and would never be permitted to.

Taking her sudden absence as a sign, Sam departed the building with his head hung but a solid sense of pride knocking on his chest for taking the leap to find Lara and listening to his gut. The fact that she recognized him ignited a hope in him that

Shiva and Céline would as well. And perhaps, with them, there would be more opportunity to talk.

He checked into his hotel room for the night and sank onto his bed, exhausted from his travels and with a sense of grumpy restlessness. Like finally getting to the end of an amazing movie, only for it to end on a disappointing cliffhanger.

He shouldn't have expected anything less. If he had found and loved Lara in his dreams, how much easier would it have been for a real man to fall utterly in love with her?

He fell asleep with his shoes still on his feet.

***

There was no mist this time.

Sam simply stood in the doorway, the heavy oak door swung open behind him.

The moment he opened his eyes, they locked onto a familiar pair in front of him.

Memories rushed through him all at once, of camels and tea and gentle laughter.

The woman standing on the other side of the door gave him a smile of tender recognition.

***

Lara stood in the hallway outside Sam's door, the carpet beneath her feet losing its pattern, fading into ruby-red threads. The walls were vacant and white, a sharp contrast to the vibrant décor Sam had grown accustomed to in Dubai. Even the ceiling seemed to be diminishing, with flecks of drywall drifting down around them like lifeless dust.

The sacredness of the space where they had first met was falling apart around them now, slowly vanishing into the furthest corners of their minds. The only thing that remained radiant and whole was her smile.

Lara reached out to Sam, her fingers stroking his face, evaluating its contours and ridges. The shyness he had bestowed upon her in his dreams had evaporated with the rest of the building, floating in the mist of his reverie.

Was this the real *Lara Khalil*?

"I've seen you in my dreams," Lara said, her palm gently cradling his cheek as she absorbed his warmth. "We had something together, something I still think about sometimes. Something I wonder about—what it would be like to live in it every day."

"I feel the same, Lara," Sam replied breathlessly, the sensation of her physical contact radiating through his bloodstream.

"Our *special* relationship taught me a lot about myself and the kind of treatment and care I need from a partner."

"Same here." His voice wavered slightly as he felt his desperation escalating. He couldn't bear the thought of her fading away, taking with her all the opportunities she represented. There was still so much he wanted to discover about her, to uncover the unique qualities that made her *Lara*.

"But... I took what I learned from you and communicated it to my boyfriend," Lara smiled softly, her hand falling onto Sam's shoulder. A friendly gesture. He almost chuckled past his sadness, but he listened to her tell her story instead. "My boyfriend and I were both failing in ways that were hurting each other. Unintentionally and not irreparably, but they had to be addressed. So, I thank you for *that*, for showing me what I was missing and giving me what I needed to find *that* in the real world."

"Are you guys—are you happier together now?"

She nodded with a quiet, mournful sort of joy in her eyes, her grasp dropping and her hands returning to her side. "Telling him about you was one of the best things I did. He didn't become angry or bitter; he just accepted my story and helped me navigate through it until we arrived at a better place. It sounds si—"

"Silly," he completed her sentence with a smile. He did know her in some capacity.

"Right," she continued with a giggle, "But it brought us closer together. I love him, Sam. I really do, and I hope you've found that within someone else, too."

Sam sighed, and he looked down at his feet, which were melting into the floor that was now turning into something grey and immaterial. "We're not going to see each other ever again after this, are we?"

"I'm afraid so."

"Well, thank you for visiting me and—and letting me know. I hope you have a life full of adventures, Lara."

She smiled serenely, her hand reaching out to squeeze Sam's one final time.

***

His eyes slowly adjusted to his surroundings, noticing the changing location each time he blinked his heavy lids.

One moment, he was in the Dubai apartment, with Lara reduced to a fragment of herself—her color drained of all animation, her face dissolving into oblivion—and the next, he was slipping toward wakefulness, still wearing the clothes from the night before. The beautiful woman from his dream remained only as a pair of eyes before vanishing entirely.

As he came fully awake, a wave of nostalgia swept over him, and his thoughts drifted to the mornings in this dynamic, electrifying city.

Now that his dream had delivered a clear message—Lara wasn't meant to be his—Sam decided it was time to shift gears. He amended his air ticket to the nearest available flight and, to his luck, found one departing in just a couple of hours. The timing was perfect, giving him enough space to shower and gather himself before heading to the airport.

He moved swiftly through check-in with his priority pass and found himself quickly settled in the luxurious business-class lounge. The pampering atmosphere was a welcome distraction as he sipped on premium cocktails at the bar on the upper deck of the Emirates A380. Chatting with fellow travelers while gazing through the small windows at the clear clouds and endless blue skies, he did his best to keep his spirits steady despite the sting of his earlier disappointment.

Around sixteen hours later, Sam was back in his seat, finishing the final scenes of a newly released movie that had helped pass the time. As the credits rolled, the long-awaited announcement came:

"This is your captain speaking," a male voice echoed over the intercom. "We'll be arriving at our destination shortly. We've begun our descent and will touch ground in Los Angeles in about thirty minutes."

Sam stretched and glanced out of the window, the sprawling city coming into view below, signaling the start of his next chapter.

Sam felt tense, barely able to recall leaving his hotel room in Dubai. As he blinked and took a deep breath, he struggled to regain his bearings, his mind pulling him in too many directions at once, as if it were scattered across different realities.

In just thirty minutes, he'd be navigating the bustling streets of downtown LA, preparing himself for what might turn out to be yet another missed opportunity.

Gathering his courage, he felt sure that he would be able to face Shiva with no regrets, even if he did have to say goodbye to her as well.

All he could hope for now was to convey how much she had meant to him in his dream—their undeniable bond, the unforgettable experiences they had shared, and the chemistry that felt so vivid, so real. Unlike the others, she had been the one who truly reciprocated his love without hesitation or barriers, sharing official dates and moments of genuine intimacy with him.

Céline, despite their strong connection, had never been truly available, and Lara remained hesitant, barely beginning to acknowledge her feelings with a kiss he couldn't even be sure it actually happened. But Shiva? She had been different, and he needed her to understand the profound impact she had left on him, both in his dreams and in his heart.

***

Sam splashed cold water on his face in the hotel bathroom sink, droplets clinging to his skin as he gripped the edges of the counter. He stared at his reflection in the mirror, his tired eyes searching for answers, and silently asked himself what the hell he was doing with his life.

Lara had been real—he had seen her clear as day and watched her as she went up to the apartment he had entered in his dreams.

She noticed him, too, and even if their final encounter within his mind was all an illusion, that couldn't and wouldn't change the reality of what he saw.

He didn't understand the mechanics behind any of it—how he knew these women yet had never met them beyond his imagination.

He couldn't jump to the conclusion that they had all been dreaming about him, too, as Lara had mentioned—or that he even shared the same exact dreams as he did. Perhaps their dreams about him unfolded entirely differently from what he saw.

He just hoped that none of their dreams about him had been nightmares…

But the possibility that Shiva and Céline would also recognize him and know some parts of himself from his dreams thrilled him.

There was something strange and cosmic going on, and it was pulling him in their directions. He wondered, not for the first or last time, what it could all mean.

Why *him*? And why *them*?

Whatever the reason was, Sam was strangely touched to be the one experiencing this miracle with them.

Despite feeling discouraged by Lara's circumstances, he decided to push forward.

He couldn't stop now, not in the middle of his journey.

Even if he had to lean into his delusions a little longer, something phantasmic was occurring, and he had to get to the bottom of it.

Double-checking the location of Shiva's art gallery, despite knowing it off by heart from his dreams, he called a car and fed them the address, pleased that he could sit back and admire the route through LA that was so familiar to him.

Though it wasn't as mystical to be familiar with an American landscape, Sam was comforted by his remembrance of the city. If anything, it just meant that Shiva was bound to remember him, too.

He brushed up on art history on his phone as the car rattled through traffic, determined to arm himself with enough knowledge to impress Shiva—just in case his usual charms fell short.

Maybe Lara didn't choose him because he gave her nothing material.

For all he knew, Lara could have easily thought he was a fabrication of *her* mind—her dream man, like she was his dream woman—and it made sense that she wouldn't abandon her life for him. Not when she figured she had filled in all of his details with her own desires.

Because he had no idea what version of him appeared to Lara or any of the other ladies, he didn't know the kind of role he played in their sleep. He didn't know the Sam Cooper they possibly saw aligned with their needs or if their dreams taught them a lesson of what they *did not* actually want in life. Lara might have been the only one who had positive experiences with Sam.

He wanted Shiva to know that he was willing to do the work outside of their dreamscape, to prove that he could live up to their expectations.

He had potential in the real world as well.

But as the car pulled up to the gallery, Sam barely had time to set foot on the property, before chaos struck.

Two women wearing name tags desperately waved down his car, and they opened the doors forcefully, disregarding Sam as he attempted to move out of their way.

"Hospital!" one of the women shouted at the driver, sticking her head inside the vehicle. "We need to go to the hospital!"

A crowd on the walkway parted for a heavily pregnant woman who was being led down the stairs, groaning as her knees collapsed under the weight of her pain.

Sam jumped into action, rushing to her side and taking over for one of the employees, Andrea—he recognized that name, that face; he had spoken to her in his sleep—who was too overwhelmed to know how to deal with the situation.

He wrapped his arm around the pregnant woman's widened waist and lifted her carefully into the car, positioning her legs gently and securing her seatbelt.

The woman placed a hand on his chest and forced him to look at her deep into her wide, teary eyes.

It was *Shiva*.

She gasped, tangling her fingers in his shirt and pulling him closer until their faces practically touched. She blinked in surprise, as if momentarily unsure whether he was real or just another illusion conjured by pain. Then, her expression crumpled with relief.

"Please, come with me to the hospital," she pleaded, her voice cutting through the air, sharp with the strain of a contraction. She let out a piercing scream, her teeth gritted tightly against the pain.

Sam felt pale. He didn't know what to say—what could he say? "Of course," he replied without hesitation.

He buckled her seatbelt, shut the door, and hurried around to the other side of the vehicle. Sliding into the backseat beside her, he gave the back of the driver's headrest a quick tap, signaling that they were ready to go.

He grabbed Shiva's hand, and they stared at each other, too stunned to do more than hold one another in silence as she panted through her labor pains.

Ch. 18

"Was It Just a Lesson?"

"I must be hallucinating," Shiva whispered. She was lying in a hospital bed, a cold compress on her forehead as she stared up at the fluorescent lights and then back at Sam. She was blinking, and Sam imagined that the light's refractions painted him with a surreal glow.

He was still processing the shock of everything happening around him, ever since they had ridden together in the cab and surprisingly to the very same hospital where he had often operated as a doctor in his dreams.

Shiva's father, Kareem, and her husband had been contacted and were already on their way. The thought of the *H* word made Sam's stomach twist.

The nurses were prompt to give her all the medication she required, awaiting her obstetrician's arrival to give instructions and move her to the operating room. Meanwhile, her employees sat anxiously in the waiting area, talking to their loved ones on the phone as they awaited the birth of Shiva's child—the child she had with another man.

His heart cracked but somehow filled with a dull sense of utter joy for Shiva. She had wanted children and a huge, happy family so badly.

It was difficult for Sam to bite back his disappointment that he wasn't the one building a family with her—especially as he stood in the very room where hers was about to begin with someone else.

It wasn't her fault that he wasn't in the right place at the right time or that the Shiva of his fantasies wasn't already connected and married to someone else.

Did he really think these women wouldn't have partners? It wasn't crazy or wrong of them to have sought out love with men who could take them on dates and move into their homes. Who could marry them without having to traverse timelines and continents just to be with each other in real life. It wasn't their fault he had let his visions disrupt his life in such tangible ways.

Sam approached the bed, where the woman he had cherished in his first vivid dream stared at him with a warm, gentle expression. *If only things had been different,* he thought, the ache of unspoken possibilities settling heavily in his chest.

"For a few weeks there," she continued, "I'd been having these dreams about someone who looked just like you. Every single night... you appeared. How funny is that? I knew childbirth would be painful, but I didn't think it'd bring you to life."

"You're not... You're not making this up, Shiva," Sam replied, his hand itching to touch hers.

"I don't remember telling you my name..." She smiled despite her wary words.

"You know mine."

"Sam?" she remarked quizzically.

He nodded.

"This is crazy," she replied with a laugh that quickly turned into a wince as she pressed her hand to her swollen belly.

"It's not." He was fully at her side, his palm wavering over her forehead as he went to stroke it. She didn't recoil or tell him to stop, but he knew nothing good could come of desiring a married woman. It would be more disastrous for him and his emotions than it would be for her. He had to resist for his own sake, so he put his hand firmly at his side. "I mean, I know it *sounds* crazy, but I've been dreaming of you, too. I met your father; I went to your art gallery. That's how I... That's how I showed up today. I remembered where you were. You and I used to love each other in our dreams, Shiva."

She sighed and reached out to him. He accepted her hand willingly, backing down from his own boundary the second she extended her warmth to him.

He needed it; he was desperate for something tangible to hold onto, something that would allow him to remember her more clearly. Something undeniably true.

"Don't get your hopes up," she warned teasingly. "I'm not leaving my husband for you."

"I know," he said with a throaty laugh. "I would never expect you to—especially now." He motioned playfully toward her pregnant belly, a teasing glint in his eyes.

"It was nice to dream of you," she mused, her voice filled with happy recollection. "I only wish that you love someone else just as much as you think you love me now."

Sam didn't have the heart to admit that—no, he didn't love anyone as much as he loved Shiva in their dreams.

All he could do was swallow dryly and say, "Congratulations on your—" He looked at her belly, which she cradled.

"Boy," she informed him.

"On your boy." Dammit. If he had been the one to be married to Shiva and waiting to bring a child into the world right now, he would have named his son after his father—Jeffrey. And he would have insisted that he take one of Kareem's middle names too, which Sam still recalled from his patient file.

Thinking like this wasn't helping him. He had to leave now before he interrupted more of Shiva and her family's happy day.

He sighed and brought Shiva's cold hand to his lips. An innocent kiss of goodbye and good luck.

Her eyes were filled with joy as he pulled away. He turned to the door as he knew that this little boy on his way would be raised with the most love, laughter, and acceptance in the world.

"And Sam?" Shiva called out just as he was about to shut the door behind him. He turned back to look at her, her hair slightly tousled, her eyes shining with the intensity of the moment. "I hope to meet you again in another life."

His quiet smile was his final wish of goodbye. He shut the door.

***

As Sam stepped just a few meters away from the door to Shiva's room, his mind still reeling from the bizarre reality of it all, he froze. Standing before him, looking perfectly at home in his scrubs, was Mike—his best friend from his dreamworld. So, he greeted him enthusiastically. "Hello, Mike!" But this wasn't a dream—this was the real world.

Mike's eyebrows furrowed as he looked at Sam, uncertain. "Hello, sir. Do we know each other?" he asked cautiously, tilting his head just enough to show his hesitation.

Sam blinked, his heart racing. He had to act fast. Of course, Mike wouldn't recognize him. They hadn't met in real life. "Oh, uh," Sam paused, collecting himself. "I—I read your name on your name tag. Doctor Mike, right? I was actually expecting you to come in here for Shiva. I just wanted to make sure you take great care of her."

Mike gave him a polite but mildly confused smile. "Of course. Don't worry, she's in good hands. Are you guys related?"

Before the moment could stretch too long or grow any more awkward, Sam quickly stepped aside. "Oh, no. I'm one of her clients who happened to be around when she needed a lift to the hospital. Anyway, great, thanks," he said, forcing a strained smile as he quickly turned and disappeared down the hallway, leaving Mike to enter the room.

As Sam walked quickly away, his mind filled with a growing sense of disappointment. The connection, the bond he and Mike had shared in a world that had felt more real than this one, meant so much to Sam. To see that it didn't translate here, into a place grounded in reality, was a cruel reminder of the distance between his dream world and the real one.

The realization hit hard—that his dreamworld, so vivid and real to him, didn't extend to everyone. He had hoped, foolishly, that Mike might somehow remember him—maybe even recognize him like

Lara and Shiva had. But that was clearly and unfortunately not the case. As he rounded the corner, Sam couldn't help but feel the weight of his isolation. Even his closest friends in his imaginings were strangers here.

***

Sam pressed his phone to his ear as the line rang, the hum of the taxi blending into his thoughts. The airport was just minutes away, and his bags, neatly placed beside him on the back seat, were small enough to qualify as carry-ons. Yet, their lightness unsettled him—a reminder of how little he was bringing along, and how empty everything felt in that moment.

He was coming back with nothing when he thought he'd be coming back with the love of his life.

How naive he'd been and how childish he felt for his previously grandiose ideas. Of course, this was how it all worked out. He should have been happy to find out that the women were real after all, thanks to his various social media searches, and maybe left it at that.

The line clicked, and Tiffany's voice gurgled through the receiver. "Sam?"

"Hey, Tiff," he replied, with an obvious sorrowful cadence.

"I saw that you cancelled Paris. Are you coming back straight home from New York?"

"Yeah, I'm heading back to Singapore after passing by my mother."

"It didn't..." she hesitated, then, in a softer tone, added, "It didn't work out?"

He rubbed his eyes. "It's no use tracking down Céline... They all have boyfriends and husbands. They all know me from our dreams together, but to them, the dreams just helped them strengthen their existing relationships."

"They... They aren't available for a real relationship with me. And I'm not mad, I'm really not. Like, I completely understand—it's just... it sucks, you know?"

"I don't wanna go through that again. I don't wanna find myself halfway across the world, just to be let down easy for the third time this week. Well, fourth."

"You and Kate?"

"We're definitely done for good, too."

"But Céline's Instagram profile was, you know, hopeful."

Sam shook his head, despite knowing Tiffany couldn't see him. "None of them were posting the men in their lives. I can't take that as evidence of potential. I need something more concrete than that."

"She's the last girl, though. You may as well see it through to the end."

"I understand that, but I can't."

"You'll always be left to wonder, Sam. Isn't that worse?"

"At the moment? No, I don't think it's worse. I think it's what I actually need. Without that, I might just give up on love entirely."

"That's a bit dramatic—"

"Nobody gets it, alright? Nobody. Not even the women who were with me in those dreams. But *I* was there, and *I* know what I felt, and I can't just let that go or beat myself down with reality. If I never meet Céline, then I'll always have my memories of her, and for me, that's enough. Besides, she was the only one who had a boyfriend in my dream. So, if she is meant to be in my life, she'll come find me. I don't always need to do the chasing. That hasn't gotten me very far."

"It's your decision, Sam."

"Yeah... it *is* my decision." His cheeks were blazing with passion. He didn't know if he felt like crying or screaming or just... sleeping.

"See you soon," Tiffany said with a sigh.

He and Céline had been such good friends despite her being with her boyfriend, but Sam couldn't imagine just being her friend forever.

He wished he could be her friend even now, but their real lives were just so different. Hopefully, like Lara and Shiva, Céline received something helpful from their time together in their dreams that helped bring her and Charles closer together. Sam couldn't expect her to actually entertain a friendship with someone she was attracted to on a long-term basis while still being in a relationship, still finding its footing in the early stages.

It just didn't feel right to burden her with the truth. It was better for her to believe that Sam was nothing more than a product of her mind.

The line dropped with Tiffany, and Sam got out of the taxi at the terminal hosting his flight to New York City.

***

Sam's dreams didn't stop.

Every single night, his mind was clouded with their faces, each of them fading into vagueness, but the outlines of their bodies, the feeling of their presence, lingered.

His multiple lives came to him in random flashes—the faint trace of Shiva's perfume, the grandeur of the Palace of Versailles, the endless dunes of Dubai.

He recalled late-night work meetings that stretched into early hours, accompanied by discussions over bottles of wine.

He thought of exhausting days in the operating room, each hour dragging as he anticipated reuniting with someone who gave him that butterfly feeling.

And then, there was the promise of an empty apartment—bare walls waiting to be adorned with fresh memories and the echoes of differing personalities.

For all of them, they represented a clean slate. A chance for Sam to become a better man, to approach love without baggage or resentment.

He thought about Shiva in the hospital bed, and suddenly, she was handing him an infant that had his blue eyes, which he had gotten from his grandmother.

He felt the weight of Lara's arm wrapped around his as she whispered in his ear about a man who had admired her, staring at her in the lobby. He didn't feel jealous, though; he was always refreshed by Lara's honesty and trusted that she'd never hurt him.

He thought about Kate as she glared at the skylight, the hollows of her immaculate cheekbones one of the last things he admired before he said goodbye forever. He thought of the lunches they shared and the warm nights spent beneath blankets on his living room floor. Eventually, Kate became an incomplete mass like the rest of them—a blurry combination of floating parts and unattached feelings.

It was Céline, however, who always stayed the same. Clear as the day he met her, her features remained intact, and her time with him never devolved into nightmarish flashes. He was still with her at the Seine, matching her steps while they walked along the water.

Things were on the horizon for them. A vast potential he grew certain he'd never disturb. He was right not to meet her, for if he had, she would have melted into his subconscious like the rest of them.

This way, they'd always be together as great friends, at least, even if it was just in the fabric of his mind.

Ch. 19

"When Destiny Strikes"

"You've served our wonderful country well, Ambassador Cooper." The Secretary of State beamed at him from behind his wiry glasses, dabbing his forehead with a handkerchief while raising his hand to flag down the waiter.

They sat across from each other at a bistro table in a high-end restaurant, a bottle of champagne resting in a bath of ice beside them as they waited for their empty plates to be filled with more appetizers.

Sam had been flown to Washington, D.C., for a meeting the Secretary of State requested at the command of the President, but nobody would tell Sam what the occasion was for.

It had been a while since Kate left, and his routine had settled into a steady rhythm.

His dreams weren't elaborate anymore, though they still offered fleeting glimpses of Céline. He continued performing his duties with characteristic dedication, and his sleep schedule had mercifully restored.

Much to Tiffany's relief, Sam no longer bore the signs of sleepless nights—his hair neatly in place, his appearance more refreshed, and the dark circles under his eyes a distant memory. Even their conversations had shifted focus, revolving around lighter, more casual topics.

He mingled with influential political figures at events and dinners, catching the dark eyes of women across the room at restaurants but never making a move. He had sworn off dating, determined to rebuild himself into someone better than he had been before. Sam believed firmly that when the right woman entered his life, she would bring with her an undeniable force and magnetism that couldn't be ignored. Of that, he was certain.

He didn't feel even a spark of attraction toward anyone he met, but he hoped it would pass with time—just as the nightly reminders of Céline would eventually dissolve into the shadows of his subconscious.

In time, those strange dreams would become nothing more than a tale he'd recount to himself in quiet moments. For now, all he could do was endure and wait for it to dissipate.

"I hope I can continue serving America's interests, sir," Sam replied to the Secretary of State, taking a cautious sip from a bowl of soup that had gone cold long ago. While he'd maintained a positive relationship with the President and his administration, he was all too aware of how unpredictable the political landscape could be.

A creeping fear settled in the back of his mind—that he was being called in to be criticized for a public announcement or speech he had given, one that might have drawn more attention than intended. He suspected this lunch was merely a courtesy, a *lead-in* to soften the blow.

The Secretary laughed. "Of course, Sam. That's why I've asked you here."

The waiter finally approached the table once again, and the Secretary ordered a second bottle of champagne while dismissing the one already at their side. "You've had an extraordinary two years in Singapore—the most successful tenure we've ever seen from an ambassador there. Our relations with the region are thriving, and now we'd like to see you work your magic somewhere else."

"Elsewhere?" His heart skipped a beat. Singapore had become more than just a post to him—it felt like a second home. He had grown attached to its bustling avenues, the comfort of his favorite takeout dishes, and the sense of routine he had built there. He had forged meaningful friendships with his colleagues and entourage and cultivated a strong, trusted relationship with the nation's political leaders. Leaving all that behind felt like a daunting prospect.

However, deep down, Sam knew he was overdue for a significant change—something to force him out of the lingering malaise his dreamworld had left behind.

"How'd you like to go to Paris?"

The Secretary chuckled as he popped open the freshly delivered bottle of champagne, the soft pop breaking the tension. He took one look at Sam's stunned expression and decided it was as good as an agreement. Pouring them both a glass, he raised his own, prompting Sam to tap their rims together. The sharp clink of crystal snapped Sam out of his daze, though his ears rang faintly, and the lively chatter of the restaurant seemed suddenly louder, pressing against his senses.

"Paris?" he asked, still stunned.

"Paris, indeed, *Monsieur l'Ambassadeur*!" the Secretary exclaimed with a grin, raising his glass in a celebratory gesture.

This move would be a significant career leap—an assignment in such a strategic country, one of the five veto powers. Yet, as he considered the opportunity, he couldn't help but think of Céline. *Don't get your hopes up,* Sam warned himself. But the thought persisted, and he couldn't stop his mind from wandering to the possibility of living so close to her.

He had promised himself to leave it up to fate—wasn't this a sign?

Regardless, the opportunity to be stationed in a country like France was much too important to pass up.

"You will continue your marvelous duties as Ambassador overseas," the Secretary added. "And you can take all your staff with you. We don't want to take you too far out of your element, as it were, and we know that your entire team is instrumental in the success of Singapore."

"I appreciate that, sir," Sam replied. He felt like his limbs were frozen while his heart thrummed with the insistence to run. To go. To leave for Paris, *now*.

"To Paris!" They raised their glasses again.

"To Paris," Sam echoed.

To a final shot at love, he thought.

***

An intimate farewell gathering was thrown for Sam back in Singapore, and everyone was in attendance. Even the Singaporean Prime Minister made an appearance, heartily thanking Sam for all his hard work.

It felt surreal to be celebrated, to have hands enthusiastically gripping his shoulders while various colleagues whispered in his ear about all the achievements he had accrued during his term with them. Men made jokes about how jealous they were of his success, while a few women, once too shy, now made bold advances.

Sam's cheeks grew red as the night wore on and the crowd became denser. The small soiree had transformed into a dinner where he was offered a podium to make a speech, and while he gave it professionally and precisely, he found himself ignoring the people before him.

There was no one he was searching for in the crowd, no familiar face whose attention he longed to catch. For once, there was nobody on the sidelines, silently supporting him—no one standing with fingers pressed anxiously to their lips, quietly rehearsing the words they had helped him craft.

It was both a relief and a reminder of what he was craving with an increasing sharpness. Perhaps things would be different—better—in Paris. Even if destiny didn't lead him back to Céline, perhaps it would guide him to someone equally wonderful.

***

After a short break in New York City with his family, Sam moved to his new post and effortlessly adapted to life in Paris—he had already experienced it in his dreams, after all.

Just as he had with Dubai and Los Angeles, he remembered all the local spots from his dreams. Though ample time had passed since he last visited Paris in his sleep, he never forgot the charming, historic alleyways and the brasseries, where neighbors met up to discuss their hectic lives.

He enjoyed taking shortcuts on his way to nearby meetings and casual *rendez-vous*, finding small efficiencies in his routine. On days off, he often took Tiffany to the city's best restaurants, sharing laughter and quiet moments of solace despite an embassy bustling with new acquaintances.

He also frequented the cafés where Céline had once surprised him with pastries during their long evenings spent carefully planning events—those glamorous nights, filled with public figures and celebrities, now little more than distant memories.

As time passed, Sam found himself no longer burdened by his past, but instead feeling hopeful about the future. He sensed a shift within—a transition from mourning his losses to embracing the possibilities before him. He was done dwelling on what could have been.

He eventually expanded his friend group and discovered intriguing places to eat and museums in the countryside to visit on weekends. He traveled to other countries in Europe, embarking on train trips to England and vacationing in Spain.

He resolved to remain open to love again. He had a great residence situated perfectly in the heart of Paris, with space thoughtfully left in his closet for someone else's belongings one day. Rather than relying on chance, he started exploring new places and attending social gatherings with a renewed sense of enthusiasm, embracing the city's vibrant charm along the way.

He went on dates that never turned into anything serious, but he didn't let it bother him. Each encounter felt like a stepping stone, shaping him into a better version of himself. The conversations were rich, and every insight into each person's uniquely fascinating life left him feeling grateful as he kissed their cheeks goodbye at the end of the night. His heart remained full, even though his bed and home were empty, occupied only by him and the companionship of Chalk.

The white dog still jogged diligently alongside Sam on their slow evenings and had a new favorite place to play fetch in the *Bois de Boulogne*. Sam loved wandering through the park himself, feeling like he stepped into another world altogether every time. He'd bring snacks for himself and an eventually tired-out Chalk, which they indulged in by the scenic little lake.

He was gradually moving forward with his life, with Céline fading into the memory he always knew she'd become—something gathered at the corners of his mind but never intruding on his present thoughts. He felt a renewed sense of clarity, a lightness he hadn't experienced in a long time.

He wanted to embody the best version of himself—approachable, polished, and, above all else, kind.

***

One morning, Sam found himself at the rustic bakery café nestled beneath the Parisian apartment he had inhabited in his dreamworld. He dipped his freshly baked bread into a steaming cup of hot chocolate, just as he had done so many times before in those imagined mornings.

He had also ordered a double espresso, unable to comprehend how some people managed to survive on the sugar rush from hot chocolate alone. Still, he didn't mind the wait, enjoying the relaxed pace of the morning.

Sam savored the quiet moment as he read the morning newspaper. Beside him, Chalk lounged peacefully, contentedly chewing on a bone-shaped plastic toy, perfectly at ease in the tranquil scene.

He had grown used to the more relaxed service in European establishments, finding the understated approach preferable to the overfriendliness of American waiters. It was refreshing not to be interrupted constantly, even if it was in the name of good service.

It was a gorgeous Saturday morning. Earlier, Sam had strolled through the city with Chalk trotting beside him and Jack following a short distance behind. The cool air carried a subtle chill—winter was brewing, visible just beyond the café's windows. Now, seated comfortably, Sam wore a soft blue sweater and a tailored pair of trousers he had recently bought.

With no plans for the rest of the day, he considered continuing his stroll through the beautiful streets of Paris. The idea of burning off the indulgent hot chocolate and French breakfast appealed to him, followed by retreating to his home for a much-needed nap.

Suddenly, he heard it. That voice. Sweet, despite being a bit rough with a thick accent.

His heart climbed in his chest, and his lungs expanded without his consent. He could feel his ears burning and his hair standing on end.

She ordered a baguette, her native tongue as familiar to him as the English she spoke just for his sake. He turned around slowly, a dumb grin on his face as his eyes fell upon her—It was *her, the one and only Céline*.

Just as radiant as he remembered, her sleek hair pulled back into a loose ponytail, her lips painted a faint red, and her skin golden and tanned even in the grey morning light. She tripped as she reached for the baguette, her movements still graceful but marked by the same endearing clumsiness he had always found charming.

He didn't hesitate to walk up to her, understanding that this was an event beyond his comprehension. The more he mulled over his options and weighed the outcomes, the more he'd lose the momentum required to capture her, once and for all. He had worked too hard on himself to abruptly worry about a woman he'd survived without, no matter how miserably, for almost a year.

But Tiffany was right—he needed to know, or he'd spend forever waking up in the middle of the night and wondering what he'd missed.

"Céline?" He called out her name plainly and without expectation.

She glanced at him out of the corner of her eye at first, but the moment she recognized his windswept hair and those unmistakable pale-blue eyes, her gaze locked onto him. Her mouth fell open gently before curving into a smile. She gaped, her eyelashes fluttering as she struggled to find the words to convey her amazement.

"Are you for real?" was all she could manage to say in response, her French accent evident. Chalk gave a confirming bark and watched her with a playful wag of his tail.

"We must have met in a dream," Sam said, his ridiculously wide grin refusing to fade.

"I—I... I thought I was losing my mind." She pressed the heel of her palm against her forehead, her voice trembling with disbelief.

He chuckled at her delighted surprise. "Trust me, I thought the same thing."

"I haven't... been with anybody but you. Since you, I don't..." Her voice faltered, and she seemed too overwhelmed to continue.

A frown crept onto Sam's face, his brows knitting together. "Wait, but... you were never with me. You were with your boyfriend—Charles."

His confusion mirrored her own. She repeated the name, completely in shock.

"You mean Charles Le Long? No! He was never my boyfriend," she laughed, as if the idea were utterly absurd. Charles... is my silent business partner. He's married and in love with his wife, Natalie—but you should have known that! Unless it seems, we weren't having the same version of our dreams."

"You're kidding me." Sam choked on his words, his voice catching in his throat. He was tempted—so very tempted—to feel frustrated over the hours he'd wasted, convinced that the French woman standing before him was like the others he'd reconnected with—taken and perfectly content with that fact.

But he caught himself. He was proud of where he had arrived in his life. He was stable, satisfied, and at peace with himself. He realized that he never would have been a good partner, husband, or father—whatever role he might have taken—if he had continued down the path he was on before.

There were moments when a slight regret lingered, especially when he thought about how their dreams seemed to help Lara and Shiva strengthen their relationships. A part of him wondered why it hadn't done the same for him and Kate. But deep down, he knew it was never meant to be.

Everything he had experienced had been preparation and growth, leading him to exactly where he was meant to be in this moment.

"I am not *kidding* you, Sam! Your name is Sam, right?" Céline smacked his arm with the end of her baguette, and they both erupted in laughter—even as she declared, "I don't think I've ever been more serious in my life than I am right now."

Sam's chest stirred with the familiar adoration he had once felt so deeply in his dreams of Céline. More than anything, he wanted to kiss her.

He had known her so deeply, so totally, he should have never doubted his own intuition.

"I'm so relieved that you are actually flesh and blood. Because it *was* like I was seeing you," she continued. "I was working my regular job, planning for—"

"Paris Fashion Week," he announced, remembering their time in the office together.

"*Exactly.* But I only ever caught glimpses. It was like I'd blink and miss you, but I still felt your ghost. It's strange, I know." She shook her head, and her shoulders fell in relief at getting the words out.

"You should hear all the things we did in my dreams..." He paused, then, with unexpected boldness and the ease of asking an old friend, added, "Do you wanna grab a cup of coffee with us?" He pointed at himself and Chalk.

She looked like she was still searching for the correct phrases to express exactly what she wanted to say. "Well, how could I say no to that now?" she said finally.

Her gaze shifted to Jack as Chalk moved to sit at the man's feet. Céline frowned slightly. "Do you have security following you? Are you in the mafia or something?"

Sam nodded, feeling a little embarrassed. "Yeah, I do have a bodyguard. But no, I'm not in the mafia—I'm the U.S. ambassador, so it kind of comes with the job."

Céline let out a frustrated sound, her eyes wide with shock. "You're *the* American ambassador? Here, in Paris? Oh my God, if I'd only kept up with politics, I might have recognized you sooner and known where to find you! This is all my fault for not keeping up with the news."

He laughed heartily. "Well, we've found each other now. Perhaps this was just the right time for us to cross paths again."

"You're right. This is beyond amazing to me," she admitted.

Sam smiled warmly and turned to pull out the seat beside him, but froze in surprise when Céline spoke. "But, Sam?"

Their eyes locked, and Sam straightened instinctively, a wave of unease stirring in his chest. There had to be a catch—some clause, some reason to keep her away from him.

But instead, she nearly tossed her baguette onto the small wooden table and closed the distance between them in a heartbeat, pressing her chest against his. Her arms wound tightly around his neck, and with a breathless urgency, she murmured, "I'm going to lose my mind unless you kiss me *right now* and prove to me that *you're real.*"

Their kiss brought a massive smile to his face, but he didn't let it break the moment. He wrapped his arms around Céline's waist, pulling her close in a hug that spoke of how deeply he had missed her—and the relief of finally being in her presence again.

She tasted like sunshine and pure joy, sinking deep into Sam's core. Every nerve in his body seemed to ignite, and for a few solid seconds, he felt as if he'd lost the ability to hear, see, or sense anything that wasn't *her*.

A few amused cheers and chuckles swam around them from the occupants of the little café, and Sam and Céline pulled away with matching shyness, waving off the attention. Chalk barked joyfully from his spot next to Jack, who smiled politely but averted his eyes.

Sam finally managed to pull out the seat beside him as Céline unbuttoned her coat and settled in.

Over shared bread and steaming coffee, they spoke as if no time had passed between them. Their lips still tingled with the lasting intensity of their kiss, but their laughter flowed easily, and their fingers intertwined naturally, like two lovers reconnecting.

And so began the next chapter of Sam's life.

"One Year Later"

Sam ran a nervous hand down the front of his classic light grey wedding suit, his fingers brushing the smooth fabric. He inhaled deeply, drawing in the sweet, heady fragrance of the flowers adorning the venue in a dazzling burst of vibrant colors.

Warm light flooded through the pristine stained-glass windows of the cathedral, casting vibrant hues across the aisle. And suddenly, Sam felt himself transported to a misty, dreamlike space, standing before a magnificent door.

This was it. This was where everything had been leading—this moment of pure, unmatched happiness.

Sam's eyes scanned the pews, meeting the gazes of dozens of people, all gathered to celebrate the day he had waited for his entire life.

His diplomatic team, some new faces, some having come with him all the way from Singapore. And, of course, the faces of Céline's media team, which Sam had gotten to know better outside of his dreams by now. A group of friends he and Céline had collected over their time together.

There was even an older couple towards the back, who owned a charming guesthouse in the little town of Colmar in the Alsace region of eastern France, where Sam and Céline had once stayed.

Colmar, known for its beautiful canals, is also the birthplace of Frédéric Auguste Bartholdi, the French sculptor who designed the Statue of Liberty—a gift from France to the United States in 1886 to celebrate the centennial of American independence and the friendship between the two nations.

Céline and Sam had spent countless hours talking with the elderly couple, who, even after 55 years of marriage, remained as deeply in love and adoring of each other as they were in their earliest days.

Inspired by the couple's enduring bond and the enchanting beauty of Colmar, they decided it was the perfect location for their own wedding.

Céline had insisted on inviting the couple to their ceremony, and Sam completely agreed. The grey-mustached gentleman, unable to speak more than a few words of English, waved warmly at Sam when their eyes met, his joy evident despite the language barrier.

He grinned back, nodding in thanks.

In the front row sat Céline's remarkable mother and her sweet Mamie, both radiant with joy. Beside them was Sam's mother, stunning in a vibrant yellow dress. Her silver hair was elegantly pinned up with a delicate hairpin that she and Céline had discovered in a tiny antique shop tucked away in the labyrinth of Paris' historic streets.

She chatted warmly with Céline's family, pausing every now and then to dab her eyes with a handkerchief Sam instantly recognized as his father's. It was a small yet meaningful piece of his old man that had made it to Sam's special day.

Sam's jaw tightened as he struggled to hold back his own tears. He knew his mother's tears were filled with pure joy, but he also understood that beneath it all lay an old grief, quietly woven into the moment.

Fixing his cufflinks—another precious relic from his family, passed down from his grandfather's own wedding day—Sam smiled at his mother.

Earlier that morning, when she had visited Sam while he was getting ready, she had patted his chest and told him, "You have a wonderful heart, Sammy. I have always been scared that you will struggle with heartbreak after heartbreak just because you love so *hard*, and that's not exactly every person's cup of tea. But I am happy to see that you have met someone who loves just as much and as fully as you do."

Sam had smiled and nodded. "Céline isn't the type to fold; she pushes right back with just as much intensity. We're a little bit like an unstoppable force meeting an immovable object sometimes."

His mother had nodded too, as if she approved. "You will keep each other stable like that, son. I'm so proud of you."

He hugged his mom close, feeling her unconditional and steadfast love fill him up and ground him for the day ahead. He hadn't been *nervous*, per se, but he felt jittery and restless with excitement. He couldn't wait to marry the literal woman of his dreams. Céline had lit up his life in every way possible. Her inescapable light had infiltrated the darkest, most scared parts of Sam and faced it head-on with no reservations or questions.

During their year-long romance before getting engaged, Sam and Céline had explored each other deeply, mapping out their future plans with the same harmony they had once brought to their *Fashion Week* presentation.

They were two elements that fit effortlessly together, turning each other to new heights. For the first time, Sam truly understood how profoundly a perfect partner could elevate your life.

Tiffany had once told him that he seemed to have transformed from a prince into a king—everything about the way he carried himself was different. "You have always been confident and charming, sure," Tiffany rolled her eyes playfully, "But it's beyond confidence now. It's peace. Like you're lighter in your shoes."

Sam had just winked at her, smiling, "That's because I have much fewer people I need to impress now."

His wonderfully caring assistant was also in the front pew, blowing her nose loudly. Sam couldn't restrain his chuckle. Next to Tiffany was his sister, sharing his dark hair and pale eyes. She blew him a kiss, which he teasingly pretended to swat away—a little game they had been playing since they were kids. Neatly dressed and perfectly patient, Sam's young nephews, Bob and Eddy, craned their necks, waiting for the beautiful bride to finally enter. Sam's brother-in-law gave him an encouraging thumbs-up, which Sam returned with a grin.

Finally, the grand orchestral music started spilling through the space.

Sam's heart felt like it was beating at a snail's pace and the speed of a rocket all at the same time.

Céline's bridesmaids waltzed into the space, dazzling in their flowing dresses. But Sam craned his neck, searching for the one person he longed to see more than anyone—his breathtaking bride.

He locked eyes with Céline, and in that moment, nothing else existed—just the two of them, destined to be for each other.

Her elegant white wedding dress highlighted every detail of her beauty, leaving Sam breathless.

Overwhelmed, he choked back a gasp, pressing his fist to his mouth in an attempt to steady himself.

Céline had the incredible cheek to grin at his touched reaction. She was radiant as ever.

When she finally left her father's side and placed her hands in Sam's, her sweet smile warming his heart, he felt complete. He let out a sigh of relief.

Chalk trotted up, wearing a dapper black bow tie, as the dog brought up the couple's stunning wedding bands.

When their rings were finally on their fingers and their hands on each other's cheeks, with permission to kiss as a married pair, they brought their lips together for the most world-changing kiss—just as perfect as their very first one in that little bakery café.

Their union spilled out into sublime eternity.

***

"Sam, lift your chin just a bit for me—yes! Perfect, hold it there. Céline, you look stunning as always, honey; don't move a muscle," Tiffany instructed, her eyes narrowing in concentration as she adjusted the camera. "Now, hold that little bundle of love up just a touch higher—let's get a clearer view of her face."

Céline giggled at Tiffany's orders, pulling the blanket wrapped around the bundle in her arms open just enough. Sam slipped an arm lovingly around his wife as his baby daughter stretched her fists into the air, turning her flawless little face into the warmth of the sun. Céline leaned more into Sam's embrace. They didn't need words to express just how perfect this moment was.

Their newborn daughter, Alba, was only a few months old, but Sam could already see so much of her mother's light shine from her. The instant he saw her sweet face for the first time, he knew that he would give his very life to protect and care for this brilliant little person with her sparkling blue eyes.

She had curled her tiny hand around his pinky finger while she was snoozing peacefully on her mother's chest. Sam had loved their baby since the second they found out that Céline was pregnant—a moment that was celebrated in shouts of excitement, with Céline jumping directly into Sam's arms and smothering him with a messy kiss.

He leaned in to kiss her cheek at the memory, and he heard the distinctive clicking of a camera shutter snapping shut.

Tiffany grinned in triumph at capturing the tender moment between the two lovers.

They were posing on the neatly trimmed green lawn in front of the Parisian U.S. Embassy, with its facade of three tiers of columns and trees swaying pleasantly in the breeze.

A little less than two years had passed since Sam and Céline's wedding, where they had danced the night away and indulged in delectable wedding cake at the reception. At the end of the night, Céline's hair had fallen loose from her intricately styled hairdo as she swayed her body to the music with Sam, barefoot and laughing. She had never looked more beautiful to him.

Within that time, Sam had fulfilled his promise to his country by strengthening the bonds between France and the U.S., making them more reliable and powerful than ever. He had reached his goals in Paris and surpassed them spectacularly—with his pretty wife and healthy newborn by his side and a stronger sense of who he is than he had ever felt.

Céline had been planning for months to expand her media agency to the States, and Sam had received a new proposal to relocate to Washington, D.C., to regroup with his country after his various posts abroad.

Sam was glad to be closer to home and happy to show Céline a part of his world in his home country too.

She was buzzing with excitement and had already treated herself to a pair of embroidered cowgirl boots and a weathered leather cowboy hat, despite Sam's amused protests that it was entirely unnecessary—it wasn't as if they were moving to the Wild West. Céline, however, had firmly declared that it was absurd not to make it a requirement for living in the United States of America.

Sam couldn't help but laugh and let it slide in the end; she carried the look with such ease and charm. It even sparked a quiet promise to himself to plan a trip to a horse ranch for her in the near future.

Despite the Cooper family leaving behind the gorgeous views of France, Tiffany had requested to stay. She had found her own magic in the City of Love, falling for her neighbor—a charmingly pot-bellied widower with three children, whom Tiff immediately embraced as her own, just as fully as she had always supported Sam.

He felt a pang of sadness. There was no doubt he was going to miss her. But seeing her luck and her own dreamlike romance unfolding ahead of her was everything Sam had hoped she would find.

Sam and Céline made their way back to the embassy, carefully bringing their golden-haired baby into the cool shade. Sam leaned down to kiss his daughter's soft head, and Céline, smiling, passed little Alba into his arms. As Sam cradled the sweet newborn tenderly, Céline nestled into his side, her affection radiating in the gentle way she leaned against him.

"I love you, Sam Cooper," she sighed, unprompted and full of sincerity. It still filled Sam with absolute pleasure and peace every time the words left her lips.

He leaned towards her, kissing her for a slow, lingering moment. "And I love you, my dream woman." A happy bark from Chalk broke the moment, his tail wagging in approval.

THE END

May your brightest dreams always find their way to you.

The Author.

Printed in Dunstable, United Kingdom